The Forgotten Family *of* Liverpool

Pam Howes

bookouture

Published by Bookouture
An imprint of StoryFire Ltd.
Carmelite House
50 Victoria Embankment
London EC4Y 0DZ
www.bookouture.com

ISBN: 978-0-34913-250-1
eBook ISBN: 978-1-78681-190-5

Printed and bound in Great Britain by Clays Ltd, Elcograf S.p.A.

Papers used are from well-managed forests
and other responsible sources.

Dedicated to the memory of my much-missed mum and dad, Joan and Bill Walton. Reunited on 31/12/16 and now enjoying that Last Waltz for ever. Writing Dora and Joe's story has made me realise how hard life was post-war for families like ours. Thank you so much for the wonderful and stable upbringing you gave me, Harold and Jill. We have lovely memories to share. All my love, Pam. xxx

Chapter One

Kirkby, Liverpool, June 1952

Dora Rodgers looped her long blonde hair behind her ears, banged on the kitchen window and wagged a warning finger. Her daughters were squabbling over the doll's pram again, with five-year-old Carol hanging onto the handle for dear life, while two-year-old Jackie screamed at the top of her voice. She turned back to the washing. It was over a year since her husband Joe's departure from the marital home, following a breakdown in their relationship, which had seen dressmaker Dora sink to the depths of despair. She had since found within herself a grim determination to prove that she didn't need him and could care for their daughters on her own. Sometimes though, like today, when she had housework and the washing to see to, as well as a skirt and blouse to finish making for one of her customers, it all felt too much to cope with. It was all right for Joe, living the life of a single man, apart from when he took the kids out for the day. He only had himself to think about.

She folded the dry towels she'd brought in from the line and laid them on the table, then picked up the basket of washing she'd just put through the mangle. One day, when she was better off, she'd treat herself to a new washing machine with an electric mangle on top, like the one her pal Agnes had. Agnes said it made washdays a doddle. Joe had told her he'd get her one, but she'd refused and said she'd buy one herself when she could afford it. Mam said she was cutting her nose off to spite her face and to let Joe pay for it. But Dora was stubborn, and she was already living in the house Joe had got through his job at the Royal Ordnance Factory; she didn't want to take anything else from him.

She went out into the garden and dropped the basket onto the small lawn. Jackie hurled herself at her legs, crying. Carol, looking smug, was pushing the doll's pram up the path towards the shed.

'Carol, share. Let Jackie have a turn, there's a good girl,' Dora said, giving her youngest a comforting hug. But Carol chose to ignore her. Dora put Jackie down and went to stand in front of Carol, who scowled and rammed the pram hard into her legs, laddering a stocking. 'Ouch,' Dora cried, jumping backwards. 'Right, you naughty little madam; go to your room, this minute.'

Carol let out a howl and stomped indoors, her plaits bouncing on her shoulders. Jackie gave a delighted squeal and ran to grab the pram. Dora watched as she pushed it up the path, her earlier tears forgotten. She turned back to pegging out her washing. Mam would be arriving soon. Maybe she'd take Carol to the shops with her. She was hard work that one, always had been, although now and again, when the fancy took her, she could be a proper little angel.

Jackie soon lost interest in the pram, just as Dora expected she would, and picked up some clothes pegs to hand to her mother. 'You're a little monkey, you are,' Dora said. 'You didn't really want that pram at all.' Jackie giggled and ran off with a handful of pegs. 'Bring them back here or *you* can go and sit in the bedroom as well.'

'Are they playing you up, gel?' a voice called from a couple of gardens further along.

Dora looked up and saw her neighbour Dolly hanging over the fence. 'Just a bit,' she called back. 'Though no more than usual.'

'Not too long now before Carol starts school. Then you'll have more time to relax with just your Jackie to see to. I miss our Alice, but I love the peace and quiet now she's at school all day. I'll pop down for a cuppa when I've finished hanging this lot out.'

'Okay.' Dora nodded, and rolled her eyes as she turned her back on Dolly. That'd be half the morning gone before she got rid of her, no doubt. Although her neighbour was kind and helped her out with the children, she could talk the hind legs off a donkey once she got going. Dora pegged the final tea towel on the line and went back inside to put the kettle on. As she spooned tea into the pot she heard the front door opening.

'Only me, chuck,' a voice called from the hallway.

'I'm in the kitchen, Mam,' Dora called back. 'Just about to make a brew. Dolly's popping round in a minute.'

'Oh, okay, well I'll nip to the shops while the pair of you have a gossip. Where's our Carol?' she asked, peering out of the back door and seeing only Jackie playing in the garden.

Dora jerked a thumb towards the second bedroom door. 'Been a right naughty girl, look.' She lifted her leg with the laddered stocking and a red mark where the metal pram had hit her.

Mam frowned. 'That'll bruise; you need arnica on it. I'll get some from the chemist, and I'll take Carol to the shops with me. We'll have a bit of dinner in the café and then I'll take her to the library. It's story time this afternoon, she'll enjoy that. Give you a break while Jackie has her nap.'

'Thanks, Mam, I was really hoping you'd suggest something like that,' Dora said. As the kettle whistled on the gas hob, Dolly knocked and walked in the front door.

'Have a seat, Dolly, while I see to Carol,' Dora said. She went into the bedroom where Carol was sprawled on the bed, her lips pouting and her cheeks red and tear-stained.

'Sowwy, Mammy,' she sobbed, holding her arms out.

Dora gave her a hug and lifted her off the bed. Her heart skipped a beat as she looked at her daughter's woebegone expression. Carol was so like Joe with her soft brown hair and big hazel eyes, while blonde-haired, blue-eyed Jackie was Dora's double. 'Right, monkey; let's have no more being naughty and I'll let you go shopping with Granny. Okay?'

Carol nodded and wiped her snotty nose on her cardigan sleeve.

Dora sighed and led her contrite daughter into the bathroom, where she washed her face and brushed her hair. 'Now no messing about, and make sure you hold Granny's hand, or else.' She lowered her voice as they left the bathroom. 'Daddy's coming for tea tonight, and he'll want to know that you've been a good girl for me. All right?'

Carol nodded again and ran into the sitting room where her granny was talking to Dolly.

'Come on then, Carol,' Granny said, giving her granddaughter a hug. 'Have you made a list, Dora?'

'It's on the table, with some money. I only want sausages, spuds and custard powder.'

'Okay, chuck, we'll see you in a bit.'

Dora closed the front door behind them and went to pour the tea. She handed Dolly a well-sugared mug, thanking God that sugar rationing was over. She offered her a ginger snap and sat down next to her on the sofa.

Dolly took two biscuits and put her mug down on the coffee table. 'So, Joe's coming for tea, is he?' She tucked a straying red curl back under her turban.

Dora looked at her in surprise. 'How do you know that?'

'I heard you telling Carol.'

'Oh.' Dora took a sip from her mug. God, the woman had ears like a bat. She'd spoken to Carol in a low voice, or thought she had. 'Yes, he's coming to see the girls. He didn't see them on Sunday because the band was playing out of town at an afternoon garden party.'

Dolly pursed her lips. 'Was *she* with him?'

'I've no idea. I didn't ask. I'm not interested even if she was. He can do what he likes now we're separated.' *She* being Ivy Bennett, who managed the canteen at the Royal Ordnance Factory where

Joe worked, and with whom he'd had a brief relationship when Dora had suffered depression after Jackie's birth.

'She's got a lot to answer for, that one.'

'Yes, so you keep telling me, Dolly. But that's Joe's business now, not mine.'

After seeing Dolly out, Dora gave Jackie her dinner and then settled her for an afternoon nap. She switched on the wireless to listen to the latest episode of *Mrs Dale's Diary* and sat down on the sofa with her sewing. Her little dressmaking business was making just enough to keep her going, along with the money Joe handed over each weekend. It was her ambition to earn enough eventually that she could tell him she didn't want or need his contribution, but for now she had no choice but to let him help her out. As the theme tune for the end of *Mrs Dale* filled the room, Dora jumped to her feet and switched off the wireless.

She glanced at the mantel clock. Her mam and Carol would be back soon with the shopping and then she could start preparing tonight's tea. It was not something she was particularly looking forward to. It still hurt her to see Joe; the overwhelming feeling of having been betrayed at a time when she was most vulnerable was still painful. She could never trust him again, no matter how much he told her he loved her and begged for her forgiveness.

She frowned as someone rapped loudly on the front door, interrupting her thoughts. Who the devil could this be? They'd wake the dead banging like that, never mind her sleeping daughter. She swung the door open and stared open-mouthed at the three men standing on the path.

One of them, a bespectacled middle-aged man, carried a briefcase and was flanked by two uniformed police officers.

'Can I help you?' Dora's stomach turned over. The last time a police officer knocked on her door had been the day of Joanie's death. Joanie, her best friend, business partner and her brother Frank's late wife, had died over four years ago in a fire at Palmer's factory where they'd both worked since leaving school. Dora caught her breath and grabbed hold of the doorframe for support.

'Mrs Rodgers?' the man in the suit asked.

'Yes.' She nodded, feeling sick. The solemn faces of the officers led her to expect bad news. 'What's happened? Is it my brother? Has he had an accident?' Frank worked at the docks and was always telling her about the men who got injured on board ships and at the dockside. It was often a dangerous place to work.

'May we come inside?' the man asked.

'Er, yes, of course.' She held the door wide, conscious of the curious stares from passing neighbours. Thankfully Dolly wasn't around or she'd be pushing past the men to get a front row seat. 'Follow me.' Her legs wobbling, she led them into the sitting room and gestured to the sofa and chairs. 'Please, sit down.' The officers remained standing behind the sofa. Dora perched herself on the chair under the window and laced her shaking hands together on her knees. 'What's happened?' she repeated. 'Has someone been injured?'

The man in the suit looked at her over the top of his glasses from his seat on the sofa, as though weighing her up, before he spoke. 'I'm Mr Oliver, from the Department for Children's Welfare,' he announced. 'You have two children, Mrs Rodgers?' He glanced at a sheaf of papers he'd removed from his briefcase. 'Carol and Jacqueline?'

'Yes, oh my God. Has there been an accident? Carol went out with my mam a while ago, but Jackie's having a nap in the bedroom. Is Carol okay, and my mam?'

'As far as I know, your mother is fine, as is Carol. However, on her return home, I have an order here to remove Carol from your care and place her in the custody of her father, Mr Joseph Rodgers.'

'What?' Dora's hands flew to her mouth. 'There must be some mistake. Why would you do that?'

'Mr Rodgers is on his way here, we contacted him at work.' The man ignored her questions. 'We are acting on information we received, and subsequent investigations, that lead us to believe that Carol's general welfare is being neglected due to you being unable to cope with looking after her as well as your other daughter following the breakdown of your marriage and the fragility of your own mental state. Therefore, for her own safety, we are removing Carol from your care with immediate effect.'

Dora felt the room spinning. The next thing she was aware of was one of the officers lifting her up from the carpet; she'd passed out and fallen from the chair.

The other officer answered the door as she regained consciousness. Joe walked in wearing his work overalls and boots. The room stopped spinning and Dora screamed at him for an explanation, but she saw he looked as confused as she felt.

He shook his head. 'I've no idea what's going on. I got a call at work from the police to make my way here. What the hell has happened?'

The man explained the reason for his visit to Joe and handed him a form to sign.

'This is ridiculous!' Joe shouted, waving the sheet of paper away. 'I'm signing nothing. Carol is well looked after by Dora. I saw her last week and she was fine, both my daughters were, in fact. Which idiot told you she's being neglected? You need to get your facts right, mate, and go after *them*, not my wife. How am I supposed to look after Carol on my own anyway? I work, it's impossible.'

'I'm afraid I'm not at liberty to disclose who made the complaint. But following investigations, I *do* have the right to remove Carol from her mother's home to ensure her safety. We have reports of Carol's behaviour deteriorating due to her mother's neglect. If *you* can't look after her, Mr Rodgers, then I'm afraid I will have no alternative but to take her into care. This could result in her being placed in a children's home or foster care and subsequently put up for adoption.' The man spoke parrot-like, as though reading from a script, with no compassion in his voice at all.

'Now hang on a minute—' Joe began as the front door opened and Carol ran in, accompanied by Dora's mam.

'Daddy,' Carol squealed and launched herself at Joe's legs. He picked her up and held her tight.

'Over my dead body,' he muttered. 'I'll find a way.'

'What's going on?' Mam stared at all the people crammed into the small sitting room.

Joe told her to sit down and took Carol into her bedroom to play. 'Stay there, sweetheart, while me and Mammy talk with Granny. Try not to wake Jackie up.'

As he came back into the room Dora looked at him, unable to speak. She shook her head and her eyes filled with angry tears as she heard him quietly telling her mam what was going on. Who could possibly have reported her to the welfare? She didn't think she had any enemies, other than Ivy Bennett, and even *she* wouldn't stoop this low… would she?

Mam burst into tears. 'I've never heard anything so daft in my whole life,' she shouted at Mr Oliver. 'My Dora's a good mother. Her children are both looked after very well. There must be some mistake.'

The police officers shuffled their feet, looking uncomfortable. One of them moved forward to pat Dora's mam on the arm but she shook him off.

'Don't just stand there, do something,' she demanded. 'And you need to get the doctor out, Joe. He'll tell them our Dora is capable of looking after her daughters and that Carol's safe and well.'

'I'm afraid the doctor won't be able to help you here.' Mr Oliver tried to regain control of the situation. 'Mr Rodgers, if you would like to get your daughter and anything you need to take with you. We'll accompany you to your car.'

Joe shrugged helplessly and looked at Dora. 'There's nothing I can do. I should probably take Carol and get to the bottom of this. I'll bring her home later once it's all sorted out.'

'That won't be possible, I'm afraid,' Mr Oliver said. 'There is nothing further to sort out. Mrs Rodgers is to have no more contact with Carol, certainly for the foreseeable future.' With that he repacked his briefcase and got to his feet. 'If you'd like to get your daughter...' he repeated.

Dora screamed that he couldn't do this. She pulled on his arm but he shook her off and looked at the police officers. 'Mrs Rodgers, don't make matters worse for yourself. I can have you arrested for assault if you persist in obstructing me in my course of duty.'

Dora dropped to her knees, crying, the man's words ringing in her ears.

Chapter Two

Dora lay on the sofa while Mam gave Jackie her tea. She felt heart-broken, all cried out and furious at the same time. Carol had been born a twin. Her sister Joanna had died within hours of their birth. Dora had suffered severe depression following her baby's death and it had taken her a while to cope with looking after Carol once she'd been discharged from a spell in hospital. But with Joe's and her family's help she'd recovered. When Jackie was born the depression had descended on her once more, but again, with time and her family's help, she'd regained control of her mind. As far as Dora was concerned, she was better now than she'd ever been and coping fine. There would be no further babies for her; one of the reasons, apart from his infidelity, that she'd insisted she and Joe should separate was that she felt she could no longer be a proper wife to him. Since their separation, her girls were her life. She would do anything for them.

'Mam, I can't believe this has happened. I mean, who would do such a thing? And why did that horrible man mention my mental state? It's all behind me, I'm better now. And if someone has reported me for being a bad mother, why have they said Joe should just take Carol? Surely they'd want him to take Jackie as well? I don't understand it.'

'It'll be somebody with a right cruel streak in them,' Mam said and pursed her lips. 'Though God knows why anybody would want to break a family up like this. Could it be one of your neighbours? Does anybody have a grudge against you?'

'I don't think so. Why would they? I hardly ever have anything to do with my neighbours, apart from Dolly, and she just wouldn't. She has her faults but she's on *my* side. She loves Carol like she's one of her own.' Dora burst into loud sobs again. 'I can't bear this, Mam.'

'I know, love, I know.' Mam sat down beside her and rocked her in her arms. 'I don't know what to suggest. I think we just have to sit it out until Joe gets in touch later.'

Not for the first time since her marriage had broken down, Dora was grateful for her mam. Despite living over in the cottage near Knowsley Hall that Dora's late dad had through his job, she was always there to help when Dora needed her. And since she'd lost Joanie and then Joe, Dora needed her more than ever. She didn't know how she'd have coped with Carol being taken away without her mam being there.

Dora's brother Frank came to pick up their mam on his way home from work and they told him the tale of the afternoon's events. Dora's heart was breaking, she felt weary and just wanted to sleep for ever.

'So where has Joe taken Carol?' he asked as he rocked Jackie to sleep on his knee. Mam had told Dora to have a lie-down but she'd refused. She'd wanted to call the doctor out but Dora said not to. She was terrified that he'd prescribe sedatives again to help her cope. Then they might say she couldn't look after Jackie and take *her* away as well.

'He rang to say he's back at his pal Don's, where he's been staying since I told him to go. Don's wife said Carol can stay there too until Joe sorts this mess out,' Dora said. 'Carol was asleep when he called. She'd been crying, poor little thing, but they have a dog so Joe's managed to distract her with it. He's taking tomorrow off work, leaving Carol with Don's wife and going to the Children's

Welfare place. He had no luck earlier. That bloody Mr Oliver sent him away; he told him there was no more to be said.'

'He'll get it sorted. It's got to be a mistake,' Frank said. 'Everybody knows what a great mam you are, Sis.' He looked down at his little niece and smiled. 'I mean, you've only got to look at the pair of them to see how well cared for they both are. Whoever made that report wants stringing up. If I get my hands on them, I'll bloody kill them.'

Devastated though Dora felt, she had a feeling things weren't going to be that easy to resolve. 'Someone must have it in for me,' she muttered. 'And I've a damn good idea who.'

'Well, you can't go making accusations until you've got some proof,' Mam said, and Frank nodded his agreement. 'You don't want to make matters worse.'

Dora sighed. There was no way of proving anything at the moment, or even *why* Ivy Bennett would do such a thing. Like Mam said, she couldn't go throwing accusations around until she had proof, and that would take time. The thought of not seeing Carol was agonising though. She'd miss her chubby little arms around her neck when she cuddled her at night, her cheeky smile and her backchat.

'What if the people at the welfare place say it's not a mistake and Carol has to stay with Joe?' she continued. 'They've probably got hold of all my medical notes from the doctor. They'll know I couldn't cope after Joanna's death, and after Jackie's birth.' Her lips trembled. Mental illness was a black mark against her and it was pointless getting hysterical. It would only make matters worse. She needed to remain calm, and even though she was breaking up inside, she would fight tooth and nail to prove they'd got it all wrong.

Mam stroked Dora's arm gently. 'By rights this place is Joe's, with it being a tied house. Why don't you and Jackie come back to live with us for a while? Then Joe can come here with Carol, and maybe

Dolly can look after her again while he works. She'll be okay with Dolly and things that are familiar. It'll be less unsettling for her.'

Dora chewed her lip. What her mam said made sense. 'Well, if you're sure it's okay. Maybe you and Frank can visit at the weekend and bring Jackie with you. It's important that Carol still sees you two as often as possible.'

'I think that's a good plan, Sis,' Frank said. 'And with a bit of luck the authorities will let you have contact with Carol again when they see that you're doing well in looking after Jackie, and letting Joe get on with looking after Carol and causing him no problems.'

Mam smiled her approval as Frank continued. 'I'll go and stay with a mate in the city and you and Jackie can have my room. It'll give you some breathing space and maybe you and Joe can work something out between you in time, if the powers that be say it's okay.'

Dora nodded slowly; it seemed the best plan and she didn't really have a choice. She looked around and shrugged. 'This house holds no charms for me anyway. I don't think I'll ever feel happy here again. There's too much sadness and bad luck. At least at your place, Mam, Jackie and me will have a roof over our heads. But it will only be temporary; something will turn up for me. I have to believe that I can stand on my own two feet.'

Chapter Three

Dora braced herself as Dolly pursed her lips together. They were kneeling on the bedroom floor, folding clothes and placing them into a suitcase. Dolly was like a dog with a bone at the moment over who was to blame for Carol being removed from Dora's care. Although she appreciated her friend's help, she could have done without the running commentary. She jumped to her feet. 'I'll make us a quick cuppa,' she said, dashing out of the room. If she heard Ivy Bennett's flipping name mentioned one more time she'd scream.

No doubt by now it would be all round the ROF that Joe had been given custody of his eldest daughter and there would be wild guesses as to why. Joe had taken both girls out for the day while Dora got on with her packing. He'd left Carol with Don's wife while he came to pick Jackie up. Dora had been hoping Carol would be in the car with him, but Joe appeared to be playing things by the book as he'd been instructed to. He didn't tell her where he was taking them and she wondered if they'd meet up with Ivy at Sefton Park or somewhere. Joe would be coming back to live at the ROF prefab tomorrow, Sunday.

Dora filled the kettle, her mind working overtime, wondering if there really *was* anything going on with Joe and Ivy. He'd told her they were just friends now and that was all, but she'd no doubts that Ivy would take advantage of the situation when Joe moved back. She'd worm her way back into his life by using Carol, Dora thought as she spooned tea leaves into the tea pot; no doubt she'd offer to babysit while he played with his band at the weekend. It was a convenient situation for Ivy and half of Dora believed that she was the culprit who'd reported her, but the other half couldn't imagine that the woman would do something like that, knowing it would hurt Joe as well as Dora to have his daughters split up. After all, if Ivy wanted to spend time with Joe he was a free man now. There was nothing standing in their way. It really didn't make sense. The kettle boiled and she brewed the tea, her mind still turning things over.

When she'd gone into labour with the twins she'd rung the factory and given Ivy the message to pass to Joe. But Ivy hadn't told Joe and he hadn't arrived home until much later. Not that it would have made any difference – baby Joanna would still have died that night. It wasn't anyone's fault, the doctor at the hospital had told her and Joe. But Dora couldn't help but resent Ivy for it, knowing she'd had designs on Joe from the beginning. And to think that now Ivy's maliciousness could be behind her losing Carol too was beyond belief. At the moment Dora felt nothing but hatred towards the woman for taking her husband away, ripping her heart out and destroying her family.

Back in the bedroom she handed Dolly a mug and perched herself on the edge of the bed.

'So, will you look for a place of your own eventually?' Dolly asked, wrapping her hands around the mug as though she were cold. 'I mean, there's not much doing in Knowsley, they're mainly private houses or tied to the hall with jobs.'

Dora shrugged. 'I really don't know. It's not fair on our Frank to take his room for too long. It might make more sense to move a bit closer to the city centre to try and get more sewing work in. I need to be where there are more people who want tailor-made clothes. I'll have to see how it goes and what I can afford, but I can't think that far ahead at the moment.'

'Well, they're building them new council estates to replace the slums. You might be in with a chance if you got something in a clearance area and then put your name on the list for a new flat or summat.' Dolly took a slurp of tea and wiped her mouth on the back of her hand.

Dora shuddered inwardly at the thought of living in a slum clearance area. That wasn't really in her plans. 'It's not done my friends Sadie and Stan much good living down near the docks,' she said. 'They've four kids now and they *still* haven't been rehoused.' Sadie, who had grown up in the same village as Dora, had been waiting patiently for ages, and her eldest child was two years older than Carol. Still, last time Dora had spoken to her there'd been hope that they'd be offered a house on the new estate at Allerton once the properties were finished.

Dora put her mug down and finished packing the case. 'I think that's it, Dolly. Just Jackie's toys to put in a bag and we're done. Joe will be back soon so I'd better start getting tea ready. Thanks for helping.'

Dolly got to her feet. 'I'll need a couple of new summer frocks for my holidays soon. Eric's booked us a week at Butlin's in Pwllheli. I'll buy some material and get him to bring me up to your mam's in a week or two for a measuring session, if that's okay.' She gave Dora a hug and made her way to the front door. 'Let me know if you need anything, gel. I'll miss you.'

'I'll miss you too,' Dora said, her eyes filling as she returned the hug. 'Thanks for all you've done in helping me with the girls. I know Joe will be glad you're nearby. I think he'll struggle on his own with Carol. She's not the easiest child to pacify when she's having one of her tantrums.'

'Carol will be fine with me, don't you worry about her. I'll keep you informed of how she's doing and I'm sure in time you'll get her back; once that bloody Ivy tells the truth. She's a nasty piece of work and she needs locking up.'

'We don't know for sure that it *was* Ivy,' Dora said, resisting the urge to agree with Dolly. 'According to Joe, she was very shocked when he told her about it and asked her if she knew anything, and seemed upset that he thought she could do something like that…'

'Huh, she's a good actress, that one. Look how she was over the message she never passed on when you was in labour. We all know it was her, no matter how much she denies it. Anyway, I've got her measure. She'll get away with nothing while I'm keeping an eye on her.'

'As soon as I've got Jackie settled in at Mam's I'm determined to pay the welfare department and Mr Oliver a visit,' Dora said. 'I need to know why my daughter was taken away. And I won't stop mithering them until I get some answers.'

'Shall we have an ice-cream?' Joe suggested as his daughters jumped around with excitement near their favourite Peter Pan statue in Sefton Park.

'Yes, please, Daddy,' Carol yelled. 'And can Roly share mine?' She giggled as Ivy's landlord's chubby little corgi dog circled around her legs, tripping her up so that she landed on top of him.

Roly yelped and Joe yanked Carol to her feet. 'Stop being so giddy. You'll end up hurting poor old Roly if you're not careful.'

Ivy smiled and picked the little dog up, giving him a cuddle. 'I've enjoyed myself this afternoon, Joe. Thank you for asking me to join you. And Roly's *definitely* had a good time.'

'It's our pleasure, isn't it, girls? To have Ivy and Roly with us, I mean.' He was grateful for their company; Roly diverted Carol's attention away from asking him why she couldn't live with Mammy and Jackie now. He'd tried to explain, but it hadn't been easy for a five-year-old to understand. Carol thought it was because she'd been a naughty girl and Mammy didn't want her any more, but he'd done his best to reassure her that it wasn't anything she'd done.

When he'd gone to work and told Ivy what had happened and asked if she knew anything about it, she'd been genuinely shocked and upset, which had immediately put any suspicions he had to bed. She tried to help him, making suggestions as to what he should do and who he should speak to, but wherever he turned, the response was always the same. Dora was to have no further contact with Carol until the authorities said she could. Otherwise, Carol would be taken into care. He felt as though he was banging his head against a brick wall. All they could do was obey the rules, sit it out and see how things progressed.

Tomorrow he was moving back into the prefab with Carol. He'd manage, no doubt. It wasn't ideal, but he'd have to make the best of a bad job. He'd give his right arm to be back with his wife, making their marriage work again. He still loved her. But Dora was adamant that it was too late and there was no going back. He still hadn't set things in motion for a divorce in the hopes that Dora would change her mind given time.

If Ivy hadn't been there to prop him up, he'd have been lost. There was no one else he could talk to. His work mates wouldn't understand. He was lonely and he missed Dora, but he couldn't see a way of winning her back. Dolly was good in that she'd help him out with Carol while he worked, but he knew she blamed him for the breakdown of his marriage. He valued Ivy's friendship and her offer to help in taking care of Carol while he played in his band at the weekend, but she seemed to need him more than he needed her. He regretted the one night they'd spent together when Dora was ill, and was careful to keep the relationship light-hearted rather than loving. But he had needs and so did Ivy. How much longer they could go on like they were before she'd expect more, he didn't know.

As they queued for ice-creams Joe watched Ivy interacting with Carol and Jackie. The girls seemed to like her a lot and she was good with them. She made few demands but was always eager to let him know, after she'd looked after Carol or accompanied him to a dance at the weekend, that she more than cared for him. Ivy saw him looking and moved over to take his arm. He stepped back and bent to talk to his daughters. The last thing he wanted was to look like a couple, and to give Ivy false hope of a future. All they could do was see what the next few months, or even the next few years, brought.

Chapter Four

Knowsley, June 1953

Dora popped her head around the sitting room door. Frank was on his knees in the corner near the window, fiddling with the television set he'd brought home yesterday. The picture was jumping up and down as he twiddled the knobs and scratched his head.

'Still not got it working?' she asked, handing him a mug of tea and staring at the test card on the screen as it slipped downwards. The BBC had reported on last night's news that the test card would be shown from nine thirty today to give viewers a chance to adjust their sets in readiness for the coronation of Queen Elizabeth II. No one else in the row of Sugar Lane cottages had a television, so their home would be packed to the rafters with neighbours later. Mam was busy in the kitchen making sandwiches and sausage rolls for her visitors. Both she and Dora had been up for hours preparing their contributions towards this afternoon's street party. Iced fairy cakes, red jelly and dishes of pink blancmange were on the table waiting to be taken across to the village hall where the party was being held in the grounds, rather than on the lane itself. The sense of excitement in the village at having something nice to celebrate after the death of King George VI in February last year was overwhelming.

The villagers were also still recovering from a murder at nearby Knowsley Hall last October; a young employee had shot Lady

Derby and four members of her staff. Two of the injured staff members had died and were buried in adjoining graves close to Joanie. The killer had been arrested and declared insane. He was now locked away for life in Broadmoor prison. It had taken a while for everyone to feel safe in their own homes again, but life was moving on and it was time to put the past behind them and look forward to a better future.

Dora's own future remained a bit up in the air. She and Jackie were still under Mam's roof and she was no closer to getting Carol back than she had been a year ago, despite all her efforts. She knew it was about time she made a serious start on trying to find them a place of their own. Space was limited in the tiny Sugar Lane cottage and she'd never be able to expand her dressmaking business until she made a move. A house with two bedrooms was a must if she were ever to regain custody of Carol. She was looking forward to spending time with both her girls at the party later; the first six months after Carol had been taken away, when she hadn't been able to see her at all, had been agony.

'It's fine for a few minutes,' Frank said, breaking her thoughts. He stood back from the television set, scratching his head. 'Then the picture starts slipping, like it's doing now.' He thumped the top of the wooden cabinet with his fist, to no avail. 'I've got to get it right for later or Mam'll go mad. She's invited half the village round to watch. Perhaps when the valves have warmed up a bit more it might settle. It would be better with the aerial on the roof but she won't have it in case it brings the chimney down.' He shook his head in despair.

The aerial Frank had got from Epstein's shop in the city, along with the television set, was an H-shaped metal contraption attached to a piece of wood that could be fastened to the chimney, guaranteeing, according to Mr Epstein, a perfect picture. There was no way it would bring the chimney down if it was fixed up properly, but Mam had said no as it wasn't their cottage to start messing with, and they were lucky to still be living in it, considering it had come with their late dad's gardening job, and she was taking no chances. So for now the aerial was propped against the wall under the window in the hope that might do the trick.

Dora lifted the aerial and propped it on the windowsill and immediately the picture stopped slipping. Frank let out a yell and she hurried back into the kitchen and took off her frilly apron, grinning to herself. She smoothed the skirt of her pale blue cotton dress down and flicked her long hair back over her shoulders. 'I'm going to start taking some of the food across to the hall,' she announced, picking up the two dishes of blancmange.

'What was our Frank yelling for just then?' Mam asked. 'Has he fixed the picture?'

'No, but I did.'

Mam frowned. 'How come *you* knew what to do when *he's* been messing around for flippin' ages?'

'Because I'm smarter than he is,' Dora teased as her brother popped his head around the kitchen door, a hopeful expression on his face. 'Looks like he's after a sausage roll. See you in a few minutes.'

Dora smiled as she walked down the lane. Everyone had really made an effort to decorate their homes with colourful bunting and Union Jacks. The outside of the village hall was decked out with them too, and banners decorated the trees and lampposts. It all looked colourful and added a bit of cheer to the village.

As Dora came out of the hall she passed a tall woman emerging from the nearby graveyard. The woman wore a long and shabby black coat; a black lacy scarf pulled over her head almost covered her face. Her shoulders were hunched and her feet were encased in shoes that were several sizes too big and flopped as she walked. Dora smiled and said 'Good morning' but the woman ignored her and shuffled past, keeping her head down. Dora shrugged and carried on her way home. She didn't recognise the woman. Maybe she was in mourning. Dora knew all about mourning and how it could make a person withdraw into themselves. It was time *she* visited the graveyard too; Dad, Joanna and Joanie would be in need of fresh flowers. So many loved ones lost, and in so short a space of time. Although the pain was easier to live with these days, it never went away.

When she arrived back at the cottage she dashed indoors, where her brother was arranging seating in the sitting room under Mam's instructions. Frank had taken Jackie to the prefab earlier to spend the morning with Joe and Carol, and he'd come back with the message that Joe would be arriving for the street party later with both girls.

'What time did Joe say he was coming?' she asked, breathless from rushing.

Frank shrugged. 'He didn't say a time. Just that he'd bring them over straight after their own street party.'

Dora nodded. Her palms felt damp and her stomach felt fluttery with excitement at the thought of seeing Carol again, not to mention Joe. She missed them both so much. In spite of her constant calls, letters and visits to the welfare department asking for a reconsideration of their decision, there had been little change in the situation. She'd never got to the bottom of why it was just Carol they'd removed either; no one would tell her. The six months she'd spent apart from her daughter with no contact had been heartbreaking and she'd relied on her mam and Frank visiting, taking photographs and keeping her up to date. Hearing their news when they arrived home with a crying Jackie had always been upsetting; Jackie asking why Carol stayed with Daddy and she couldn't.

Six months ago the authorities had started allowing Dora weekly meetings under Joe's supervision. Carol had been shy on the first visit and they'd taken the girls to Sefton Park and done all the nice things Dora knew they'd enjoyed before her daughter had been snatched away. She was careful to take things at Carol's pace and not push her too much. Dora remembered the look on her daughter's face when she'd produced a dolly from her bag with a dress that matched the one Carol was wearing, which Dora had made her for Christmas. She'd clapped her hands with excitement. 'Is that for me, Mammy? Her dress is like mine,' were the first words she'd heard Carol say for ages. She treasured that memory.

Although Jackie had seen her sister each Saturday since they were separated, they had grown apart. Dora just hoped that as time went on a bond would grow between them again. It broke her heart at first when she and Joe took the girls out and her daughter pushed her away and asked to go back home to Aunty Dolly, but she tried not to let it show. It would take time for them all.

As promised, Dolly had kept Dora informed with the goings-on at the Belle Vale prefab and, surprisingly, Joe hadn't moved Ivy in with him. Dolly said Ivy babysat on Saturday nights while Joe played in the band but she never stayed over. She always left in a taxi shortly after Joe arrived home. Dora felt pleased about that, but wasn't sure why. She knew that if she gave him the least bit of encouragement, Joe would come back to her, but she also knew that she couldn't forgive him for what had happened, and it would never work. She could never trust him again.

Soon the neighbours, many of whom had never seen a television set before, began piling into the small sitting room and Mam took orders for tea and squash. Dora kept the kettle on the boil and the tea pot full. Frank handed plates of food around and conversation flowed as everyone found a space to sit, the younger ones on the floor. Thankfully the television picture behaved itself as orchestral music filled cavernous Westminster Abbey while the dignitaries filed in and took their places. The party in the small sitting room got under way as a neighbour dropped in with two bottles of sweet sherry he'd been saving to toast the occasion. There was a mad dash to various houses to collect a few glasses as Dora's mam only had half a dozen, not nearly enough to go around. When Princess Elizabeth arrived at the abbey, Dora gasped as she caught sight of the stunning gown that had taken eight months to research, design and create.

She'd devoured every magazine article she could find as details of the dress had emerged. Designed by royal dressmaker, Norman Hartnell, the fabric was reported to be rich ivory satin embellished with silver and gold threads and precious stones. It was hard to tell from the tiny television screen, but Dora had read that emblems representing Scotland, Wales and Canada, amongst others, had been hand-embroidered on the panels of the skirt. She'd have to wait until the first photographs emerged to see the full colour and beauty of the low-necked gown, and the crimson, ermine-trimmed velvet mantle that was attached to the shoulders.

As the ceremony began, glasses were filled and raised, food consumed and tears shed as the young Elizabeth was crowned with accompanying fanfare. As 'God Save the Queen' blasted from the tiny speaker on the front of the television cabinet the whole room rose and joined in singing the national anthem with its new title. Dora swallowed the lump in her throat and sang along with their visitors. She felt quite moved. Elizabeth was the same age as she was and her children were only tiny; Charles not yet five and Anne almost three. Being queen was an enormous task to take on, and it wasn't one Dora envied. She hoped the young royal couple would still find time for each other and their children. The ceremony finished with Elgar's 'Pomp and Circumstance March' – just as the picture on the screen began its ritual jumping up and down.

Frank got up from the floor and switched the set off. 'Well, that was grand. I think we should make our way over to the village hall for the party. I believe there's more sherry and some ale just waiting to be supped.'

Mam and Dora cleared the empty plates and glasses and washed up before following the others, carrying the rest of the party food with them.

'Does Joe know to bring the kiddies straight to the hall?' Mam asked as Dora locked the front door and slipped the key into her dress pocket.

They normally didn't bother locking doors, but one or two neighbours had mentioned they'd noticed a few things missing recently. Nothing of value, mainly food taken from kitchen tables where it had been left to cool, and the odd pint of milk, so Dora was taking no chances.

'Yes, Frank told him. Dolly has organised a street party for the prefabs on the Belle Vale estate so they're coming here after that,' she replied as they strolled down the lane. 'Oh, look at that big cloud, I hope it doesn't rain. They forecast it, but said mainly down south.'

'We'll have to whizz everything inside if it does,' Mam said, squinting up at the cloudy sky. 'It'll soon blow over, hopefully. Be nice to see our Carol again.'

Dora nodded and stopped as she caught sight of the woman in black from that morning. She was walking ahead of them, her head down.

'Who's that woman, Mam? I saw her hurrying out of the church grounds this morning when I took the blancmanges across to the hall.'

Mam shook her head. 'I've no idea, love. Can't say as I recognise her from the back. She looks poor though, with her shoes flip-flopping off her feet like that.'

The woman shuffled past the entrance to the village hall and didn't look round, keeping her head down.

'Well, she's obviously not coming to the party – she's walked right past,' Dora said. 'Oh look, there's Sadie and Stan and the kids.

They must have come up to see her mam.' Dora yoo-hooed her friend Sadie, who turned and waved, a delighted smile on her round face. 'I've not seen her for ages; it'll be good to have a catch-up.'

They caught up with the couple and Dora hugged Sadie. 'How are you? It's been a while.'

'I'm okay, thanks,' Sadie said. 'It's good to see you. Where are the girls?'

'Joe's got them. He's bringing them over later.'

'Oh, lucky you. Stan, you see to our lot while I go inside and help Dora and her mam with the food,' Sadie ordered.

'It's okay, Sadie, we can manage,' Dora said. 'You've got your hands full.'

But Sadie was adamant. 'And that's precisely why it'll be nice to take a break, buttering bread and making sarnies,' she muttered, following them inside. 'I need a bit of peace. Little 'un was up all night. She's cutting her back teeth. I'm that tired, I could sleep on a washing line.'

Dora laughed. Sadie and Stan had four under-sevens and, by the looks of things, were well on the way to producing number five. 'Are you...?' She nodded in the direction of Sadie's swollen stomach.

Sadie puffed out her cheeks. 'For my sins. It's the last one, and this time I mean it. Doctor thinks I should get sterilised afterwards. I can't take any more. I'm so worn out. I mean, look at you, all fresh and slim as a rake and I look old enough to be your mam. I wish we'd have stopped at two, like you.'

Dora chewed her lip and looked away.

Sadie's hand flew to her mouth, her cheeks flushing bright pink. 'Oh my God, Dora, I'm so sorry. I forget at times that Carol was a twin, and you having to deal with all your troubles. Me and my big mouth.'

'It's okay, Sadie, really. Please don't upset yourself. Come on, let's get cracking and put the kettles on.'

Sadie waddled across to the sink and filled the kettles while Dora got the large tea pots out of the cupboard.

'I was going to write to you later this week if I didn't see you today,' Sadie said, once the kettles were on the gas hob. She wafted a hand in front of her warm face and looped her dark hair behind her ears. 'My next-door-but-one neighbour, Elsie, is moving in a couple of weeks. The council have offered her a new ground-floor flat. She can't manage the stairs any more, her knees have gone. Anyway, her house is up for grabs until the full clearance happens in our area. As fast as people are being rehoused the landlords put somebody else in the old properties.'

Dora frowned. 'How come they haven't offered you and Stan anything yet?'

'Ah well,' Sadie began. 'With this new one on the way they now say we'll have to wait for a four-bedder, but they're few and far between. Fella from the housing said we'd move up the list as soon as I drop this baby. Anyway, what do you reckon? I can ask the landlord to hold it for you if you're interested. Elsie keeps it spotless. It's a nice little house.'

Dora nodded slowly. 'Tell you what, I'll have a good think about it and discuss it with Mam and Frank. And I'll have to talk with Joe, of course, in case I get Carol back eventually. Don't say anything to them just yet, but it sounds perfect and just what I need.'

Sadie smiled. 'I won't. It'd be great having you as a neighbour and Carol could go to school with my Philip and Heidi. You'd be in with a good chance of a nice new place eventually, Dora. It's well worth thinking about.'

'And I definitely will,' Dora promised, feeling a little thrill of excitement at the thought of having her own home again.

Chapter Five

Joe and the girls arrived and Jackie ran to Dora for a cuddle. Carol hung back, her arms around Joe's leg. He tried to loosen her grip, but she clung on until Uncle Frank crept up behind her and made her jump by pulling on her plaits. She squealed and flung herself into his arms. He swung her up onto his shoulders and, grabbing Jackie by the hand, led them towards a long trestle table where Mam was supervising the little ones into place. Frank sat Carol down with Jackie next to her. He gave them plates of sandwiches with the promise of cake, red jelly and pink blancmange to come, and went back to Dora and Joe.

'Thanks, Frank,' Dora said. 'They look happy enough now.'

'Fancy a pale ale?' Frank asked. 'I've got a stash hidden away.'

'Don't suppose you've got any sherry?' Dora asked hopefully.

Frank winked and dashed inside the hall, coming out with three full glasses.

Dora gasped. 'Frank, I'll be flat on my back at this rate. I only wanted a drop.'

'Get it down you, Sis. Not every day we celebrate a new queen on the throne. Start of a fresh era. We can put the war stuff well and truly behind us now. All the scrimping and scraping, and move on. This country's in for big changes. There are better things to come, you mark my words.'

Joe nodded. 'Yep, there are. I'm thinking of applying for a new job soon.' He took a sip of his drink as Dora looked questioningly at him. The breeze blew strands of hair into her eyes and she brushed them away.

'Where?' she asked. 'And how will that affect where you live? The prefab comes with your job.'

'Oh, it won't be for a while, and by then I'm hoping to have enough put away to buy my own little place. I've been saving for a deposit and my mum might help out a bit too if I ask her. The ROF can't keep going much longer. The country doesn't need arms any more. I'm looking at jobs in the motor trade. That's where the money is going to be for the future. The only thing is, I may have to move out of Liverpool.'

Dora felt her jaw drop as he looked away and took another sip of his drink. He had a shifty air about him, as though he were keeping secrets. Was he going to announce that he wanted to marry Ivy? A shiver ran down her spine and she looked at Frank, who raised his eyebrows.

'But what about Carol? I'll never see her if you move away. Who'll look after her? Dolly won't be around. And where will you go anyway?' Dora's questions tumbled over one another.

'Er, I'm not sure yet. There's nothing in the city at the moment, but time will change that. Like I say, cars are going to be big business for the future. Bentley and Rolls-Royce at Crewe are advertising, but I need to get other things into place before I do anything.'

Dora folded her arms. 'What other things?'

Joe looked at Frank. 'Can you give us a few minutes, mate. I'd like to talk to Dora in private.'

'Of course. I'll go and join the kids for jelly.' Frank hurried away, leaving the two of them alone.

'Shall we go inside the hall?' Joe suggested.

'I suppose so, but there'll be women coming in and out to refill the tea pots. We can go and sit at the bottom end on the stage.'

She led the way through the room where they'd held their wedding reception seven years ago; such a happy day with a wonderful future to look forward to. How could something so promising go so wrong? She sat down on the edge of the stage.

Joe sat down beside her. He drew a deep breath and looked at her closely.

'I need to ask you something, Dora. Whatever answer you give me, that's it; I promise never to ask you again.'

Dora felt butterflies in her tummy as she gazed into his eyes. She remembered how he'd made her feel exactly the same in their early courting days.

He took another deep breath and began. 'I'm going to be totally honest with you.' He stopped and cleared his throat, looking embarrassed. 'I still love you, I think you know that. And in spite of everything, I think *you* still have feelings for *me*.'

She chewed her lip. Although they'd agreed to remain fairly friendly and amicable for the girls, this was the last thing she'd been expecting to hear today. He took her hand and laced his fingers through hers. She was tempted to pull away, but resisted as he started speaking again. 'Us being apart is just stupid. The kids need us, this to-ing and fro-ing with Carol isn't good for her. She's getting really naughty in school now and I've had complaints from her teacher recently about her not paying attention and being lippy when spoken to. She needs stability and I can't do that on my own. If we were back together I'm sure the welfare would raise the ban on her being with you full-time. You can't keep living with your mam, Dora, there isn't enough room. Jackie needs her own bed now, and not sharing with you. And it's not fair on Frank, sleeping on the sofa or at his mates'. It's not right for any of us. Why don't you come home, love, make us a family again?'

Dora swallowed the lump in her throat. She was tempted, so tempted. No more struggling and both her daughters under one roof, back in her own little house. They could move on from Joe's infidelity. But when she looked up and saw the hunger in his eyes, she knew she couldn't risk it. Another pregnancy would finish her off.

The doctor had warned of the likelihood of falling into depression again after giving birth, even of the risk of suicide and the possibility of her harming any further babies. There was no guarantee that she wouldn't fall pregnant again, no matter what they did to try to prevent it. Sterilisation was the only solution and she'd already turned that idea down. She was glad she had as well, because she'd recently read a magazine article about a woman who'd had her womb removed to prevent further pregnancies after a sterilisation operation failed and she'd almost lost her life giving birth.

Dora couldn't take any chances; she had to let him go. They'd never be able to live together like a proper man and wife, and he might stray again, if not with Ivy then another woman. She couldn't expect him to live like a monk for ever. He was too young for that and he was an attractive man. It wasn't fair. But the choice had to be hers and although it would further break her heart she had to tell him.

She pulled her hand away from his. 'I'm sorry, Joe. I… I don't love you enough to give us another try,' she lied as his hazel eyes clouded with hurt. 'We need to start getting that divorce sorted as soon as possible. We've been apart for ages now so it shouldn't take too long. You should move on and start afresh.'

'But, Dora, I love *you*; I don't want to start afresh. Surely you can see how much better it will be for the girls *and* for us. If I change jobs, Carol will have to go to strangers after school and in the holidays. She's struggling as it is. And there's no way you'll get her back while you're at your mam's. There's no spare bedroom for starters. The welfare takes all that into account, you know. You're being selfish. You should think about the kids. Okay, you say you don't love me enough. I don't believe you, but even if it's true I don't want to be apart from you. I'm happy enough to put up with it if you'll come back to me.'

Dora chewed her lip. '*I'm* not the selfish one, Joe. You ruined it for us when you slept with Ivy. I can't trust you. Don't you see that?

I'm sorry, but I just can't do it. I'm probably going to be leaving Mam's place in a couple of weeks anyway. I'll write to the welfare people and let them know as soon as I've got my own house, with two bedrooms. I'm going to carry on fighting tooth and nail to get custody of Carol again, Joe. And I'm determined to get to the bottom of who reported me. If I find out it *was* that bloody Ivy, I'll kill her.' She turned and stormed out of the hall, leaving the two ladies who were filling tea pots staring after her and shaking their heads at Joe, who was following on her heels.

He grabbed her arm and pulled her round to face him. 'What was all that about?' he demanded. 'It wasn't Ivy who reported you. I can assure you of that. And what do you mean about a house? Where is it? How come you haven't told me until now?'

Dora pulled away from him and pointed in Sadie's direction. 'It's Sadie's neighbour's house. She's just told me about it. The neighbour's moving out and all being well, I'm going to take over the tenancy. I'll be moving in with Jackie as soon as I can and then she and Carol can share a room when I get her back.'

Joe frowned. 'You can't take the kids to live down there. It's like a bombsite still. Half the houses are falling down. It's bloody dangerous, Dora, and there's rats as big as dogs running around.'

Dora shuddered inwardly at the thought of rats of any size, but stubbornly stood her ground. 'It's only temporary. We'll get rehoused quite quickly, I'm sure,' she said, with more confidence than she was feeling. 'And hopefully I'll get some work, living in the city. More than round here anyway. I'll try a few of the drapers' shops to see if there's any out-work available.'

Joe shook his head wearily and followed her back to the girls, dancing on the lawn with a crowd of other children to the Boys' Brigade band, who were playing a rendition of 'The Sailor's Hornpipe'. 'Look, can we just agree to be friends, for their sake?'

She nodded, hating arguing with him in full view of all their neighbours. 'Of course.' She lowered her voice. 'Look, I'm sorry

I can't be more than that to you, Joe. Let's just try and enjoy the rest of the day with the kids.'

Jackie was dancing in rhythm to the happy tune while Carol tried her best, but she wasn't a natural. Frank waved Dora and Joe across to where he was standing.

'Our Jackie's good, you know,' he said proudly, watching his little niece weave and swirl in time to the music, her long blonde hair, escaped from its restraining ribbon, flowing freely on her shoulders. 'I'd like to pay for her to have dancing lessons, Sis, if that's all right with you two.'

Dora beamed. 'It's more than all right. She'll love it. She's always dancing and singing when the wireless is on. Thank you.' She gave her brother a hug and Joe shook his hand.

'No point wasting money on our Carol, she's got two left feet,' Joe joked.

Frank nodded. 'True, but we'll find something she'll enjoy. Maybe swimming lessons. See if you can get Jackie a place at Marjorie Barker's dancing school, Sis.'

'I will. I'll do it next week.' Dora was conscious of Mam waving her arms and trying to catch her attention. 'Mam wants me. Won't be a minute,' she said to Joe. 'The Punch and Judy show will be starting soon, so take them over to that if I'm not back.' She walked over to where Mam was helping to clear the tables. 'What's up?'

'That woman in the long black coat's over there,' Mam said, pointing towards the gate. 'She's just helped herself to all the leftovers from the tables and rammed them into her pockets, crusts and all. Poor bugger must be starving. I've asked around but no one knows who she is or where she's come from. I'm just wondering if I should offer her a brew. She's got a bit of an unwashed pong when you stand downwind of her though.'

'Mam!' Dora stifled a giggle. Her mam never minced words. She always spoke as she found, sometimes embarrassingly so. People in the village were used to Mary Evans and her outspoken manner, but heaven help a stranger who crossed her.

'Well, she could do with a good wash if you ask me. Anyway, I'll try and find out a bit about her if I can. Very strange how she's just appeared from nowhere though.'

Dora nodded. 'I'll go and ask her if she'd like a cuppa.' She made her way towards the woman, who stared at her and then hurried out through the gate and onto the lane without looking back. Dora shrugged in Mam's direction and made her way back to Joe and the girls. The woman's face didn't look familiar and her eyes looked blank, as though she wasn't quite all there.

Ivy Bennett walked slowly down the road, Roly on her heels and her thoughts in a jumble. She wondered how Joe was getting on at the Knowsley village street party. She'd avoided the party on the avenue where she lived – too many noisy kids for her liking – although she'd watched the coronation ceremony on her landlord's telly with him and his elderly wife. Would Joe be playing happy families now with Dora and their daughters? The thought sickened her and no matter how hard she tried to push it away, it wouldn't go.

Joe and Dora had been living apart for ages now and although they showed no signs of getting back together, every time he told Ivy they were having a family weekend she was sure it wouldn't be too long before they'd be announcing their reconciliation. Keeping a low but supportive profile wasn't really working in her favour. She felt no further forward than she had done a few years ago when they'd spent their one and only night together. She needed a plan of action to force his hand, but at the moment she had no idea what that could be.

Chapter Six

Dora linked her hands around her knees and sighed. She and Mam were sitting on the sofa, mulling over the day's events, which had been a great success with the rain holding off right until the end. Frank had gone down to the docks to celebrate with some mates and he said he'd stay over to save him having to get up too early for work. Joe and a very tired Carol had gone back to Kirkby and Jackie was asleep upstairs after crying for her sister to stay. Dora choked on her own tears as she pacified her youngest with the promise that one day Carol would be able to sleep over. They'd just watched the news on the television, reliving the morning's ceremony with Dora trying again to get as close a look as possible at the dress on the tiny screen.

'Mam,' Dora began. 'Sadie told me about a little house near her and Stan's place that's coming up to rent soon…'

'What, down near Scottie Road?' Mam shook her head. 'Oh, I don't know, chuck. You'd need to grow a thick skin down there with some of them women. Tough as old boots, a lot of 'em.'

Dora smiled. 'Sadie's not tough and *she's* survived. Anyway, she says I'd probably get rehoused into something brand new eventually. I need to let her know if I'm interested as soon as I can though or it'll go to someone else. It's time I got out of your hair. We've been here long enough.'

'Well, it's up to you, love. I suppose you can give it a try. You'll have to keep a close eye on our Jackie, though. She'll be like a fish out of water.'

'She got on well with Sadie's lot today. I'm sure she'll be fine. And if I have my own place and show that I can manage all right I might be able to get Carol back eventually.'

'Aye, if Joe'll let her go.' Mam pursed her lips. She fiddled with the hairnet that was keeping her curlers in place. 'I think you'll have a job on your hands there, my love. She's still no nearer getting close to you than she was last year. She's spent so much time being looked after by Joe in her young life it's not surprising. If you want my honest opinion, and I'll give it to you anyway, you'll have your hands full with Jackie and work, and living on your own. Carol's best left with Joe where she's settled, and maybe the authorities will let her have a few weekends with you in time.'

'We'll see, but I have to fight to get my daughter back. It's unfair that she was taken away in the first place.' Dora chewed her lip before continuing. 'Joe asked me to take him back earlier.'

Mam sighed. 'It'd be the best thing all round if you got back together. You'd have your nice home again and the kids would soon get used to it. And you'd only need to work when you wanted to, not because you have to. Personally, I think you're making a big mistake in not having him back, my girl. Marriage is supposed to be for life. Couples get over things given time. Joe's always been sorry for what he did with Ivy. You need to think carefully about giving him another chance. Somebody else will snap him up soon and then that'll be it and you'll be sorry.'

Dora raised an eyebrow. 'Well I've given him my answer, and I'm not going back on it. It's not fair on him or me.' She got to her feet. There was no point in arguing. Mam would never understand. She was of the *you make your bed and you lie in it* generation. 'I'll go and make us some Horlicks.'

In the kitchen Dora waited for the milk to boil and considered her options, of which there were few. She was certain she'd made the right choice. If she could manage to keep her head above water she'd be fine. Living alone wasn't something she was looking forward to, especially in a tough area. Okay, she'd had a few months alone at the prefab after Joe left, but she'd always felt safe and secure there *and* she'd had both girls with her. She'd just have to get her head around things and toughen up a bit more. It was *her* life and she was determined to make something of it. She'd either sink or swim trying. Anyway, she'd go and take a look around the house as soon as possible before she talked herself out of the idea.

Dora hoisted her bag up onto her shoulder and crossed over Scotland Road. She looked at the piece of paper with the address she'd written down. She'd left Jackie with Mam while she came to look around the house that Sadie's elderly neighbour had recently vacated. Turn right as you get off the tram, Sadie had told her, go past St Anthony's church and then turn into Wright Street. Sadie's house was at the bottom end of the terrace. She looked around as she hurried along the cobbled street and her spirits soared a little. The area didn't look *too* bad. Not a patch on Knowsley village. It was fairly quiet as the local kids were at school. No doubt be a lot noisier later. She could hear the seagulls in the distance and a couple flew overhead, screeching, on their way to the nearby River Mersey.

A lot of houses had been damaged in the Blitz and had been cleared, leaving grassed-over spaces in-between, although there were still a few standing that were boarded up. Most of the windows of the occupied houses looked decent enough, with net curtains to deter prying eyes. Some of the nets were brighter than others. Mam always said you could tell a woman's standard of housekeeping by whether she dolly-blued her nets regularly and kept her front steps and windowsills donkey-stoned. Dora grinned to herself. Mam would have a field day when she visited, judging who best to get pally with and who to leave well alone.

She knocked on the door and stood back. The dark green paintwork was peeling slightly, but the brass knocker and letterbox gleamed and the spotless step would pass Mam's muster any day. A child shouted 'Mammy' and then the door creaked open and Sadie, looking slightly harassed, greeted her and welcomed her inside. The little boy who had shouted smiled shyly and shot off upstairs.

'Peter, don't get all your soldiers out, I've just tidied them away,' Sadie yelled up the stairs. 'Please excuse the mess,' she apologised as Dora followed her down the narrow hallway and into the back room. 'Pull one of the dining chairs out and I'll put the kettle on. I've some Camp coffee in if you prefer it to tea.'

'Tea's fine,' Dora said, smiling at the little dark-haired girl sitting on a rag rug in front of the fireplace. All Sadie's kids had her dark hair and brown eyes. There was no mess evident at all. The room was spotless; and although the furniture showed signs of wear it was well-polished and cared for. Sadie seemed to manage very well with four children, despite being heavily pregnant again. It suited her and she always looked content. 'Hello Belinda.' The child beamed and crawled over to Dora. She pulled herself up by the chair leg and held out a well-chewed soggy crust. Dora took it and put it on the table as Sadie came in with two steaming mugs. She set them down and dashed back into the kitchen, reappearing with a packet of lemon puffs. Belinda pointed and smiled.

'You can share one with me,' Sadie said, breaking a biscuit in half. 'Help yourself, Dora. Sit back down again, Belinda. Aunty Dora doesn't want your messy paws on her nice clean skirt.' Sadie lifted her daughter and sat her at a distance with her snack.

'I'll pop them both in Vi's next door while I take you to look around the house,' she said. 'Vi's a nice neighbour, another one that lives alone since she was widowed, like Elsie did. Her sons live miles away, one in Southport and the other in Crewe. They don't visit as often as they should, but that's lads for you. My lot are her substitute grandchildren and she's dead good with them. They run to her when I start yelling if they've misbehaved. Your Jackie will love her. She's always reading them stories.' Sadie smiled and took a sip of tea. 'Elsie was lovely too. I'll miss her but it'll be great having you so close by. There's a couple of women across the street that I don't bother with. Gloria and Freda Smyth. Sisters married to brothers, strangely enough. Thick as thieves and hard as nails, they are. Don't do them any favours. If they come knocking to borrow anything say no from the off. And they quite often send one of their kids over. One little lad has big sad eyes and makes you feel sorry for him, but he's a slippery little sod so don't ever let him in your house. He'd rob his own grandmother, that one.'

Dora frowned. 'Thanks for the warning. I'll keep myself to myself until I get the measure of them all.'

'Best way,' Sadie said. 'The landlord dropped the keys in this morning so I can show you around, he apologises that he can't do it himself today, but he's left a rent book for you just in case and a lease to sign if you decide to take it. I told him you're a respectable lady with a little girl and your own business. He said that's the type of tenant he likes. The rent's nineteen and six a week, payable on a Saturday morning. He or his son comes to collect it between ten and eleven. You'll need a bit of money for decorating and some floor coverings because Elsie took her carpet squares with her.'

Dora nodded. 'I've got some put away and our Frank said he'll help me out.'

Sadie finished her tea and swung Belinda up into her arms. 'I'll take her and Peter to Vi's. Won't be a sec.'

The rent was very reasonable for a house with two downstairs rooms as well as a tiny kitchen and two equal-sized bedrooms, Dora thought. It was identical to Sadie's house, with the narrow entrance hall and steep staircase going up between the two rooms. Dora tried not to wrinkle her nose at the stale smell of a closed-up house. Once the windows had been opened for a while and the place aired through it would smell fresher. The walls needed a coat of distemper and the scuffed woodwork would need painting too. But Dora could see beyond that and imagine herself and Jackie living here, certainly for the foreseeable future. The cream and brown tiled fireplace in the front room was modern with no evident chips; and in the back room a black-leaded range, like Mam's at Sugar Lane that she baked her bread in, would heat the room as well as the one above. She'd soon have it all looking nice. Joe could bring Carol here for her Saturday visits. The kitchen had a white pot sink and wooden drainer set under the frosted glass window and three shelves near the back door. Frank would probably be able to get her a couple of cupboards for pots and pans. Elsie had left a gas cooker that was clean, if not old-fashioned, but if it worked it would do for now and save her having to buy one.

She nodded at Sadie, who'd followed her around while she took everything in. 'I like it. What's the backyard like?'

Sadie rolled her eyes. 'If anything will put you off, this will.' She unlocked the back door and led the way into the communal backyard. The cobbles were free of weeds and a few window boxes with marigolds adorned the donkey-stoned sills. Sheets, towels and nappies hanging on a line blew in the stiff breeze coming up from the Mersey. 'Although we're a short walk from the river here,' Sadie began, 'it's good for drying your washing. Always a breeze in this yard, even on a nice day like today.' She led Dora across the yard to a low outbuilding with a slate roof and four black-painted doors.

'Only four between all the street?' Dora's jaw dropped. Her mam had warned her there'd be shared lavatories.

'I'm afraid so,' Sadie said. 'We all keep them clean and well-bleached though, so you won't catch anything.' She opened the middle door and waved her hand. The white toilet bowl was topped with a wooden seat, faded from regular bleaching, and on the wall, hanging from a nail, sheets of neatly cut newspaper awaited their next recipient. The red quarry-tiled floor looked freshly painted and clean and there was a hint of Dettol in the air. 'Because some of the neighbours have already gone, you'll only be sharing with us and Vi, so that's not *too* bad, is it?'

Dora shook her head. Her parents had always had their own lavatory in the private back garden, and then the prefab she'd lived in with Joe had a proper bathroom, so sharing wasn't something she was used to. It was a wake-up call.

'I was hoping each house would have its own lav, but Mam did warn me I might be sharing.'

'I know. It was a shock to me too when we moved in. But we got used to it pretty quickly. I use a chamber pot for the little ones at night, and we don't use newspaper either. Those squares are Vi's. I buy rolls of Izal cheap from the market. The kids use it for tracing paper as well. But if you *do* buy it, don't leave your rolls in there, or they'll get pinched by them across.'

Dora looked aghast. What was she letting herself in for?

'Come on, I can see you're in shock. Let's go back to mine while you have a think about it,' Sadie said, linking her arm through Dora's. 'It's really not that bad once you get used to it. And think of the future, when we'll have nice new places with indoor lavs and baths and hot running water.'

Back at Sadie's, Dora sat and mulled things over while her friend went next door for Belinda and Peter. She had three choices. Stay with Mam in Knowsley, go back to Joe or move down here and stand on her own two feet. She thought about the house. She and Jackie could live in the back room and she'd make it nice and homely and then keep the front room for best and use it as a sewing room too. There was plenty of space for a table and her sewing machine. She could make it nice so her customers would feel welcome – that's if she could persuade any to come down to this street. Parts of it were kept nice by the residents but other parts left a lot to be desired. Well, she'd work hard and make her little house stand out from the others by getting Frank to give the front door a nice lick of black gloss and maybe even paint the step and sill red, to give them an edge over the donkey-stoned steps. Save her time each week as well, they'd only need a wipe over. Frank could also come straight here from work some nights and maybe sleep over. They'd be company for one another. She knew he got lonely and a bit down at times. He was also reluctant to talk about Joanie unless he was pushed.

By the time Sadie came back she'd made up her mind. 'I'll take it,' she said. 'Give me the lease to sign.'

Chapter Seven

When Dora arrived back at Sugar Lane Mam and Jackie were finishing their tea and Frank had just come in from work.

'How did it go, Sis?' he asked, swilling his face and hands at the kitchen sink.

Dora smiled. 'I'm taking it. It'll do us fine until I get offered a new place. Needs a bit of tidying up, painting and carpets and stuff, but I reckon I'll soon have it looking okay. I've got the keys.' She dangled them in front of him. 'The landlord told Sadie to give them to me if I signed the lease. So there you go. I'm now officially a tenant of Wright Street.'

'Smashing. We'll get stuck in at the weekend. I'll ask a couple of mates from the docks to help with the painting in exchange for a pint or two. I can get my hands on some distemper, and I'll ask around if anyone's got any carpet squares they want rid of. Are there any oilcloth borders around the outer edges of the floors?'

'Yes,' Dora replied. 'All the rooms have them, and they're sort of a brown pattern like the dance floor in the village hall.'

'Parquet-floor style. That'll look nice. I'll try and get carpets that will go with it.'

Mam smiled. 'And I'll treat you to some curtains, chuck. We can perhaps do what we did when you moved into the prefab. Get some good-quality second-hand pairs from Paddy's market that you can alter to fit.'

'Thanks, Mam, that will be lovely. I'm sure we'll get something nice.'

Mam nodded. 'I'm sure we will, and I'll ask around the village to see if anyone is getting rid of any bits of furniture. It's the WI meeting next week – bet they'll all want to help when I tell them.'

'Oh aye.' Frank laughed. 'Give 'em a chance to offload some junk.'

'Cheeky.' Mam swiped at him with a tea towel. 'Right, you two sit yourselves down. It's liver and onions with mash tonight. Your plates are in the oven. Use a cloth to lift them out, Frank,' she warned.

Frank lifted out the plates of food and placed one in front of Dora.

'Get stuck in while it's hot,' Mam ordered. 'Me and Jackie will have a story before she goes to bed while you two have your tea. By the way, make sure you lock that back door if you go out to the carsey I was cleaning my front windows outside this afternoon and when I came back in the door was wide open and two of my loaves had gone.'

As Dora and Frank looked up in surprise, she folded her arms and continued. 'I'll kill the thieving bugger, when I get my hands on them. That's at least half a dozen of us who've had food pinched in the last couple of weeks. I'd report it to the police but they've better things to do than chase after a pie and bread thief. We just need to be more careful and keep a look-out, see if we can't catch them at it.'

By the time Joe brought Carol for her first visit to Wright Street, Dora and Jackie were settled in. As Dora opened the front door to greet them the two identical gossipy sisters from across the road were standing on their adjacent doorsteps, arms folded, bleached blonde hair up in curlers, cigarettes dangling from their red-painted lips. Both stared at Joe, eyeing him up and down and nodding approval. One of them smirked at Dora and yelled, 'Hey, gel, didn't know youse gorra fancy man. Bit of all right 'im, ain't 'e? An' he's gorra nice car too.'

'Bloody hell,' Joe said, blushing and ushering Carol inside. 'You didn't tell me the Ugly Sisters lived opposite.'

'You know them?' Dora asked, shocked.

'I don't know them personally, but I know of them,' Joe said. 'They come to one of the social clubs we do regularly, the Eldonian. Always make a right show of themselves. Loud and drunk for most of the night, cavorting around on the dance floor. The steward's always threatening to chuck them out, but I think they put the fear of God in him, plus their husbands put a lot of money over the bar. Hope they didn't recognise me then.'

'Well we'll just ignore them,' Dora said. 'They're common as muck, as Mam would say. They were the same when Frank and his mates were painting the house. Wolf-whistling, even. Jackie won't be long. Frank's taken her to her dancing lesson. I had to stay behind to finish a dress that someone's picking up tonight and I knew you and Carol would be arriving soon.' She dropped to her knees and held her arms out to Carol, who hung back and looked up at her father.

'Go on, chick, give Mammy a hug. She's been waiting for you,' Joe encouraged and gently pushed her forward.

Carol stepped into Dora's embrace, but Dora felt her stiffen as she hugged her tight, and her heart sank. This wasn't going to be easy; her daughter was clearly uncomfortable with their close contact and there was no point in forcing her to share hugs and kisses. That would come in time, and if there was one thing Dora had plenty of, it was time. She desperately wanted to rebuild a relationship with Carol. She took a deep breath.

'I've made some little cakes, and when Jackie gets back we'll put some icing on them.' She smiled encouragingly. 'And I've got some of those special tiny biscuits that I know you love. Shall we go through to the back room and make Daddy a cup of coffee while we wait for Jackie?'

Carol nodded shyly and followed Dora.

'Have you settled in then?' Joe asked, looking around. 'You've got it nice. Feels quite cosy in here.'

'Yes, sort of,' Dora said. 'I miss having Mam and Frank around, of course, and it's a bit quiet once Jackie's in bed. But I have the wireless for company and my sewing work to keep me occupied.' She was conscious of him looking closely at her, his eyes speaking volumes. 'Have a seat. Won't be a minute.' She dashed into the kitchen and filled the kettle before her pink cheeks gave away her feelings. She missed him more than she'd ever admit to anyone, except for Joanie, her best friend who'd died in the factory fire five years ago. She had Joanie's framed photo on the mantelpiece in her front room and when she worked she often chatted to her as though Joanie was in the room with her. It felt comforting and made her feel less lonely. But this was her life from now on and she'd better get used to it. She made two mugs of Camp coffee and poured a glass of orange juice for Carol. She emptied the bag of iced gems she'd bought especially for today onto a small plate, then loaded up a tray and carried everything through.

Carol smiled happily and rammed several gems into her mouth at once. 'Save some for Jackie,' Joe said, laughing. 'Greedy girl.' They sat in companionable silence for several minutes until he took a deep breath. 'School holidays soon,' he began.

'Yes, I know. Er, Mam and Frank were wondering if they could have Carol occasionally so they can do something nice with both girls. Frank's got time off the second week and he suggested New Brighton and Southport for trips out.'

Joe scratched his chin thoughtfully. 'It would certainly help me if they did. Dolly's away for that second week and I've booked my holidays off at the end of August. So I'm a bit stuck. If your mam and Frank could have her the week Dolly's away it would be great. She could even sleep over. Nobody needs to know. That bloody fella from the welfare doesn't check up. The only thing that bothers me is, whoever reported you is still out there, and until we find out who it is we won't know if they're watching and will tell tales. So just be careful if you stay at your mam's when Carol is sleeping there. Might be best not to. I don't for one minute imagine it's any of your mam's neighbours, but you never know.'

Dora nodded. 'I doubt it is too, but you're right about me not staying at Mam's just in case. I can't take the risk of not being able to see Carol again. Have you any plans for the weeks you're off?'

Joe lit a cigarette and threw the spent match into the grate. He took a long drag and blew a cloud of smoke into the air above his head. 'Sort of, but nothing's set in stone yet.'

'We're going to Morecambe with Aunty Ivy,' Carol, who'd been absorbed in her juice and biscuits, blurted out. 'And we might be taking Roly with us.'

Dora nearly dropped her mug as Joe coughed and spluttered on his ciggie. 'Carol, nothing's been decided yet,' he said.

Dora stared at him, this man who still looked at her with hunger in his eyes. To say she felt shocked was an understatement. 'You're going away with Ivy?' she said. 'After everything you said to me at the street party?'

He raised an eyebrow. 'You gave me your answer that day. And you told me to get on with my life. So that's what I'm trying to do.'

'Yes, but *Ivy*,' she whispered, feeling close to tears.

'We're just good friends, that's all. *I* get lonely too, you know, Dora. So does Ivy. She knows someone with a caravan and we're hoping we can use it for a week. But like I say, nothing's set in stone. Look, maybe we shouldn't be talking about this in front of…' He inclined his head towards Carol, who was now rooting in Jackie's box of puzzles and books.

Dora shook her head. 'Fine. But it's okay for you and Ivy to discuss it in front of *my* daughter, is it?' She got up and took his half-finished coffee and hurried into the kitchen with the tray. As she rinsed the pots at the sink her eyes filled and she blinked the tears away. Why was she crying? This was her choice and Joe was free to do as he pleased. So why the heck did it hurt her so much?

'Dora,' he said softly from the doorway. 'Please don't get upset. Ivy's just a pal. There's nothing between us other than friendship. She knows I still love you.'

'Yet she's happy to go away with you? She's the sort who doesn't care whether a man's married or not as long as she gets her claws in him. She's no better than those two across the road. I'm surprised at *you*, Joe.' She wiped her eyes on her hanky as Joe shrugged and walked back into the sitting room to Carol. Dora followed him.

She composed herself and smiled at Carol, who was staring curiously at her. She took a deep breath and turned back to Joe. 'When Jackie arrives home will you look after the pair of them while I nip to the market for some cotton and stuff, please? I won't be too long and we'll ice the cakes when I get back, Carol.'

'Of course,' Joe said. 'Grab yourself a bit of free time. Then maybe we could take them out for a stroll to the Dock Road and Pier Head and treat ourselves to an ice-cream at Stan's café. We can watch the big ship go out, eh Carol? The *Queen Mary* sails off to America this afternoon. They'd love that, I'll bet.'

Chapter Eight

July 1953

Dora took a pen from her handbag and scribbled down an address on a bit of paper she found in her jacket pocket. Samuel Jacobs Drapery Store on Homer Street was advertising for a seamstress, with hours to suit. The postcard was fastened to the inside glass of the front door, but the shop was currently closed until Monday. She wondered why until she remembered that Saturday was the Jewish Sabbath day and, with a name like Samuel Jacobs, the proprietor was most likely Jewish.

Hours to suit, too. Dora smiled. Jobs like that were few and far between in her line of work. She could still make clothes for her regulars but a bit more money coming in would help until she built up her customer list again. She hurried back through North Hay Market and down Scotland Road. She'd been a bit longer than she'd intended to be, but Joe had told her to take her time. With a bit of luck, Sadie might look after Jackie on Monday morning while she popped back to Jacobs' and made enquiries about the job vacancy. Fingers crossed, if she went early enough she might be first in the queue.

Back at the house Joe was looking perplexed as Carol sat in the armchair, her arms folded and a mutinous expression on her face, while Jackie lay on the rug crying her eyes out.

'What's going on?' Dora asked, dropping her shopping bag on the floor and holding her arms out to her youngest daughter, who jumped up and ran into them, throwing baleful glances at her sister.

Joe held his hands up in a gesture of helplessness. 'I popped outside to the carsey, and came back to find Carol pulling Jackie down onto the rug by her plaits. She's had a smack on the bottom and Jackie's had a cuddle, but she wants her mammy, not me.'

'Oh, dear.' Dora shook her head. 'Carol, it really hurts when you pull hair. It's not a nice thing to do. Come and say sorry to your sister.'

Carol reluctantly slid off the chair and stood in front of Dora and Jackie. 'Sorry,' she mumbled. 'Want to go home now, Daddy,' she directed at Joe.

'Say sorry like you mean it, Carol,' Joe said. 'And we're not going home yet. Mammy said she'd ice the cakes with you, and then we're all going for a nice walk.' He raised an eyebrow at Dora and nodded towards the kitchen.

She put Jackie down and followed him, pushing the door half-closed while still keeping an eye on the girls.

'I'm sorry,' Joe began. 'Like I've said to you before, she needs stability. She's jealous of Jackie because she's with you and she still thinks you don't want her. No matter how much I tell her that's not the case, she doesn't understand. I find it difficult to deal with at times.' He ran his hands through his hair and lit a cigarette. 'I come home from work knackered, pick her up from Dolly's and I don't always have the time to play with her. We read the book that she brings home from school and by the time she's had her tea she's tired and ready for bed. She's missing out on the time she should be spending with you and her sister after school.'

Dora blew out her cheeks. 'So it's all down to me again, is it? If *your* bloody girlfriend hadn't reported me to the welfare people we wouldn't be in this situation. Carol would still be with *me*, I'd be living in the prefab and life would be fairly normal for them both, with you dropping in when you can. Instead of which I'm stuck down here in a place I don't want to be, but I have no choice.'

'Dora, you did have a choice, and it *wasn't* Ivy. She's not my girlfriend. How many times?' Joe took a long drag on his ciggie while Dora got a glass from the cupboard and filled it with water. She drank slowly and looked at him.

'Maybe it wasn't Ivy who reported me, but it *was* her you slept with.'

Joe shook his head and went back into the sitting room. The girls were sitting quietly together, looking at a book, their earlier spat forgotten. 'Carol, come on, we're going home.'

'But what about our walk?' Dora said.

'What's the point? I'll see you next week. Phone me if you need anything.' He threw an envelope down onto the coffee table and pulled Carol to her feet. 'Your money,' he said, pointing to the envelope.

Dora chewed her lip, close to tears as he slammed the front door behind him. She turned as Jackie tugged on the hem of her skirt. She lifted her up and gave her a cuddle. 'Shall we ice the cakes? We can take them to Granny's tomorrow when Uncle Frank comes to pick us up.'

Jackie smiled and snuggled into Dora's neck. Dora carried her through into the kitchen and pulled a stool out for her daughter to stand on near the drop-leaf front of the cabinet. If only Carol would let her get close and cuddle her like Jackie did.

'What you lookin' at, yer nosy cow!'

Dora peered through her bedroom nets across the street at the show the Ugly Sisters were performing in the middle of the road. A woman from the house next to Gloria's had stuck her head out of the window and was yelling at them to stop carrying on. Gloria, in full voice, was warbling Guy Mitchell's song 'She Wears Red Feathers' with Freda joining in.

'Come on, gel, you're makin' a right holy show of yerself. Gerrin the bleedin' 'ouse.' Freda's husband, who was struggling to stay upright, dragged his wife by the arm up onto the pavement. She kicked and screamed until he let go as more windows opened and voices yelled for a bit of bloody peace and quiet.

Dora let the curtain fall back into place and sat down on the edge of her bed. Their first Saturday here and so far it had been a disaster. Jackie was curled up with her teddy bear, fast asleep, thumb in mouth. She refused to sleep in her own bed. Mam had warned her that would happen. She was so used to sharing a bed with Dora. Tears trickled down her face as she thought of how different her life was now to how it should have been. When they'd worked at Palmer's factory, both she and Joanie had had such high hopes for their wonderful futures filled with children and happy times with the men they loved and running their own dressmaking business. Now Joanie was dead, Frank got upset if anyone even mentioned her name these days, Joe was no longer Dora's. Add two confused little girls to the mix and it was all such a mess.

The racket outside stopped and the slamming of doors heralded a peaceful silence. Dora sighed and wiped her eyes. Tomorrow she planned to take some flowers from Mam's garden to the graves of her dad and Joanna, who were in the same plot, and Joanie's grave nearby. She moved Jackie across to her own side of the bed and slid in beside her, hoping she'd get a few hours' sleep at least. Frank was coming to pick them up at ten thirty. She'd leave Jackie at her mam's while she visited the graves.

Dora tidied the dead flowers away and put fresh sweet peas and sweet williams into the vase on her dad and baby Joanna's grave. She blew a kiss at the headstone inscriptions and got to her feet.

As she made her way across to Joanie's grave she caught sight of the woman in black, hurrying out of the churchyard. So she *was* a mourner after all – but who was she mourning and where did she come from? Dora frowned. It was very odd. No one from the village had passed away for some time, otherwise Mam would have known all about it.

She knelt down at Joanie's graveside and picked up a large bunch of dead flowers. She wondered who'd put them there; they looked professionally arranged, with a faded red bow around the dirty paper wrapping. Joanie's mam wouldn't have bought them – she always brought flowers from her garden – and Frank found it hard to visit the grave and left it to Dora and Joanie's family. There was a card stuffed into the flowers and Dora pulled it out. On the front it had the message, *To Grandma, Happy Birthday, from Billy, Harry and Enid. xxx*

Dora looked around, wondering how the bouquet had ended up on Joanie's grave. Maybe it had been blown there from a nearby plot, although the weather had been mild and calm lately, so that was unlikely. Then she saw a scribbled message on the other side of the card and the words turned her stomach.

You got what you deserved and so did the bitch you worked with. Hope you like your *dead flowers.*

Dora's hand flew to her mouth. She felt sick. Who would put such a horrible message on Joanie's grave? And did 'the bitch you worked with' mean *her*? But why? What had they ever done to deserve this? It didn't make any sense at all. She felt a trickle of fear run down her spine and looked over her shoulder and all around, but she was the only one in the churchyard. Earlier in the morning there would have been the usual service, but people had long gone home for their Sunday dinners. Dora pushed the card into her jacket pocket and threw the dead bouquet into a nearby bin. She placed fresh flowers in the little vase on Joanie's grave and topped it up with water she'd brought in a mineral bottle, at Mam's suggestion.

*

'And you say there was no one around when you got there?' Mam asked, turning the small card over and shaking her head. 'Only I always pop by the graves and say hello to them all as I pass through the churchyard on my way back from Sunday service. It wasn't there then, I'm sure of that.'

Dora had waited until they'd finished their dinner, Jackie was upstairs having a nap and they were sitting comfortably with a glass of sherry before she showed them the card. Frank was sitting stony-faced on the sofa with a glass of pale ale. A pulse flickered in his right cheek as he snatched the card from Mam's hand and threw it onto the fire.

'Why did you do that?' Mam asked. 'Someone might have recognised the handwriting.'

'And what good would that do?' he snapped. 'It won't bring her back. I'll kill whoever wrote it if I get my hands on them. I'd like to know what they meant by it.'

Dora took a sip of her sherry as a thought struck her. 'The only person I saw this morning was that woman with the black coat. The stranger we saw at the street party. She was hurrying out of the churchyard and she didn't look round or anything and let on to me. I just assumed she was a mourner visiting a grave.'

Mam pursed her lips. 'Hmm, well that's funny, because a few people have reported seeing her recently. We were all wondering if it's her who's been stealing the food from our kitchens. You remember how she crammed her pockets with leftovers at the street party? She's obviously going hungry and just helps herself when an opportunity presents. I bet it was her put them dead flowers and that nasty message on Joanie's grave.'

Frank looked at Mam as though she'd gone mad. 'Don't be so bloody daft. Why would a complete stranger do something like that? How could the woman possibly know who Joanie is, and who our Dora is, come to that? She might be guilty of nicking a bit of scran, but we can't know she was behind the flowers, surely.'

Dora shrugged. 'It is a bit odd though. That she should be the only one around before I saw them, I mean. We need to find out who she is and where she lives.'

Mam shook her head. 'We've had no joy with that, chuck. Like I say, no one knows her or where she disappears to when she leaves the village.'

Frank topped up their glasses and Dora told them about the events of Saturday, her fall-out with Joe and the noisy neighbours and their antics. 'Oh, and I saw a job for a seamstress advertised in a shop window yesterday. I'm going to call in on Monday morning to find out a bit more about it.'

Mam frowned. 'And who will look after our Jackie if you get the job? Sadie's got enough on her hands with her own brood and *I* can't come into the city every day. It's too much for me.'

'Mam, I wouldn't expect you to do that. My next-door neighbour Vi might have her for a few days. She's really good with Sadie's little ones and our Jackie seems to have taken a shine to her as well.'

'Hmm, and how old is this Vi? It might get too much for her, looking after a kiddie all day.'

'She's not elderly. I would say late forties. Her boys are grown up and left home. So she's on her own, and I can offer her some money depending on what I earn. I'll still do my own customers' clothes at night to keep me afloat.'

'Well, I suppose all you can do is see what the job involves and then take it from there. But it'll be hard work for you.'

Dora nodded and changed the subject before her mam put further mockers on her plans. She told them about Joe needing a helping hand in the school holidays with Carol, and Mam beamed.

'We'll sort something out with him. Frank can go round one night after work and make the arrangements.'

Chapter Nine

On Monday morning Dora fixed her hair up into a French pleat. She put on her only unladdered pair of stockings that she saved for best, and a pale green tweed two-piece she'd made last year. The skirt flared gently just above her knee and the close-fitting jacket was finished with a neat peplum around the bottom edge. Her brown court shoes and bag finished the look. Jackie was already round at Sadie's having breakfast with Peter and Belinda and they were all going into Vi's for a story while Sadie got on with her washing. Dora slicked her lips with her favourite Tangee lipstick and smiled at her reflection in the bedroom mirror. The suit made her feel professional and confident and she hoped that feeling would convey itself to Samuel Jacobs.

As she locked her front door a loud wolf-whistle blasted in her direction. She glanced across the street and saw a gangly youth leaning against the window ledge of Gloria's house, ciggie dangling from his mouth, dripping paintbrush in his hand. Lenny Smyth; the eldest son, a cocky and arrogant lad, Sadie had told her. He appeared to be painting the sill in the same colour red as hers. Gloria appeared at the open front door and gave him a clip around the ear.

'Gerron with it,' she yelled. 'If it's good enough for Lady Muck over there then it's good enough for us. And youse can do yer Aunty Freda's when you've finished mine.' She went back inside and the lad shot Dora an embarrassed smirk.

Dora tried her door handle, making sure it was locked before she went on her way. You couldn't leave your doors unlocked and go shopping here like you could in Knowsley. It was a bit unnerving but no doubt she'd get used to it. She smiled at a half-dressed toddler wandering along the pavement. She presumed it was a boy. He wore a grubby blue top and his wet nappy hung down almost to his knees. She wondered where he'd come from. The door of the last house on the street stood ajar. Maybe he'd slipped out of there without his mother noticing.

As Dora looked back at the child, who was crossing the street now and going towards Gloria's son, a young woman shot out of the open door and screeched at the top of her voice, making Dora jump.

'Mikey, get back here, yer little bugger!' She ran past Dora and grabbed the child, dragging him by the hand back to the house. She scowled as she caught Dora's eye. ''Ere, are youse from the welfare come to spy on me? My eldest lad must have left the door open when he went to school. I was feeding my baby and Mikey slipped out without my seeing him. I don't neglect my kids, yer know.'

Dora took a small step back as the front door opened further and a fetid smell wafted out. Another small child of around four stared at her, his blue eyes round in his dirty little face. She shook her head. 'I'm sure you don't. And no, I'm not from the welfare. I live down there.' She pointed up the street.

'Oh, right. Well I'm Della,' the woman introduced herself. 'I thought you were somebody important with you being dressed up posh like that. Nobody dresses up posh around 'ere. You must be Sadie's new neighbour, the one that makes frocks. I'd best get back inside and finish feeding my little fella. Nice to meet you, er…?'

'Dora.' She smiled and hurried on her way. That poor woman. She had her hands full with her four boys. But Sadie had four kids and another on the way, yet her house and children were spotless and well-cared-for and Sadie was always neat and tidy herself. Maybe Della's husband had no job to bring in a decent wage to keep them all. Cleanliness costs nothing but a bar of soap, as her mam was always saying. She'd ask Sadie about Della later when she picked up Jackie. It made her feel so sad to think of the welfare ordering her to give up Carol when she had looked after her, kept her clean, loved and well fed. She'd always done her best. It didn't seem fair that kids who lived in squalor down here were allowed to stay with their parents. Surely health visitors would raise an eyebrow. She blinked rapidly as her eyes filled, and carried on her way.

As she walked down Homer Street Dora's confidence started to ebb. What if the job had already gone? It was half-past nine; somebody might have got there earlier and been waiting for the owner to open.

Thankfully the card was still on the door. She took a deep breath and entered the shop. A little brass bell positioned above the door rang out and a plump, pleasant-faced woman standing behind the large counter smiled. The woman wore a navy dress and her dark hair was fastened up like Dora's in a neat French pleat.

'Good morning, madam,' the woman greeted her. 'How may I help you?'

'Good morning,' Dora replied. 'I've, er, I've come about the job.' She pointed to the card on the door. 'The seamstress's job.'

The woman's face lit up. She gestured to a wooden chair near the front of the counter. 'Take a seat, my dear. My husband is upstairs in the workroom. I'll go and fetch him.'

Dora smiled and sat down. She glanced around the large shop. It was bright and airy, with the double windows letting in a lot of light. The shelves were well-stocked with boxes, all labelled with various haberdashery requirements: zips, bias-binding, fancy lace, buttons, hooks and eyes, needles and threads in all colours, each colour allocated its own box. Dora always felt a buzz of excitement whenever she walked into a haberdashery store; the smell of new fabric and the anticipation of choosing something she could make into a pretty dress or skirt. She heard footsteps on the stairs and a tall man with a bushy beard appeared behind the counter, followed by his wife.

'Samuel Jacobs.' He extended a large hand and gripped Dora's in a firm handshake.

'Dora Rodgers,' she said, smiling broadly. The man had dark brown twinkly eyes and a neat little black skull-cap on top of his head, partly hiding hair that was sprinkled with grey, like his beard. His black clothes were covered in bits of thread and there was even a length of white cotton dangling from above his left ear. She immediately felt comfortable in his presence. His wife was nodding her head as though pleased by what she saw.

'Would you like to follow me, Dora, and I'll explain what we do here. Esther will make us tea – or do you prefer coffee?'

'Tea would be lovely, thank you,' Dora replied and smiled at Mrs Jacobs, who disappeared into a back room. Dora followed Mr Jacobs up a flight of wide wooden stairs and stepped into a huge, well-lit room that held dressmakers' dummies in various stages of undress, two tables with sewing machines and another large table where a length of fabric was laid out ready for cutting, a paper pattern pinned onto it.

'This is a wonderful work space,' she said. 'So bright and well laid out.'

'Yes, it is a nice place to work,' Samuel Jacobs said. 'I take it you have experience in the trade, Dora? Is it okay if I call you Dora?'

'Yes, of course.'

'Then you must call me Sammy. My wife and I don't like to stand on ceremony. Ah, and here she is with our tea. Thank you, Esther, my dear.'

Esther placed a tray, set with a lace cloth and flowered-sprigged china, onto one of the sewing tables. 'You must try my biscuits, Dora. Lemon and ginger. I made them yesterday. By the way, your outfit is lovely. Such an attractive shade of green. No doubt made by your own fair hands?' Dora nodded and replied that it was indeed designed and made by her. Esther smiled and left them to it.

Sammy pulled out a chair for Dora. 'Quality work,' he said approvingly. He sat on the edge of a table and listened as Dora told him about her sewing background.

He looked at her closely when she stopped mid-sentence and took a deep shuddering breath. 'So, you and your friend decided not to go ahead with your business plans then?'

She sighed. 'Sadly Joanie died before we got the business off the ground properly. I've been trying to build things up by myself, but my marriage broke down and I've only just managed to find a place of my own to work in again. I have a few regular customers, but I'm not as busy as I'd like to be; which is why I'm looking for a job.'

He nodded and silently stroked his beard. 'I'm sorry about your friend. It's always hard to lose someone close.'

'Joanie was more than a friend.' Dora sighed again. 'She was family, married to my brother. It was a tragedy all round.'

'You said you both worked in a clothing factory? She wasn't the young lady who perished in Palmer's, in that fire? The boss and his accomplice were arrested for involuntary manslaughter. Terrible business.'

Dora nodded. 'Yes, that was Joanie.' She swallowed the lump that had risen in her throat. Joanie's death was hard to talk about, but if she were to end up working here, in close proximity to Samuel Jacobs, it was best that he knew something of her background. There was a wireless playing quietly in the room and Dora knew that certain songs could trigger tears, no matter how hard she tried not to cry. He may as well know about her history, warts and all, before he made up his mind to employ her. One thing she wouldn't talk about to a stranger, though, was her bouts of post-pregnancy depression. She hadn't even told him she had children yet.

'Are you living in this area now, Dora?'

'Yes. I've just taken a lease on a little house not far from the Dock Road – well, it's in-between there and Scotland Road. I'm hoping to be rehoused into something new eventually. I, er, I have a young daughter who will be looked after by family and neighbours while I work.' She crossed her fingers on her lap, hoping that would turn out to be true. 'So I can be quite flexible with the hours.'

'Ah, that's splendid to know. You see, apart from outfits that we make for the lady and gent in the street, we also design and make costumes for shows. Pantomimes, musical shows, that sort of thing. The local theatres are our biggest customers. I would need you to be available to visit the theatres to take measurements and to deliver garments, often at short notice. Sometimes we get a frantic phone call minutes before curtain-up that a seam has split and it means an immediate journey with a sewing kit to do a temporary fix if there's no handy needlewoman on site. Then you would need to remain at the theatre until the end of the show and bring the garment back here for a proper repair. It can be quite exciting and you will get to see a show for free as well while you wait. How does that sound? We will of course provide a taxi for you. We don't expect you to carry costumes on trams and buses. Some of them can be quite bulky. We will look after you.'

Dora sat open-mouthed as he explained the business to her. It sounded fabulous to her ears. But she'd struggle to get Jackie looked after at night if there was a last-minute theatre visit to make. Maybe Frank would be able to help out and stay over to look after her. Or Joe could pick her up from Vi's if she called him at work. It would all need to be carefully thought out, but if she was offered this great opportunity to expand her sewing skills, she was going to grab it with both hands. 'It sounds wonderful,' she said.

'Good. Our last seamstress married and emigrated to Canada a few months ago. I've struggled to find a suitable replacement for her. I think you might be just what we're looking for. We'll work with you to make the hours as suitable as possible. Now drink your tea and don't forget to try Esther's biscuits while I pop downstairs and speak with her.'

Chapter Ten

On her way back to Wright Street, Dora nipped into the market and bought three vanilla cuts, by way of a celebration, and four two-penny slabs of Cadbury's Dairy Milk. Sadie and Vi would appreciate the treat, the kids would love the chocolate and there was one for Carol for next time she came over. Dora knew she should be watching the pennies so that she wouldn't be short for rent day on Saturday, but she'd manage somehow. Vi had the kettle on ready and waiting. Both she and Sadie were anxious to hear the news. Belinda was sitting on the rug trying to chew the ears off a toy bunny, her cheeks bright red from teething, but the room was otherwise empty of kids.

Dora shouted, 'I got the job,' and waved the white paper bag in the air. Sadie and Vi cheered. The back door stood open and she could hear childish voices in the yard. She popped her head around and called out to Jackie, who ignored her, her attention taken by a spinning top that Peter was showing her. 'Hey, madam, come here and give Mammy a hug.'

Jackie turned and grinned and hurtled towards her. The two little boys belonging to Della were also in the yard, but playing near their own back door. At least they were dressed now, in shorts and T-shirts. Dora scooped her daughter up and gave her a kiss.

'Who'd like some chocolate?' she said. Della's sons looked across. Dora chewed her lip. She'd bet those kids hadn't ever seen or tasted chocolate. Rationing of sweets hadn't long been over. Jackie and Peter followed her inside. 'The two little lads from the end house are out there,' she said to Sadie. 'I've got some chocolate for these three. Shall I offer some to the boys?' She could always pick up another bar for Carol later in the week.

Sadie nodded. 'It would be a rare treat for them. But go and ask Della if it's okay first.'

Dora took the small slab of chocolate with her and strolled up the yard. The boys stared at her, their blue eyes wide with expectation. She rapped on the open back door.

Della came running, a baby in her arms and a worried look on her face. She had fastened her dark hair up, and bits were escaping from the pins and dangling into her eyes. Her wrap-over apron was faded and her feet were encased in peep-toe sandals that had once been white. 'What's up? Are the little sods misbehaving?'

'No,' Dora replied. 'I wondered if they'd like to share this between them. I've just got some for mine and Sadie's kids and I bought one too many.'

Della's jaw dropped and a smile lit up her tired face. 'Oh, thank you, Dora. They never get treats. I can't afford it. And they've *never* had chocolate before either.'

Dora smiled as the two little boys eagerly snatched the slab she broke in half.

'What do you say, Mikey, Donald?' their mother prompted.

'Fank you,' Donald managed, his cheeks bulging, while Mikey nodded, a blissful look in his eyes.

'I'd better get back to my little one.' Dora turned as Della called out her thanks again.

Back in Vi's kitchen a mug of tea waited on the table and the vanillas were out on plates. The kids were quiet, sitting on the rug and enjoying the chocolate.

'Don't make a mess on Aunty Vi's rug,' Sadie warned. But the chocolate vanished quickly with not a scrap wasted. 'Well that didn't touch the sides,' Sadie said with a laugh. 'Greedy little monkeys. Was Della okay with you?'

Dora nodded. 'Yes, fine. I feel a bit sorry for her.'

'Me too,' Sadie said. 'She doesn't have much luck with her menfolk. Her husband was killed in an accident with a motorbike and the one she's taken up with now, father of her two youngest, is a waste of time. He'll still be in bed until the pub opens. He drinks every penny he earns doing casual labour wherever he can get it.'

'Well how does she pay the rent and put food on the table?' Dora said and took a sip of tea. 'Oh, that's a good brew, Vi.'

Sadie pursed her lips and lowered her voice. 'She earns a living down the Dock Road while me and you are sleeping. Sailors and dockers are her customers.'

Dora frowned. 'What, you mean…? Oh God, the poor woman. What a mess to get into. She mustn't earn that much either; she doesn't look as though she has two halfpennies to rub together.'

'Most of what she earns, that lazy bugger she lives with takes,' Vi said, shaking her head. 'We never used to have such common neighbours in the old days. Everyone was kind and they were decent, hard-working folk. We all looked out for each other. But now, what with them noisy buggers across the street and Della, it's getting a right bad reputation round here.'

Sadie sighed. 'Never mind, we'll look out for us three and ignore the rest. I worry for her kids though. Della leaves them home with him and he's always drunk. Poor little devils. Anyway, we can't be responsible for how people choose to live their lives, can we? Come on; let's have some good news. Tell us all about the new job.'

Dora soon settled in at Samuel Jacobs'. She loved the variety of work the job brought with it. The theatre costumes were a challenge but she was an eager pupil and Sammy a great teacher. When she told him that she'd made her own and various friends' wedding dresses his eyes lit up. 'And would you be prepared to make them for us? We could have one on a model in the window and see if it brings in any enquiries.'

'I'd love to. I'll bring my sketches in and then you can see the styles I designed.'

'I think we've found a little gem in you, Dora,' Esther said. 'We're so lucky.'

'No, I'm the lucky one. Thank you for giving me this chance. I'm really enjoying the work. I love the challenge of trying something new with the theatre costumes, all the lovely trims and beading. And it's just so nice to get out of the house and away from that street for a few hours a day. It's not the nicest place to live, but it's all I can afford for now, so I'm making the best of it.'

It was early days, but so far things had worked out fine in getting Jackie looked after. Vi had agreed to mind her three days a week. Dora had offered to pay her but Vi refused. 'She's absolutely no trouble and I enjoy her company. She keeps me entertained with her singing and dancing when we have *Housewives' Choice* on the wireless. How about I get some material and maybe you can run me up a new frock as payment?' she said.

Dora smiled. 'I'd love to. Whenever you're ready, Vi.'

Mam came over on the other two days. Frank brought her on his way to the docks. And while she was there she insisted on doing a bit of washing and cleaning, as Dora was finding it hard to keep on top of her housework at night when she'd brought sewing home to finish. It was hard work but at least she could pay her rent and the coalman, put money in the gas and electric meters and food on the table without having to open the envelopes of money Joe gave her. She was determined not to use his money and was saving it for Jackie's future. Saturday and Sunday were her days off, although Sammy told her she might occasionally be needed at one of the theatres. So far it hadn't happened and it was nice to have her weekends free. Joe brought Carol over on Saturday afternoons still and they did their best to have nice family times.

School holidays began and Mam took Jackie home with her on the week she and Frank were looking after Carol for the odd day. Dora set about creating a wedding dress while she had the house to herself. It had to be really special for the window display and Sammy had told her to help herself to any trimmings, as well as the white satin fabric she'd picked for the main part of the dress. The sleeves were to be made from unlined lace with bell-shaped ends. There was a child-sized dummy in the workroom and Dora suggested she should make a bridesmaid's outfit too, and said she'd be happy to dress the window when she'd finished the clothes.

On the third Saturday in August Joe arrived with Carol as arranged. They'd planned a picnic in Sefton Park and he'd promised to take the girls on the boating lake. Dora didn't like being on water in such a small boat, so she sat on the grass with the picnic laid out ready for when they'd finished their sail.

As she lay down to soak up the rays of the sun a shadow fell across her. She shaded her eyes and looked up to see her friend Agnes's smiling face, and behind her Agnes's husband Alan and their daughter Patsy, who was a couple of weeks younger than Jackie. Dora jumped up and they hugged one another. She hadn't seen Agnes for weeks.

'Joe's on the lake with the girls,' Dora said as Agnes sat down on the picnic rug.

'Oh, why don't you take our Patsy out in a boat while I have a natter with Dora?' Agnes suggested to Alan, who had no choice when Patsy grabbed his hand and dragged him across to the lake.

'It's so good to see you,' Agnes said. 'We've brought a picnic too, so can we join you?'

'Be my guest. It's lovely to see you too. I hate not having a phone and being able to keep in regular contact.'

'I saw your mam yesterday and she told me you were coming here today, so I was hoping we'd bump into you. I need a couple of sundresses for Patsy for the holidays, but we're not going until the end of September. It's just a week in Southport for us this year. Alan's so busy at work; he can't take any more time off until the season is over. You wouldn't believe the amount of people who go flying to places these days. It's not something *I* fancy but I've heard the weather is better abroad than here. Any chance of you fitting us in?'

Dora nodded. 'Of course there is. If I make them to fit Jackie they'll fit your Patsy no problem. We've got some lovely spotty cotton fabric in at work and some nice gingham too.'

'I'll leave the fabric choices up to you, but make sure it doesn't clash with her red hair.' Agnes laughed. 'As you can see, it's redder than mine these days. Anyway, how's the new job going? Your mam said it's all working out well for you.'

'I love it. Sammy is so nice to work with and his wife is really sweet. Keeps trying to feed me up. She makes the most gorgeous cakes and biscuits.'

'Has Joe found a new job yet? We heard he was looking for something else. And how are the pair of you getting along these days? Rumour has it he asked you to take him back…'

Dora felt her cheeks heating and she looked across to the boating lake where Joe and the girls were waiting on the bank for Alan and Patsy to finish their turn. 'He did, yes. But I can't, and you know why.'

Agnes shook her head. 'Dora, if you had that sterilisation operation they offered you it would all be fine. The kids are older now, so you wouldn't need as much help from your mam afterwards as you might have done when they were little. You're young and healthy and you'd recover quite quickly. You're throwing such a lot away. He loves you. It seems such a waste for you both not to be together.'

Dora shook her head. 'I can't do it. It's not just that; what if he cheated on me again?'

Agnes blew out her cheeks. 'I honestly don't think he would. He's mad about you, everyone knows that.' She changed the subject. 'How do you like living down on Wright Street?'

Dora screwed up her face. 'It's okay, it has its moments, more good than bad, I suppose. My neighbour Vi is lovely. She's in-between me and Sadie and she looks after Jackie for me while I work. The three of us are lucky to be next to each other. But if I'm honest the rest of the neighbours leave a lot to be desired.'

Agnes raised an eyebrow. 'That alone would make me think about going back to Joe.'

Dora shrugged. 'I suppose it would for most women. He's going away for a few days with Ivy and Carol soon. They're staying in a caravan, so you see, he's not pining for me as much as he makes out.'

'What?' Agnes gasped. 'And you don't mind? You must be mad. I don't understand you at times, Dora. If you give Ivy the chance to get her claws in him again you'll always regret it.'

'He claims they're just good friends.' Dora knew that sounded lame and unconvincing, even to *her* ears, and was glad to see Joe and Alan and their girls heading towards them. Jackie flopped down beside her and plugged a thumb in her mouth. Dora cuddled her close and kissed the top of her sweaty head. 'You need your sunbonnet on.' She beckoned for Carol to come and sit with them, but Carol hung back and sat down next to Joe. Dora swallowed hard. It upset her that Carol was still so uncertain around her even after all this time.

She turned back to Agnes. 'I'll give you a call from work when Patsy's dresses are ready, it won't take me long to make them. I'll ask our Frank to give me a lift over to your place to drop them off.'

'And you and Jackie must stay for tea, and then Alan can run you home afterwards.'

'We'll look forward to it,' Dora said.

*

Back at Wright Street Joe placed his usual envelope on the table. Carol had taken Jackie outside to the lavatory. He stood with his back to the range, lit a cigarette and threw the spent match into the grate.

'We need to talk,' he began, turning towards Dora and pulling a large buff-coloured envelope from his inside jacket pocket. It was folded in half lengthways and he opened it out and handed it to her.

She looked at him. 'What's this?'

'Divorce papers,' he replied, taking a long pull on his ciggie. 'You told me to get on with it, remember? You need to read them and, if you agree, you sign your copy. I've gone for desertion and adultery with an unnamed party, all my fault. It's far easier if we both agree; and I don't want to drag Ivy's name through the mud – it would take for ever if she objected to being named. I'll pick up all the costs. I don't want you struggling to find the money. I was in the wrong, even though it was you who deserted me, strictly speaking. *I* wanted us to get back together and start again and you didn't.'

Dora stared at him as though he'd gone mad. 'I didn't desert you. We simply couldn't be together after what you did. It was impossible, and you know it,' she snapped. 'Oh, just leave it on the table, Joe, and I'll read it when Jackie goes to bed.'

He nodded. 'Right, well thanks for the picnic. I'll pop in after work on Friday next week to pick up the papers and see Jackie and then I'll probably be away from Saturday in Morecambe. It's looking likely, but only for a few days.'

'So, does Ivy know about the divorce then?' She practically spat out the woman's name.

'No. It's not her business to know what goes on between me and you. That's why I didn't name her, and then she's got no reason to know.'

'Hmm, she'd be rubbing her hands together with glee if she did.'

Joe shook his head. 'Well, she doesn't. And like I told you, we're just good friends so it wouldn't make any difference if she *did* know.'

'Joe, you're so naïve,' Dora said.

He shrugged. 'You can reverse this situation any time you want to. You know that. The ball has always been in your court, Dora.' He threw the end of his ciggie into the fireplace and went to the door to call Carol and Jackie inside. He shook his head when he saw what they were up to. Carol was poking her finger through a tar bubble that had appeared with the heat in-between the cobbles and Jackie was rolling a lump of tar between her fingers. There was tar stuck to their legs and the skirts of their dresses.

'Get in here, now,' he roared. 'Look at the state of you. You look like two street urchins. That mess will never come off your clothes. Naughty girls.' He slammed the door closed as they ran into the kitchen. Dora appeared behind him.

'Oh dear. All over your nice new sundresses too. Better take them off and then I'll find Carol something to wear from upstairs while you get her home. Otherwise there'll be tar on your car seats. I might be able to get it removed. I'll see if Sammy at work can suggest anything that won't damage the fabric. Try and scrape it off Carol's legs, Joe, while I get a couple of towels.'

By the time Joe and a weeping Carol had left after having her legs scrubbed, Dora felt exhausted. How easy it would have been to just pack a bag and go with him in the car and send for the rest of her stuff later. She heated some water in the kettle and pans and lifted Jackie into the sink for a bath. And later, while Jackie was in bed, she'd heave the big tin bath off the wall hook outside the back door and steam the house up while she filled it to take a bath herself. Then there was the emptying of it, a pan at a time, when she'd finished, as she couldn't lift it up to tip it down the sink. It was a right performance. She thought with regret of the lovely bathroom with hot running water in the prefab that she'd left behind.

And it was Saturday night again, so no doubt the Ugly Sisters would be making their usual drunken racket outside. She shook her head as she rinsed Jackie's hair. How long she'd be able to stand living here, she really didn't know. She needed to write the letters she'd been meaning to since she moved in; one to the council to get her name on the rehousing list and the other to the welfare department to ask for custody of Carol again.

Chapter Eleven

On Sunday morning Dora opened the front door to an ashen-faced Frank. He was a bit earlier than usual and she led him into the back room where Jackie was sitting waiting patiently with her teddy and the three bears book on her knee. 'What's wrong?' Dora asked. 'You look dreadful. Has something happened?'

Dora made Frank sit on a chair and got him a glass of water. His hands trembled as he took it from her and sipped slowly. She waited until he'd composed himself and then he nodded and took a deep shuddering breath. 'It's Mam. I've taken her to the hospital. She was in the kitchen preparing veg and I nipped out to the paper shop. The lad had left the wrong paper so I took it back to swap it. When I got home she was on the floor, her head was bleeding at the back and she couldn't remember what had happened. I think she must have been knocked out for a few minutes. I wrapped a towel around her wound and took her straight to Fazakerley hospital.'

Dora's hand flew to her mouth. 'Oh my God. Do you think she had a dizzy spell and fell, or something? We'd better get over there. Oh, we can't take Jackie with us. What am I going to do with her? Vi's away at her son's for a few days, he came for her earlier, and I saw Sadie and Stan go past with their lot a while ago.'

'Let's think about it on the way,' Frank suggested. 'Come on, lock up and let's go.' He lifted Jackie up and hurried out to the car with her while Dora picked up the bag she'd packed earlier for their day in Knowsley, dashing outside and putting it on the back seat next to Jackie. The gangly youth, Lenny Smyth, was sitting on the doorstep opposite, watching every move through narrowed eyes. She ran back to the door and checked to make sure it was locked. All the windows were closed. She'd done them before Frank got there. As he started up the engine and shot off down the street, Dora had a thought. 'We can take Jackie to Agnes's. It's on the way and I'm sure she'll look after her.'

Frank nodded as he drove up Scotland Road. 'I think Mam might have caught her head on the corner of the table as she went down,' he said. 'It wasn't a big cut, but it might need a couple of stitches. The nurse that took her off me said they'd clean her up and take her to X-ray to make sure she's not fractured her skull or anything. They put her in a wheelchair and I said I'd come and get you. We've to go back to the accident department.'

Frank screeched to a stop outside the bay-windowed house on Second Avenue and Agnes came out. She was only too pleased to help. 'I hope your mam's okay,' she said, giving Dora a hug after her hurried explanation. 'Don't you worry about Jackie now; I'll give her some dinner with Patsy and they can play nice in the garden. You get yourselves off and see to your mam.'

At the hospital they found Mam on a trolley in a curtained-off cubicle, her head swathed in a big bandage; her face was devoid of colour and her eyes closed. But as Frank banged into a chair she opened them and half-smiled. 'Always the clumsy one, our Frank,' she croaked through dry lips.

'Mam, oh Mam, what happened?' Dora sat beside the trolley and held her hand. 'Did you faint or something?'

'I'm not sure, chuck. One minute I was peeling spuds, next thing I'm on the floor with our Frank calling my name and slapping my cheeks.'

A nurse bustled into the cubicle and smiled. 'We're going to keep Mrs Evans in for a couple of days,' she told them. 'She's got mild concussion, so we need to observe her for a while. There's no skull fracture, but we've inserted three stitches in the wound. Would it be possible to bring her some nightclothes and toiletries at visiting time? It's at two o'clock, so you've got an hour to dash home. She'll be up on the first floor, ward B2.'

Dora nodded. 'Of course. We'll be back in a bit, Mam.' She dropped a kiss on her cheek.

'Don't bring that tatty white nightdress that's on the chair,' Mam said. 'I'm cutting it up for dusters. I've a nice blue one in the top drawer, and there's a new pink one in a TJ Hughes bag next to it. I was keeping it for best in case I go away, but it'll do nicely for in here. My slippers are on the floor by the bed.'

Dora sighed with relief. Her mam giving orders even though her face was so pale was a good sign. 'Don't you worry. We'll make sure you look nice. See you in a while.'

Dora looked around the Sugar Lane kitchen. All seemed to be in order. The abandoned carrots and potatoes were in the sink, but there was no sign of anything else to go with them. 'Frank, did Mam make a beef and onion pie for dinner? She bought some mince from the butcher on Friday when she was down at mine looking after Jackie.'

'Yes, she did,' Frank replied, coming into the kitchen. 'She baked it after she came back from morning service at the church. It was cooling on the table with an apple pie when I popped to the paper shop. She was muttering about putting them in the sitting room oven to keep warm.'

Dora hurried into the sitting room, but the bread oven was empty and the fire almost out. 'Where the hell are they then?'

Frank shrugged and went to try the back door. It was unlocked and the gate at the bottom of the garden was swinging open. 'Shit, looks like the phantom pie thief has struck again while we were at the hospital.' He ran down the path to close the gate; he checked first to make sure there was no one on the narrow dirt lane beyond it, but there wasn't a soul in sight.

Dora shook her head as he came back inside. 'Maybe they struck before Mam had her accident. Oh God, Frank, what if they came in, attacked her, pushed her over or something and stole the pies? Shall we call the police?'

Frank chewed his lip. 'Let's get back to the hospital before we jump to conclusions. See if Mam's remembered anything.'

As they made their way out to the car, Dora carrying a bag packed with Mam's things, their elderly neighbour from across the lane came limping over. 'Is Mary okay?' the old lady gasped. 'Only I was cleaning the upstairs window when I saw Frank come out with her. By the time I got downstairs again you'd driven off. I saw she had her head all wrapped up. Has there been an accident?'

'Yes,' Dora said. 'She's had a fall, Maisie. I'll pop over later and let you know how she is.' She got in the car beside Frank and they set off back to Fazakerley.

The ward sister, who introduced herself as Sister Ashton, called them into her office as Dora and Frank arrived on ward B2. She gestured to a couple of chairs in front of her desk.

'Is everything okay?' Dora asked, sitting on the edge of her chair and clutching the shopping bag.

Sister tapped her teeth with a pen as she looked at the notes in front of her. 'Your mother is settling down with us, but she's having a few flashbacks as to what happened this morning. Now I'm not too sure whether she's confused because of the bang on her head – delayed concussion can cause a patient to ramble a bit – or whether she's affected by the strong painkillers we've administered, but she told me there was someone behind her in the kitchen and she thought it was Frank come back from the shop. She says she can't remember anything other than that. If you would like to chat with her, see if she says anything else that might help us to understand how she got her head injury.'

Frank nodded. 'I definitely wasn't back – it was me that found her on the floor. But we have reason to believe someone may have been in the house. A couple of items are missing and the back gate was open. It never is, no one ever comes in that way except for the dustbin men on a Wednesday and the coalman on a Monday.'

Dora got to her feet, feeling sick. If someone had attacked their mam, it didn't bear thinking about. 'We'll let you know if Mam says anything significant. But if someone *was* in the house, they could've caused her injury.'

Sister nodded. 'And in that case we will need to report it to the police.' She patted Dora's arm. 'Just see how you get on now and we'll take it from there.'

Mam had her eyes closed as they sat either side of the bed. Her face looked sunken and Dora realised she hadn't got her teeth in. She always looked older without them. She stroked her worn hands, feeling tears welling. She couldn't bear it if anything happened to Mam. She'd always been the rock Dora depended on, getting her through those awful times after Joanna and Joanie died – and then it had been Dora's turn to be the strong one for *her* following Dad's death from lung cancer the following year. She looked across at Frank, who was chewing his lip, his eyes moist with unshed tears.

'She's a tough old girl. She'll be fine, you know. She has to be.'

He nodded. 'Her eyelids are flickering; I think she's waking up.' As he spoke Mam's blue eyes opened slowly.

'I wasn't asleep,' she mumbled, trying to focus on the two of them. 'I was just resting my eyes. Have you two had your dinner? Where's our Jackie?'

'Jackie's with Agnes, and we'll get something to eat later,' Dora said.

'The pie'll be cold by now. I was going to put it in the bread oven to keep warm. You'll need to reheat it and finish peeling the spuds.'

'Mam. Stop fretting. We'll sort ourselves out,' Frank said, raising an eyebrow in Dora's direction. 'Just concentrate on getting yourself right.'

'Did you bring my nighties?'

Dora lifted the bag onto the bed. 'I'll put them in your locker and maybe later one of the nurses will help you get changed out of that hospital gown. There's a nice bar of soap, a flannel and towel and the Polydent and pot for your teeth as well.'

'Mam, can you remember what happened?' Frank probed gently. 'Sister said you thought I was behind you in the kitchen. But I wasn't there.'

Mam screwed her eyes tight shut for a few seconds. 'I heard you coming in at the front door,' she said. 'I called out that you'd been quick and you came into the kitchen and I didn't turn around because I was busy with the vegetables. But you came up close behind me and then…'

'And then what, Mam?' Dora prompted.

She sighed loudly. 'I don't know. Next thing I recall is Frank slapping my cheeks and calling "Mam". But if it wasn't *you* that came in, Frank, who the heck did?'

'That's what we need to find out,' Frank said. 'Mam, listen carefully now. We need to tell the police about this. From what you say, it sounds as though someone was watching as I went out earlier. As soon as I was out of sight they came into the house by the front door. They either assumed the house was empty or that you were in there alone. When I left you those pies were definitely on the table. And now they've vanished. So it looks like our mystery bread thief is getting bolder and more dangerous.'

Mam chewed her lip, looking frightened. 'Do you think I was attacked, son?'

Dora clutched Mam's hand and nodded. 'It is possible, and we've got to stop this person from hurting anyone else. So me and Frank, along with Sister Ashton, are going to speak to the police.

They may want to ask you a few questions, but don't be scared. We need to catch whoever did this to you.'

'I can't believe that anyone would attack your mam in her own kitchen for the sake of stealing a couple of pies,' Agnes said, handing out cups of tea and sandwiches to a starving Dora and Frank. 'What's the world coming to?'

'It's very worrying,' Dora agreed. 'The police have asked us not to touch anything from the scene of the crime, as they put it, so that they can dust for fingerprints. They're meeting us at the cottage at seven. All we've done is lock the back door to secure it and grabbed some bits for Mam.'

'I tell you what. Leave Jackie with me and she can sleep top to tail with Patsy tonight. She'll be tired and cranky when the police are there and you don't want that. I've got spare pyjamas that will fit her and something to dress her in tomorrow. You'll need to give work a call to let them know you're not able to go in for a couple of days while you get your mam settled at home, Dora. You can come over and make the call from here in the morning.'

Dora nodded. 'Thank you. And it had gone completely out of my mind with all this happening, but Mam was supposed to be looking after Jackie early in the week because Vi is at her son's until Wednesday. They were going to swap their days over.'

'Sis, you need to work. Just have tomorrow off, I'm not going in either, and then I'll take a couple of extra days to look after Mam and Jackie.'

Dora frowned. 'Frank, you can't do that. It'll be too much. It should be me looking after Mam, after everything she's done for me.'

'We'll manage,' Frank insisted. 'Tomorrow I'm going to call at every house in the village, see if anybody has seen anything that might help find this weird thief. I mean, what sort of burglar just nicks food and nothing else? It doesn't make sense.'

Dora blew out her cheeks. 'Somebody who's hungry, I guess. There's the strange woman in the long black coat that hangs about occasionally. She helped herself to all the street party leftovers. And I can't help wondering if there's any connection with that nasty message left with the dead flowers on Joanie's grave.'

At the mention of Joanie, Frank shook his head and went outside to join Alan and the girls in the garden. Agnes leaned forward, a questioning look on her face, so Dora told her what had happened.

When she'd finished Agnes looked shocked. 'You must make sure you tell the police everything you've told me. There could be something significant in there.'

Dora nodded. 'I think there could be too, although I couldn't tell you why. It's just a gut instinct.' Telling Agnes the tale, it didn't seem half as daft as she'd first thought it sounded.

Chapter Twelve

Frank dropped Dora at Agnes's on Monday morning while he went to knock on doors in the village to make his own enquiries. The police officers who had come to the cottage last night had taken statements from both him and Dora and this morning they were visiting their mam in hospital to see if she could help any further. There was little evidence to go on, but they informed the police that several neighbours had reported having food stolen, and people living down Old Mill Lane, opposite Palmer's now demolished factory, had also complained that food left out cooling in kitchens had gone missing. One woman had even had a saucepan of lamb scouse lifted from her stove last week while she was out in her back garden bringing in the washing. She'd gone back inside to find her tea missing and the front door wide open. But not a single neighbour had seen a thing.

The police could offer nothing at the moment other than advising everyone to keep all their doors locked, even when someone was in the house. Now Mam had been injured, possibly by the intruder, they were taking the matter more seriously and making door-to-door enquiries. They said they would be in touch as soon as they had something to report. Frank wasn't holding his breath. He thought he might be able to get more information from their neighbours than the scuffers would.

Maisie across the road waved him over as he parked the car. He remembered that Dora had told her they'd let her know how Mam was, but by the time they'd got back from Agnes's last night and the police had been and gone, Maisie's house had been in darkness, so they'd assumed she'd gone to bed. He hurried across the lane as the old lady leaned on her gate.

'How's Mary doing?' she asked.

'She's okay, needs to rest,' Frank replied. 'We're going to see her later.'

Maisie dug in her faded apron's pocket and pulled out a small bottle of 4711 cologne. 'Take her this. Sprinkle it on a hanky and dab it on her forehead. It smells lovely and it's quite soothing. And give her my love.'

'Thanks, Maisie. I'll do that. I don't suppose you saw any strangers hanging around near the house yesterday, before I took Mam to the hospital?'

Maisie shook her head. 'No, chuck.' She screwed up her face as though thinking. 'But there was a woman I didn't recognise in church yesterday morning. She was sat right at the back and I was with your mam near the front. Funny though, 'cos as we were coming out, she dashes away sharpish like, and then Mary says, "There's that woman who pinched food from the street party." She'd gone when we got outside. Mary said her usual hellos at the graves to Jim and the babby and your Joanie and then we walked back up here.'

'Okay, thanks, Maisie. I'll let you know how we get on and when Mam comes home, you can pop over for a cuppa with her.'

Frank brought his motorbike round the front. It would be easier to observe things if he rode slowly along the lanes, rather than if he was in the car. He called at houses in the immediate vicinity on foot, but got the same answer from each one. No one had seen anything out of the ordinary, although a few reminded him that they'd had bread, cakes and pies stolen over the last few weeks. He covered the rest of the village on his bike with the same results.

He drew a deep breath as he turned into Old Mill Lane. Since Joanie's death he'd been unable to face coming down here and would go out of his way to get where he was going rather than drive this way. But since Dora had found that strange message on her grave, he'd almost felt like he should face his demons. He parked his bike against the sandstone factory wall: all that was left, apart from the brick-built bike shed nearby, to mark Palmer's once-thriving clothing business – a business that had survived the war, only to be brought to its knees by the feckless son-in-law of the late owner. Once orders for clothes ceased and debts began piling up, George Kane had paid his foreman Jack Carter to commit arson by burning down the factory that Frank's lovely new wife and his sister had worked in since leaving school. Kane had promised Carter further money when the insurance company paid out.

Joanie had stayed behind to use an over-locker for a private job. She'd snuck upstairs to the unused second floor on that fateful night. Jack Carter had set fire to rags soaked with lighter fuel on the first floor and, thinking the place empty, locked her in, leaving the place ablaze. Joanie had been pregnant with their first child. She hadn't stood a chance.

People often told Frank it was time he found another girl, but he was heartbroken. He knew that he'd never find another Joanie and nor did he want to. He'd dedicated his life since to looking after Dora the best he could and caring for Mam, and enjoying seeing his little nieces growing up.

He'd thought about moving abroad a few years ago, to America or Canada, but apart from filling in forms for a passport, he'd done nothing about it. Now Dora was living apart from Joe, and Mam was becoming frailer since the death of his dad, he felt it was his place to be here for them all. He sat on the perimeter wall and looked across to where the remains of the sandstone factory walls still lay. Most of the debris had been cleared away and it had been rumoured in the *Echo* a while back that houses were to be built on the site, but so far nothing had been confirmed.

Jack Carter and George Kane were arrested soon after the fire and both were now serving life sentences for arson, fraud and involuntary manslaughter. Frank hoped they'd both rot in jail for the pain they'd put him and his family through. Hanging would be too good for them, but they couldn't be charged with murder as Carter hadn't killed Joanie deliberately. His shock the following day when he'd found out she was missing in the burnt-out shell of the factory was genuine, and he'd not hesitated, once questioned, to confess all.

Frank felt an overwhelming sadness at his loss; life would never be the same again. He lit a cigarette as a bus drove up the lane and stopped on the opposite side of the road. The passengers alighted and a couple of women with shopping bags crossed over. One of them smiled at him, but the other looked like she was sucking a lemon. Frank smiled back, ignoring the miserable-looking woman. 'Good morning, ladies.'

'Good morning to you too, chuck,' the pleasant woman answered. 'Are you looking for something? Can I help you?'

'I was just passing,' Frank said. 'Thought I'd stop here for a few minutes. Memories, you know.'

'Yes, very sad what happened to the old place. I used to work here years ago, before the war. I packed it in when the babbies came along.'

Frank nodded and took a deep drag on his ciggie. He blew a cloud of smoke above his head. 'My wife worked here too, and my sister.'

The woman nodded and turned to her miserable friend, who was sighing loudly and swapping her bag from hand to hand. 'Go home, Beryl, and put the kettle on. I'll join you in a minute or two.' She rolled her eyes as Beryl shuffled off up the lane. 'She's been a right misery all morning. Had stuff pinched from her kitchen earlier, so we've had to go into town to do some extra shopping that she wasn't planning on. But she'd nothing in for tea – it had all gone.'

Frank raised his eyebrows. 'We've had stuff go missing from our house too and so have a lot of our neighbours. I only live up the road on Sugar Lane. Actually, apart from a bit of reminiscing, the reason I'm down this way is to ask around if anyone has seen anything or knows who the thief might be. I mean, it's a bit odd that all they steal is food. Yesterday my mam was knocked unconscious in our kitchen and two pies were stolen. When it was just a bit of food disappearing it seemed almost like a sketch in a comedy film, but when people get hurt, it stops being something to joke about.'

'Get away! And is she okay, your mam?'

'She's still in hospital, had stitches in a head wound. She's trying to remember what happened but she's still a bit foggy. She's certain someone was standing behind her though, and then that's it.'

'Well, I never.' She looked closely at Frank and sighed. 'Aren't you Mary Evans' lad? Lost your wife in that dreadful fire?'

Frank swallowed hard and nodded that he was.

The woman touched his arm. 'I'm so sorry, son. Tell you what, leave your bike here and come down to Beryl's with me and have a cuppa. Wait till I tell her about your mam. I hope Mary's going to be okay. Beryl had a lucky escape there. She was down the carsey when she was robbed. I'm Joyce, by the way.'

'Frank,' he said, and followed her the few yards up the lane.

'Wait until you hear this young man's tale, Beryl,' Joyce began as they let themselves in at the back gate. Beryl had taken off her coat and was sitting on an old wooden bench in the garden.

'Kettle's on,' Beryl said, looking Frank up and down. She managed a half-smile and got one back.

Joyce sat beside her on the bench and told Beryl the tale Frank had just told her. 'His poor mam. *You* were lucky you'd gone down the carsey. Florrie over the road had her pan of scouse pinched a few days ago.'

Frank tried to keep a straight face. It was all so bizarre. 'I know. The police told me.'

'Police? Are they involved now, then?' Joyce asked.

''Fraid so. Well after Mam was found on the kitchen floor we had to report it. Can I ask you something, ladies? It might sound a bit odd, but no odder than what's already going on.'

'Ask away. Let me just go and make the tea first. I'm spitting feathers.' Joyce got to her feet. She was soon back outside with a tray and three mugs of tea. She rummaged in her shopping bag and produced a packet of Gypsy Creams. 'Now help yourself,' she said, opening the packet.

Frank took a swig of tea and then asked if either of them had seen a woman in a long black coat wandering around.

Beryl's eyes lit up and she almost choked on her Gypsy Cream. 'I have,' she said. 'Don't you remember, Joyce, last Friday when we were coming back on the bus from Paddy's market? A woman wearing a black coat stepped out in the road and the driver had to bip his horn proper loud.'

'Oh yes,' Joyce said. 'We thought she must be deaf or a bit simple in that she didn't notice the bus was almost on top of her.'

'Where was this?' Frank asked.

'Down the bottom of the lane. Just before our stop opposite the factory. Don't know where she went from there. We looked down as we got off the bus but she'd vanished. God knows where, there's no houses down that end of the lane.'

'Well there's the farm, but she's not from there, because we know the farmer's wife and it wasn't her.'

Frank chewed his lip. 'Thanks for that. Might be useful, I'll let the police know.'

He finished his tea and got to his feet. Joyce saw him to the lane. She gave his arm a gentle rub.

'Hope your mam is better soon. And I'm so sorry about your young wife. It must have been a dreadful time for you all. Take care and let us know what happens.'

*

'Here's Uncle Frank,' Dora said as her brother pulled up outside Agnes's house. 'Put your sandals back on, Jackie, there's a good girl. Thanks for having her, Agnes, and for letting me use your phone to ring work.'

'You're welcome. Any time. Now keep me up to speed with what's going on. Give your mam my love when you see her later. You can drop Jackie in any time that you need help.' Agnes gave Dora a hug and patted Jackie on the head. 'See you soon, sweetheart. And keep doing your dancing and singing. We loved it. She's kept us entertained,' she said to Dora. 'I'll have to enrol our Patsy in the dancing school at some point.'

Frank helped her with the bags and settled Jackie on the back seat.

'Did you get any joy from the neighbours?' Dora asked as they set off for Wright Street.

Frank told her about his encounter with the two ladies on Old Mill Lane.

'Oh, Frank, it must have been hard going back there. That was brave of you. I know you don't like to be reminded.'

'Actually, I feel better for doing it,' he said. 'A bit easier in my mind. And it could be that your black-coated woman and the pie thief might be one and the same. She certainly gets about in the areas where the food keeps going missing. I'll let the scuffers know and they can work it out for themselves.'

Chapter Thirteen

After a quick sarnie and mug of tea, Dora hurried up Homer Street towards Samuel Jacobs'. Frank had taken Jackie down to the docks. He needed to speak to his boss about taking a few days off and he'd promised his niece an ice-cream from Stan's café if she was a good girl. Dora was going to pick up some work she could do at home. A couple of costumes for a show at the Empire needed finishing and delivering, which she could do while she was off, and she would take Jackie to the theatre with her. She'd enjoy that, especially if there was a rehearsal for the show, which was a musical review.

Since Jackie had started her Saturday morning dance classes at Marjorie Barker's dancing school, Dora had been surprised by the way she sang in tune to most songs she heard, especially her favourite Shirley Temple songs. She picked up the words without a problem and remembered them, and her tap dancing skills were coming on a treat. She wasn't as keen on the ballet class as it meant being serious and Jackie was a giggler, but she was persevering. Dora felt proud of her girl. Maybe she had her own little star in the making.

'Dora, it's good to see you,' Esther greeted her from behind the counter. 'How is your mother, my dear?'

Dora smiled. 'She was doing okay when I rang the hospital this morning from my friend's. My brother and I are going to visit again tonight and then hopefully they may let her home in a day or two.'

'Well, it's very kind of you to offer to do some work at home for us. It will help us out so much. And then, if you can manage it, will you take the outfits to the Empire for us? Just check they fit okay before you leave.'

Dora nodded as Sammy appeared, his beard covered in bits of thread as usual, and placed a large bag on the counter. He rummaged in the boxes on the shelves and put some beads, white lace and velvet ribbon into a small paper bag, then popped the bag into the larger one. 'That should do it,' he said. 'The instructions about what goes where are inside the big bag with the outfits. How is the wedding dress coming along?'

'It's lovely,' Dora said, 'though I say it myself. Once I've got the theatre costumes out of the way I'll get the wedding dress finished and bring it in to fit on the model while I turn up the hem. I've made it to my size and it fits really well.'

'And how is your mother?'

'I was just telling Esther, we're hoping they'll let her come home very soon. Not too much damage done. Just a few stitches and mild concussion. She was very lucky, though we're still trying to find out who's responsible. I'll definitely be in work on Wednesday. My brother is going to look after my daughter for me. I don't want to let you down.'

'Dora, you're not letting us down. Family must come first. And that was a nasty thing to happen to your mother. I hope you get to the bottom of how it happened soon. Don't worry if you can't make it in on Wednesday. It's a big help to me that you're taking the outfits to the Empire.' Sammy went to the till and took out some coins. He handed them to Dora. 'Make sure you get a taxi to the theatre.'

'Thank you. But I'm sure my brother will take me in the car.'

'Well, just in case he can't, you keep it for the fare. And we'll see you soon. Now are you sure you can manage the bag? It's quite heavy.'

Dora lifted it down. 'It's fine, and I haven't got far to go. Thank you. See you soon.' She walked towards the door as Esther, who had disappeared into the small kitchen area, reappeared with a tin.

'Take this for when your mother is allowed home. It's just a cake and a few biscuits.' She wrapped the tin in some brown paper from under the counter.

Dora opened the outfits' bag and Esther sat the tin on top. She gave Dora a hug and opened the door for her.

'Goodbye and thank you,' Dora said. 'You are both so good to me.'

'Will you stay here with us tonight, Frank? You've got to bring me back from Fazakerley, so you might as well. We can pop into Mam's and make sure everything is okay before we come back over here.'

'Yes, I'll stay,' Frank said, taking the empty plates into the kitchen and putting them on the drainer. He'd brought some fresh plaice back from the fish shop at the docks and Dora had made chips to go with it. Even Jackie had tucked in, enjoying a rare treat mid-week. Fish was usually a Friday tea from the chippy. 'I'll sleep on the sofa in the front room. Have you got any spare blankets?'

'Not really. We'll have to grab a couple from Mam's and you'll need a pillow as well. Right, come on, Jackie, let's get your nighty on, then I'll take you over to Aunty Sadie's for a couple of hours. Be a good girl, because Sadie has a lot to do at night. Just sit and be quiet with your book. We won't be long.'

As Dora hurried back from Sadie's, Gloria Smyth, standing on her doorstep, called out, 'Got yerself another fella, gel?'

'He's my brother, actually,' Dora replied.

'Ooh get youse, *actually*,' Gloria mimicked, flicking ash onto the pavement from her ciggie. 'Who do yer think you are, the bloody queen?'

Dora ignored her and slammed the door as she went indoors.

'What's up? You look a bit narked,' Frank said, putting on his jacket. 'I've boiled a kettle and put the plates in to soak in the sink.'

'Thanks, Frank, you're a good one. It's that bloody woman across. Gobby cow that she is. Thinks you're my fancy man. She was the same with Joe the other week. He knows her and her sister from the clubs. Right pair of tramps according to him.'

Frank grinned and rooted in his jacket pocket for his car key. 'Right, let's go and see Mam.'

Mam was awake, a bit of colour in her cheeks tonight. She seemed glad to see them and smiled as Frank produced the little bottle of cologne from Maisie. 'Tell her thanks, love.'

'I will. How are you feeling?'

'A bit washed out, but I'm all right.' She gestured a hand at her surroundings. 'Be glad to get out of here. Oh, they're nice enough and it's very clean, but there are some right miserable beggars around. You can't have a bit of a laugh and joke. The police came today and Sister pulled the curtains around my bed while they asked me a few questions. They made me laugh out loud. Then all eyes were on them as they left and then all on me afterwards. This lot think I've done something wrong, I'll bet. They haven't said, but I can tell.'

Dora laughed. The ward was neat and tidy, the pink and white striped curtains pulled back from around the beds in a precise manner with matching cotton counterpanes on each bed. The elderly occupants, white- or grey-haired ladies, attired in their best nighties, like Mam. But not one smile. Too prim for their own good, a bit like her ex mother-in-law in fact. For a fleeting moment she wondered how Joe was getting along with Ivy and Carol in Morecambe, and then pushed the thought away. 'We'll speak to Sister before we leave,' Dora said. 'She might be able to tell us when you can come home.'

Mam nodded. 'I'll be glad to get back in my own bed.'

'Could you tell the policemen anything you couldn't tell us yesterday, Mam? Has anything come back to you?'

Mam chewed her lip. 'Yes, but I'm wondering if I imagined it. There was a smell. Like an unclean sort of smell. I know that

I've smelt it before and I can't think where. But I'll tell you this: whoever came into my house was a dirty beggar. I told the police and they wrote it all down.'

Dora stiffened and caught Frank's eye. At the street party Mam had mentioned that the woman in the black coat had a bad smell about her. 'She's got a bit of an unwashed pong when you stand downwind of her.' Those were the words she'd used that day. She'd tell Frank when they were outside. But if it *was* that strange woman who'd hurt her mam, why had she done it? And more to the point, who on earth was she?

The bell sounded for end of visiting and Dora and Frank made their way to Sister Ashton's office. She'd been watching out for them and waved them inside, gesturing for them to take a seat.

'I'm pleased to report that your mother is showing great signs of improvement,' she began. 'The police popped in earlier and took a short statement and they asked me to let you know that they'd like you to call in to the station at your earliest convenience. Now, with regards to your mother's discharge, we're thinking maybe Thursday. She might appear lively tonight, but she's been sleeping a lot off and on and that's a good thing. She's resting. We'll get her up tomorrow and sit her in a chair and then on Wednesday we'll get her walking up and down the ward at intervals. All being well, we'll let you know at Wednesday night visiting if you can take her home on Thursday. How does that sound?'

Dora breathed a sigh of relief. 'That sounds just fine. I'll get everything ready and we'll make sure she rests. What about her stitches? Who'll take those out?'

'Your own doctor or a district nurse. We'll let you have that information when she leaves here. It will all be done in her own home.'

Chapter Fourteen

'So, you can definitely identify them as your mother's?' The police officer held up two plates with the remains of pie crust around the edges.

'*Definitely*,' Dora replied. The enamel plates had been in the family as long as she could remember. Mam always made her pies in them. The plates were white with a dark blue rim that was chipped in places. 'Where did you find them?'

'Ah, well that's the odd thing. These, along with at least a dozen other assorted plates, a saucepan and some cutlery, were found in the old bike shed on the land where Palmer's factory used to stand. There were some old blankets and a few items of clothing as well. Someone has been living rough in there for a good few weeks, it would seem.'

'Flipping 'eck,' Frank said. 'Two women I spoke to earlier on Old Mill Lane said they'd seen the woman in a black coat near there, but she vanished. I was going to report the sighting to you next time we came in.'

'Well, we've a couple of officers down there now keeping a low profile. Hopefully an arrest will be made very shortly. We'll keep you informed.'

Dora chewed her lip. 'Do you think Mam's attacker *was* the woman in black, then?'

'There's a strong possibility,' the officer replied.

'But why would a complete stranger hurt an old lady in her own home?'

'We'll get to the bottom of it, Miss, don't you fret yourself. We'll be in touch.'

Dora linked Frank's arm as they walked back to his car. 'We need to call at Mam's house now, make sure it's all locked up and get you some bedding, then we'll head back over to Wright Street and pick up Jackie.'

Frank sighed. 'I'm knackered, love. Be glad to get my head down tonight. Been a funny sort of day.'

It certainly had, Dora thought. There must be more to this than food stealing, though. The woman had obviously done that to survive. But who was she and was it also her who had targeted Joanie's grave and left that horrible message? It didn't make any sense. Dora was really uneasy about the whole thing.

On Wednesday afternoon Dora felt Jackie's grip on her hand tighten as they made their way into the Empire Theatre. A uniformed concierge approached them and smiled.

Dora smiled back. 'I'm from Samuel Jacobs'. I've brought some outfits for the show.'

'Follow me.' He led them into the theatre, where a dress rehearsal was in full swing. 'Sit on the front row there.' He pointed. 'When they stop for a break the choreographer will come over to you.' He caught the eye of a man and pointed to Dora, who held the clothes bag aloft. The man nodded and carried on organising his dance troupe into line.

Dora took a seat and Jackie sat down next to her, her eyes wide as she took in the on-stage activity. When the music struck up and the little girls began to dance to Shirley Temple's 'On the Good Ship Lollipop', Jackie was on her feet, copying the dance movements and actions and singing along with them. Dora tried to get her to sit back down but she was having none of it and threw herself into the routine as though born to it. The man on stage turned to look at her halfway through; he smiled and nodded his approval.

Dora's cheeks were hot with embarrassment as the routine came to an end and the man left the stage and joined her. 'I'm so sorry—' she began but he held his hands up to silence her.

'There is no need to apologise. Your child is talented.' He lowered his voice. 'Much more so than a few of them up there! She must be encouraged at all costs. Do you have her enrolled in a dancing school?'

'I do, yes. She attends Marjorie Barker's in Kirkby on a Saturday morning.'

'Ah, sometimes I use Miss Barker's pupils for my reviews. What is your daughter's name? I shall ask for her for the Christmas show.'

'Jacqueline Rodgers,' Dora said proudly. Wait until she told Frank, Joe and Mam. They'd be so thrilled. 'I'm from Samuel Jacobs', by the way. I've brought the outfits for the show.' She held out the bag.

'Ah, lovely, my principals' outfits. If you'd like to wait a moment, I will ask them to try them on and make sure they fit.' He hurried away as Jackie tugged at her sleeve, her eyes bright.

'I like it here, Mammy,' she said. 'Can we come again?'

'Of course we can. I'll bring you along each time I need to do a theatre visit, as long as it's not your bedtime.' If Jackie indeed had a talent then she would make certain they all encouraged her as much as possible.

On the way back to Jacobs' to report that all was well with the outfits, Jackie hung onto Dora's hand and sang 'The Good Ship Lollipop' all the way down Lime Street. People stopped to stare and smile at the giddy little blonde, doing her Shirley Temple impersonation.

Esther welcomed them in. It was the final hour before closing time and she produced the biscuit tin and let Jackie have first pick. She poured tea for them all and Dora took Sammy's upstairs.

'Ah, Dora, how did it go?'

'Fine. Everything fitted well and my daughter showed off her dancing skills and might be chosen for a Christmas show.' Dora laughed. 'She's a one. Full of herself.'

Sammy chuckled. 'Always nice to encourage confidence and talent from a young age. My son has two left feet, even now in his twenties he still can't dance. He trod on his poor bride's feet throughout the first dance at their wedding.'

Dora smiled. It wasn't often he and Esther mentioned their only child, Sonny. Maybe they weren't as close to him as she and Frank were to their mam. Sonny didn't live in Liverpool like his parents; he'd moved to London and worked in a bank. Perhaps there was disappointment that he hadn't followed in his father's footsteps.

As she hurried back downstairs she could hear Jackie's piping voice as she sang for Esther. She was also dancing, holding out the hem of her dress at each side, just like she'd seen the performers do earlier.

'She makes a grand Shirley Temple,' Esther said, clapping as Jackie took a bow. 'Dora, if you're ever stuck for a babysitter you can bring her in here to keep me entertained. The customers will love her too. Now I mean that. While your mother is laid up, it could be ideal.'

'Thank you. That's wonderful. I hate to let you down. You've been so good to me, but I can see it will probably take Mam some time to get right.'

As Dora and Frank were leaving the ward after visiting a much-improved Mam that night, Sister Ashton beckoned them into her office.

'We're going to keep your mother with us for one more day and then discharge her on Friday afternoon following doctor's rounds. I also wanted to let you know I have a message here from an officer at the station: he and a fellow officer would like to come round to see you. They've been to the house in Knowsley but there was no one there. I said I'd ask where you're staying tonight and let him know.'

Dora gave her Wright Street address and Sister said she would pass it on.

'They must have some news for us,' she said as Frank drove them home. 'I wonder if they've arrested someone.'

'Well, let's hope so. You go and get the kettle on and I'll nip and get Jackie from Sadie's. I just want a quick word with Stan. He asked if there are any jobs going down at the docks; his hours have been cut and things are looking a bit dodgy at the moment. Don't mention it to Sadie though. He doesn't want her worrying with her expecting.'

'I won't. Can you help him, though?' Dora asked, unlocking the front door.

'Aye, I think so. He'll need to go down and see the boss as soon as he can.'

Dora threw a shovel of coal on the fire in the back room and filled the kettle. Frank was back in minutes with a sleeping Jackie in his arms.

'She was spark out on the rug,' he said. 'Shall I carry her up to bed?'

'Yes, but put her in mine. She'll only scream the place down if she's in her own. You might as well as sleep in it, Frank, because *she* won't. She'll be tired out with all the singing and dancing she's done today.'

Dora jumped up at a knock on the door and let in two police officers. She led them into the front room where Frank had lit a fire. 'Please take a seat.' She gestured towards the sofa. Frank sat down on the floor and Dora in the armchair under the window.

'The sister on Mam's ward said you needed to see us,' she began as one of the officers took out a notepad and pen.

'Does the name Myrtle Carter mean anything to you?' The officer looked at Dora.

She frowned as Frank blurted out, 'That's Jack Carter's missus, I think. Am I right, officer?'

'You are, sir. The woman we arrested earlier, the person seen wearing a black coat and stealing food, is indeed known as Myrtle Carter, wife of Jack Carter who is serving a manslaughter sentence. She's been living rough in the bike shed on Palmer's land for several weeks now. But, according to our investigations, prior to that she was in a mental institution for several years. We are still investigating her movements and she *will* be kept in custody until we get to the bottom of things.'

Frank nodded slowly. 'You do know that my wife Joanie,' he nodded towards the framed photo Dora kept on the mantelpiece, 'was the girl who died in the fire?'

'We do, sir. I know it was a few years ago now and we weren't on the force at the time, but please accept our condolences.'

'I don't understand the connection to us,' Dora said. 'Could she be the one who left the horrible message on Joanie's grave out of some sort of spite? But I still don't understand what it meant. She said Joanie got what she deserved and so did I. And she called me a bitch. But I have no idea what she meant by *so did I*. It's almost like she carries a grudge.'

The officer nodded his head. 'That will be part of our investigation over the next day or so.'

'Why was she living in the bike shed?' Frank asked. 'She and Jack had a house and family. Where are the kids?'

Dora nodded. 'They had four young children. I remember Jack telling me that.'

'I've no idea,' the officer replied. 'Possibly in care or with relatives if she'd been admitted to an institution.'

'Bit of a sorry state of affairs,' Frank said. 'Well, thank you for coming to let us know. I'll be staying here with Dora and my niece until Friday and then I'll be back in Knowsley with Mam. She's being discharged on Friday.'

'And I'll be staying there too from Friday,' Dora said. 'So you know where to find us.' She saw the officers out and scowled at Gloria Smyth, who just happened to come to her door at the same time. Probably hiding behind her filthy nets and spying, Dora thought.

''Ere, gel, what did the scuffers want?' Gloria squawked as Frank came to stand behind her. 'What you bin up to then?'

'Mind your own bloody business,' Dora shouted as Frank pulled her out of the way and yelled across, 'They've been looking for the murder weapon for that body they found down the docks. But I'm hardly going to hide it in my sister's house, now am I? So they still can't pin anything on me!'

Dora grinned and shut the door, but not before she saw Gloria's jaw drop and then run to her sister's door and hammer on it. Dora drew the curtains across in the front room, but couldn't resist a peek through the nets to see Gloria gesticulating across at her house and Freda nodding her head and waving her cigarette in the air as she ooh-ed and aah-ed. Ha, bet it wasn't often a police car came down Wright Street unless it was going across the road. Makes a change, Dora thought.

Frank patted the sofa and she sank down beside him. 'So what do you reckon then?' he said. 'Myrtle Parker… but why target us? If anything, it should be us making her life difficult after what her bloody husband did to our family. I thought she'd moved away. I haven't heard anything of her for years.'

'I don't get it,' Dora said. 'Okay, I can understand her stealing food if she was hungry and maybe she hung around our village because she knows it well and has some idea of who's in and out. But what I don't understand is the message on Joanie's grave. And why did she attack Mam?'

Frank blew out his cheeks. 'I have a feeling that may have been accidental. She'd been in the church that morning, according to Maisie across the lane. She saw me go out, might have thought Mam was still out too and took her chance. Perhaps she got a shock when she saw Mam in the kitchen and lashed out when Mam spoke to her, thinking it was me. Mam would have recognised her if she'd turned and seen her face. That would have given the game away so she wasn't taking chances, and remember, she's most probably not all there if she's been in an institution.'

Dora sighed. 'Well I know all about mental health problems, don't I? They make you do stuff you wouldn't normally do. No doubt we'll get to know a bit more tomorrow.'

'Yep. When are Joe and Carol back from Morecambe?'

'Friday. I'll need to let him know that I'll be at Mam's when he brings Carol to see me on Saturday.'

Chapter Fifteen

Dora opened the official-looking envelope that popped through her letterbox on Thursday morning, and held her breath. It was a reply to her recent letter to the welfare department, with her request that Carol be returned to her care as soon as possible now that she was living in her own house. She read it quickly. It was signed by Mr Oliver, who had previously instructed that her daughter was to live with Joe. He wanted to make a call to the house next week to discuss the matter with both her and Joe, who would also be in receipt of a letter, and had given the date of Wednesday at eleven thirty.

Dora sighed. Was nothing ever straightforward? Joe would be back at work. He wouldn't be very happy at having to take extra time off. *She'd* be back working by then too, and how the heck could she ask for more hours off? Sammy and Esther didn't even know she had another daughter. She'd been too ashamed to say that she'd lost custody of her. If she told them now they'd think she had something to hide and might judge her to be a bad parent. Another problem that she'd need to face in having Carol back was school and getting her settled in properly. And then who would take her and pick her up? She couldn't rely on Sadie, whose baby would be arriving in the next few weeks, and Sadie's mam would be busy popping over to help her. And yet, as a mother, she knew she had to fight for her rights. But would Carol even *want* to live with her and Jackie? What if she hated it and played up and caused problems?

Frank came inside from his visit to the lavatory and washed his hands at the sink. She read him the letter and he frowned when she told him she and Joe would be at work then. 'They don't make it easy, do they?' he said. 'Why not ask Sammy for a couple of hours off? You could tell him you need to take Mam to the doctor's or something, unless of course you tell him the truth. Make it simpler all round.'

'I don't want them to think badly of me,' she muttered, shoving the letter back into the envelope and putting it up on the fireplace behind the clock.

'They don't sound like judgemental people to me, Sis. And have you thought about how you'll explain Carol away if she does come back to live with you? I'd get it out of the way now, before it becomes a problem too big to deal with. Either of the kids could be poorly at any time and you'll have to take days off to look after them. I don't think Mam will be able to do as much as she did for you. She's getting older and quite frail now and this head injury will have set her back a bit too. If you want to keep working, you need to get it sorted.'

Jackie looked up from her bowl of Weetabix. 'Will you play jigsaws with me, Uncle Frank, while Mammy goes to work?'

'Uncle Frank needs to go out soon, you'll have to go to Vi's,' Dora said. She turned to Frank. 'I'm just going to knock on Vi's door to make sure she's okay to have Jackie. She only got back from her son's last night. Won't be a minute.'

Vi answered the door at her knock and invited Dora inside. She seemed a bit flustered, and she wasn't even dressed yet. That wasn't like Vi, who was always up early and dressed promptly. Today a hairnet covered her curlers and she wore a blue quilted dressing gown over a long nighty with matching blue slippers.

'I'm glad you're here, Dora, I need to talk to you.' She poured Dora a mug of tea from a brown tea pot and pushed it across the table.

Dora wrapped her hands around the mug and frowned. She had a feeling that what Vi was about to say was not what she wanted to hear.

'I'm, er, I'm giving up my house and going to go and live with my son and his wife in Southport,' Vi began. 'They've had a little annexe built onto the side of their house for me. It's got its own private entrance and it's lovely, just like a little bungalow. They're expecting their first baby and when Sheila goes back to work I'm going to be in sole charge. It's my first grandchild and I'm that thrilled to bits about it, I can't tell you.'

Dora tried to look happy for Vi, who looked so excited, but inside she felt sick. There would be no one to look after Jackie now. She'd have to give up her job and go back to trying to scrape a living from her own occasional sewing jobs that were few and far between, and accept Joe's money with good grace. Sometimes it felt like the fates were conspiring against her; all she wanted was to be able to work and have her girls with her again. Then she pulled herself together; it was selfish of her to feel this way. Vi needed her family around her. She just hoped they wouldn't take too much advantage of her lovely neighbour and would appreciate everything she did for them. 'That's wonderful news, Vi. I'm so happy for you.'

'Thank you, dear. I'm sorry I'll be letting you down over having Jackie. I hope you'll be able to find someone else to mind her.'

'Oh, don't worry about us. We'll be fine. I've just popped in to tell you I'll take her with me today, so you can have a rest after your trip,' she fibbed. 'When will you be leaving us?'

'On Saturday. Our Colin phoned my landlord and gave him a week's notice. I have to be gone by twelve o'clock. Colin's booked a van to come and take my things and he's picking me up. So it's all arranged, barring the packing and clearing out. But I've got today and tomorrow to do that.'

Dora finished her tea and got to her feet, feeling sad. Apart from losing a lovely friend and neighbour, there was the worry of who would be moving into Vi's house. She said goodbye and dashed into Sadie's, knocking and entering without being asked.

Sadie popped her head around the kitchen door, looking flustered. 'Won't be a minute. Just making Peter and Belinda some breakfast. Park yourself on a chair.'

She hurried through with a plate of toast and hoisted Belinda into the high chair and bellowed up the stairs for Peter, who came hurtling down and took a seat at the table. 'What's up? Do you want a coffee? I'm going to have one. I didn't get time before I rushed the other two up to school.'

And although she'd just had tea at Vi's, Dora nodded. 'Please.'

When they were seated in opposite armchairs in Sadie's neat-as-a-new-pin front room, two mugs of Camp coffee to hand, Dora, suddenly feeling overwhelmed, took a deep breath and put her mug down on a small lamp table.

'Right, now tell me what's wrong,' Sadie said. 'You look proper mithered to death.'

Dora's eyes filled as she told Sadie the morning's events. 'I don't know how I'm going to cope and I feel so selfish saying that because Vi deserves a bit of family time.'

'She does,' Sadie agreed. 'I just hope Colin and his wife value her and look after her properly. I'll miss her. She's always been there for me. The kids will miss her too. Don't worry, Dora, I'm sure you'll find a way to manage. This letter you got, do they want to come and see you?'

'Yes, me *and* Joe,' Dora replied. 'And they'll take one look around this street and the outside lavs and make a decision based on that. I told them in my letter that I hoped to be rehoused in a new property in the not-too-distant future.'

'Well I expect they've taken all that on board. Er, don't think I'm being nosy, but I saw the police car outside last night. Was it to do with your mam?'

Dora nodded and told her about Myrtle Carter and how they were waiting for more news on the matter. 'I still don't understand what she was up to though and why she attacked Mam or put that horrible message on Joanie's grave. It's all so muddled.'

Sadie sighed. 'I'm sure they'll get to the bottom of it in time. But at least she's locked up now and won't be harming anyone else. Are you going into work today?'

'Yes, and I'm going to take Jackie in with me. Frank said I should tell them about Carol too. I know I should have done that right away, stupid of me not to. Now it looks like I had something to hide.'

'I'm sure they'll understand.' Sadie finished her coffee. 'I wonder who we'll get next door. Unless they just board it up until they demolish the street. Vi would have been going very soon anyway, like we will once this little bun is out of the oven. Did you do anything about getting your name on the list? If you do get Carol back you'll get more points.'

'Well, that's all in the lap of the gods for now. I've applied and I'm playing a waiting game, like you. Can I leave Jackie with you later while we pop in and see Mam?'

'Of course.'

'She's being discharged tomorrow and I'll be staying up in Knowsley for a few days, but I'll be back here to see Mr Oliver next Wednesday. Will you just keep your eye on the place for me, Sadie? I really don't trust that lot over the road.'

'No problem at all, don't worry. Now go and get it over with at work. Esther and Sammy sound lovely, so I'm sure you're worrying over nothing. Just explain that someone must have had it in for you and you're still trying to get that sorted out.'

Dora gave Sadie a hug. 'Thank you. I'll see you later.'

Mam looked pale as Dora tucked a blanket around her knees. Although it was warm outside the house felt chilled from being closed up, so she'd lit the fire earlier. 'Right, you stay there and rest and I'll get you a cuppa,' Dora ordered. 'Frank will be back shortly from the shops with Jackie and then he's promised to take her to the park. I'll need to pop out to the phone box to ring Joe later. He can bring Carol over here tomorrow.'

Mam looked worried. 'Will you ask Maisie to come and sit in with me while you nip out, chuck? I don't fancy being left in on my own.'

'I will.' Dora smoothed Mam's grey hair from her face. 'But you don't need to worry. That woman is locked up. It won't happen again.'

She made Mam her cuppa and then busied herself in the kitchen, washing the things Mam had worn in hospital. The district nurse would be calling in the morning to check her wound and hopefully take out the stitches. All being well, her mam would be on the way to recovery and her confidence would come back. The shaky old lady in the sitting room was a shadow of the independent woman she'd been. Bloody Myrtle Carter had a lot to answer for. What had she been thinking? Dora hoped the police were making some headway with their investigations. Surely it wouldn't take long.

Yesterday she'd taken Jackie into work for a couple of hours. She'd spoken to both Esther and Sammy and explained the situation with Carol and that she had lost her regular child-minder for Jackie. She'd said that if she was given custody of Carol again it might be difficult to work as many hours as she had been doing, but that she would happily take work home and do the running about to the theatres while Carol was at school. They had both been extremely understanding and Dora had never felt such relief. They said they would work around her available hours. They didn't want to lose her. Esther insisted that Jackie was no trouble to have around and had cleared an area off the kitchen and put a small table and a couple of chairs in. Jackie could sit in there and draw and do her jigsaw puzzles while she and Esther listened to the wireless. Next year Jackie would be starting school, so there would just be the holidays to worry about.

The only problem to overcome now was telling Joe about Wednesday's visit from Mr Oliver, although he'd no doubt have read the letter by the time she rang him. Dora knew Joe wouldn't be very happy and would put as many obstacles in her way as he possibly could. He and Carol were as close as she and Jackie were.

Chapter Sixteen

Ivy Bennett swanned into work half an hour early on Monday morning, a wide smile on her chubby face. She busied herself getting the frying pans on the gas hobs and tossing several rashers of bacon into each in readiness for the hungry nightshift. She cracked two dozen eggs into bowls and sliced two large loaves of bread. She liked this bit of peace and quiet before Flo, her assistant, arrived. It gave her time for reflection.

She'd just enjoyed five days in Morecambe with her lovely friend Joe and his little girl, Carol. They'd taken her landlord's dog Roly as company for Carol and the pair had played on the sands while she and Joe had relaxed in deckchairs. The weather had been fine and she'd caught the sun on her face, giving her a healthy glow. It had been too good an opportunity to turn down when she'd been offered the chance of borrowing the caravan from someone her landlord knew, and thankfully Joe had accepted the offer when she'd asked him to accompany her.

She'd told Joe there were two bedrooms in the caravan when in fact she'd known there was just the one, and they'd settled Carol into that each night while they sat and enjoyed a couple of drinks outside on the lawned area. She'd feigned surprise at the lack of bedrooms and told Joe they'd have to make do with the seating area, which, when pulled out with the table folded away, made up into a double bed.

Joe had avoided intimacy with her since their one and only time together years ago, telling her they should just remain good friends as it would cause less hassle if he decided to get a divorce. Ivy had been supportive and patient, helping him with Carol, while all the time plotting to win his love. A few drinks, a relaxing atmosphere and close proximity to each other's bodies, even though she'd placed a pillow between them, did the trick. Joe had said very little on the drive home and he hadn't invited her to stay over on the Friday night, but dropped her and Roly off at their home. All day Saturday she'd worried herself that he regretted making love to her again. But on Sunday he'd come over to see her and, while Carol took Roly into the garden to play, told her that Dora had applied for custody of Carol and that there was to be a meeting on Wednesday. He hadn't been happy about it, but she'd reassured him that maybe it was time Carol spent at least a few days a week with her mother and sister. There'd also been mention that someone was being held in custody for attacking Dora's mother, but Ivy hadn't taken much notice as she wasn't the least bit interested in anything to do with Dora and her family. He'd given her a real kiss as he'd left her, not just a peck on the cheek like she used to get before the holiday.

She was keeping her fingers crossed now that if Dora *did* get custody of Carol, it would leave Joe at a loose end and he'd hopefully spend more time with her, especially at the weekends when she could accompany him to shows with the band, instead of babysitting for him and having to be grateful for ten minutes of his company before he put her in a taxi home. Being lovers again put a whole new perspective on things as far as Ivy was concerned. And if she and Joe did make a go of it, the last thing she wanted was to be lumbered with either of his kids on a regular basis. Once a week would be more than enough. She'd waited long enough and wanted him to herself.

She nodded at Flo, who lurched in and took off her coat, put on her white overall and black and white check pinny like Ivy's and washed her hands at the sink.

'Did you have a good time, Ivy?' Flo asked as she slid slices of bread under the grill. 'You look like you've caught the sun a bit.'

'Yes, it was lovely, thank you. Beautiful weather.'

'And did Joe enjoy himself?'

'Oh, I can safely say that Joe really enjoyed himself.' Ivy lifted the bacon rashers out of the pans and dropped the eggs in. The fat splattered over the sides onto the gas flames and she wafted a tea towel to dispel the rising smoke. With a bit of luck she could pack this job in and become a lady of leisure soon. Making a nice home and looking after Joe's needs would keep her occupied and happy.

Dora got the bus and tram home on Wednesday morning, leaving Jackie with her mam and Frank, who had taken another few days' holiday to look after her. Sammy and Esther had been kind enough to let her take the day off, but she was calling in to see them later and to drop some work in. As she neared her house a little shudder ran through her to see all the windows in Vi's had been broken, including upstairs. A man with a handcart filled with pieces of wood was busy hammering slats into place across the frames, watched by a smirking Lenny Smyth and his mother.

'Morning, Dora,' Gloria called. 'Been stoppin' over at yer fancy man's again?'

Dora ignored the woman as Sadie called from her doorstep and beckoned her inside. She stepped through broken glass that crunched beneath her shoes and went into Sadie's house. 'What's up, well apart from that lot out there?'

'I'm glad you're back. Those bloody lads of Gloria's have smashed Vi's house up. She'd not been gone more than two hours and they were inside. Stan tried to get them out but they threatened him so I told him to come back in. Can't afford for him to get injured with our lot to look after. The sink is out in the yard. They chucked it through the window. Stan said it was lead piping they were after. He's been inside since and turned off the water at the stop tap, otherwise we'd have had damp coming through the walls. That man boarding up said the scuffers had arranged for him to come and do it. Someone must have been on the phone to them.'

Dora sighed. 'I can't believe it – the man from the welfare is coming this morning and there's glass all over the pavement. I'll get my brush out when that fella's finished and sweep it towards the wall for now. So, looks like we're not getting another neighbour.'

Sadie shrugged. 'I doubt it. The landlord won't want to be replacing windows now when it's so close to him offloading to the council. In a way it might be good in that the welfare man can see the houses are getting close to being demolished. He'll be able to work out for himself that you'll be out of here soon.'

'Maybe.' But Dora wasn't convinced. 'I'd better go and light a fire in the front room, so it looks at least half homely. Then I'll sweep the street and get myself ready for the visit. Joe's coming at eleven. He's not happy about it, but we'll see.'

Dora rubbed her sweaty palms on the skirt of her dress and looked at Joe for reassurance as he sat next to her on the sofa. Mr Oliver took the armchair under the window. Joe gave her a half-smile, which didn't quite reach his eyes and did nothing to quell the butterflies leaping around in her stomach.

Mr Oliver shuffled a few papers around on his knee and looked at the two of them over the top of his glasses. 'Mr and Mrs Rodgers,' he began, 'I've given this matter a great deal of thought. I know you've been building up a relationship with your daughter, Carol, Mrs Rodgers, while she's been under the supervision of Mr Rodgers.'

Dora nodded, clasping her hands together around her knees to stop them shaking. She was terrified that he'd say something like she couldn't keep Jackie either now.

He continued. 'However, we are not certain that it is in Carol's best interests to remove her from Mr Rodgers at this time. She is settled with him and in her school, although I have a report from her teacher that expresses a bit of concern about her behaviour. Now, if we were to uproot her, she would need to change school to one closer to this address, but as you will no doubt be rehoused away from here shortly, Mrs Rodgers, it is likely she will need to change schools again. For a child already showing signs of being unsettled, that isn't a good thing.'

Dora pursed her lips. Before she could control herself she blurted out, 'You enforced your stupid rules on me and unsettled our daughter who was just fine before. What you did caused her and my family a lot of harm. It's taken ages to build up our relationship again.'

'We only do what's best for the children we believe to be at risk, Mrs Rodgers.' Mr Oliver shuffled the papers on his knee again.

'Really?' Dora got to her feet, her eyes blazing. 'So who's responsible for kids who are neglected, who go hungry and walk around in rags? Whose mother is a whore by night and leaves them alone with a drunken father? Eh? Go on, answer me that if you can, Mr-bloody-Oliver!'

Joe grabbed her hand and pulled her back down beside him. 'Dora, stop it. That's not helping.'

She snatched her hand away and glared at Mr Oliver, who now had two small red spots high on his cheeks.

He cleared his throat. 'If you have reason to believe that children of your acquaintance are being neglected then you should report it to the authorities, who will investigate further.'

'You should already know about these kids. Check with the health visitor for this area. I'm not grassing on anybody. Look what it's done to us. But you, Mr Oliver, need to do a bit more of your so-called investigating and get your facts right before you ruin people's lives.' She stopped as someone hammered on the front door. Joe got up to answer and let in a flustered-looking Frank.

'Oh God, Frank, is it Mam? What's happened? Where's Jackie?' Dora gasped.

'It's okay, Maisie's sitting in with Mam and I've taken Jackie round to Agnes's. I've got something very important to tell you and I wanted to make sure *he* was still here. Er, I'm Dora's brother.'

He nodded in Mr Oliver's direction and sat down on the arm of the sofa next to Joe. 'This is something you all need to hear,' Frank said, all eyes on him. He took a deep breath. 'The police have been to see me and Mam again this morning. Turns out that Myrtle Carter has confessed all. After Jack was sent to prison she couldn't pay the rent and was evicted. Her kids were taken into care and she was on the streets. She started drinking and was arrested for disorderly behaviour and it was decided she was going off her rocker, so she was sent to a mental institution. While she was in there she plotted revenge for when she was allowed out again. Once she was free to go she wanted to make someone pay for losing her kids who she couldn't get back, having no home or money to take care of them.

'She was angry that Jack had been arrested for Joanie's death, but blamed Joanie for being on site the night of the fire, and she blamed you too, Dora, for daring to have a business that needed Joanie to be using Palmer's over-lockers. Joanie died but you were still around and she assumed you were living the perfect life. She didn't know that you had two kids, just thought you had Carol. It was her that reported you for neglecting Carol. She knew about your mental health history from Jack and she played on it, wanting Carol to be taken into care just like her kiddies had been. It was to punish you for all that she lost.' Frank paused again. 'She moved recently from the rooming house they put her in, made her way to the bike shed at Palmer's, lived rough and stole food to stay alive. And the rest, as they say, is history.'

Dora, Joe and Mr Oliver stared open-mouthed at Frank. Mr Oliver spoke first. 'This woman, this Myrtle Carter, you say the police told you all this?'

Frank nodded. 'Yep, you can get a report from them. I expect this throws a new light on our Dora getting Carol back now, Mr Oliver?'

'Well, the case will certainly need to be reinvestigated now.' Mr Oliver placed his papers inside his briefcase and stood up. 'I'm sorry for all the upset you've been through, Mr and Mrs Rodgers. What I was about to suggest, before Mrs Rodgers' outburst, is that Carol spends weekends with her mother and sister, no need for supervision unless you feel you need the help. I'll be in touch shortly when I have spoken to the police and filed a new report. I bid you all good day.'

Dora saw him out, her legs shaking so badly she could hardly walk. She couldn't believe what Frank had told them. Myrtle Carter. She couldn't even feel sorry for the woman who'd caused such pain. She didn't think she'd ever forgive her.

Chapter Seventeen

March 1954

On Saturday morning, Dora helped her mam out of Frank's car and up the path of the Belle Vale prefab. Jackie and Frank carried in bags and boxes of party treats between them. Jackie was high as a kite with excitement. Her fourth birthday yesterday had been celebrated at the Jacobs', with Esther providing a little afternoon tea party and a birthday cake, in-between serving customers. And today the family and a few friends were gathering for further celebrations. Joe had suggested holding the party here as he had a bit more room than anyone else and if the weather was dry the kids could play outside in the garden. Mam wasn't well enough to host anything at the moment, although she'd insisted on making a cake with pink and white icing and candles. Dora had been too embarrassed to invite anyone to Wright Street, as most of the houses now stood empty and boarded up or vandalised. When Joe said they should all come here, Dora had jumped at the suggestion.

Carol let them in and seemed as excited as her sister, pulling Jackie into the sitting room and pointing at the balloons that Daddy had blown up and hung on the walls. Dora hoped the good mood would continue. The weekend sleepovers advised by Mr Oliver had been a bit difficult, as Carol always screamed blue murder when Joe left her. After three weeks of it Joe said they should do the visits a day at a time; he'd bring Carol over each morning. He'd also suggested they go out as a family occasionally so the girls got to spend time together with both parents. So far it had worked out well and she and Carol had grown a bit closer, a comfortable truce drawn between her and Joe for the sake of their daughters. She still couldn't envisage a day when Carol would be returned to her care full-time, though. As Mr Oliver had pointed out, there was the problem with changing schools. During the reinvestigation of the case following Myrtle Carter's confession, Dora had been told that the authorities would wait until Dora was settled in her new home before any further decisions were made. But until she had Carol back, she was told by the council that the need to rehouse her with just the one child was not as great as that of other families on the waiting list. Dora felt like she was going round in circles in a no-win situation.

'Look after Granny, girls, while I go and find Daddy.' Dora sat Mam on the sofa in the sitting room and went into the kitchen, where Joe was washing up. Frank brought the bags and boxes through and put them on the table.

'I'll make a start on the sandwiches,' Dora announced. 'Put these eggs on to boil.' She handed a paper bag to Joe, who did as he was told, a little smile playing at the corners of his mouth.

'What's so funny?' Dora asked, tying a frilly apron over her blue floral dress and looping her hair back behind her ears.

'Nothing.' Joe grinned. 'You're as bossy as ever, giving orders like you still lived here.'

Dora raised her eyebrows. 'Cheeky.' She unpacked a tub of potted beef and sliced a loaf that Mam had made yesterday. 'What do you think of Jackie's cake? Pink and white icing, she'll love it. Esther made her a beauty yesterday but most of it got eaten and I took the rest home to Sadie and her lot. There are some biscuits and little fancies in one of those boxes from Esther.'

'That's kind of her. How *is* Sadie?' Joe asked.

'She's fine. New baby's doing well. He's huge and Belinda is walking now, so that makes things easier when Sadie takes them all out. She's still waiting for the bigger house, but I can't see them waiting too much longer. Stan's working down the docks with Joe now. He seems to be enjoying it. More hours, better money and right on his doorstep.'

'That's good. And *you* haven't heard anything yet, about a new place I mean?'

'Not yet.' Dora sighed. She was dreading the day Sadie moved out. The thought of being on her own in Wright Street wasn't something she was looking forward to. 'The council would rehouse me quicker if I had Carol with me, but like they say, she'd have to change schools twice. I can't win, can I? I just wish they'd hurry up though. There was a huge rat in the backyard the other day. It terrified Jackie as it ran past. Stan chucked a brick at it, but he missed.' She glanced out of the window at the lovely little garden with its pristine lawn and flower borders. How she missed it. The girls pushed past her and made for the garden swing. 'Granny's shutting her eyes,' Carol yelled.

'Jackie loves it here.' Dora smiled, looking proudly at her daughters, each dressed in a new multi-coloured floral party frock that she'd made, their hair fastened up with matching ribbon bows. She shook her head before the wish-I-still-lived-here thoughts crowded her mind, and began to spread margarine on the bread. Frank squeezed her arm and went outside to play with his nieces, who clamoured for him to push them high on the swing.

Joe smiled. 'He'd have made a great dad. Such a bloody shame he never got the chance. I hope he meets someone else soon. He needs to settle down.'

'Like you have, you mean.' Dora couldn't keep the sarcastic edge from her voice and immediately regretted it as she saw his eyes cloud. 'Sorry, I promised myself today would be a nice family day. No bickering.'

Joe nodded. 'We'll do our best. I'll make Mam a drink. Do you want one? Then I'll nip to Dolly's and get the stuff she's made for the party. She's a good one, mithers me to death, but she's a great neighbour when I need her.'

'I will have a cuppa, thanks. Is Dolly bringing Alice up later?'

'Yep. A couple of Carol's little pals from school that Jackie's met are coming too and Agnes is bringing Patsy. I called Agnes last night and invited them.'

'Oh, I'm glad you did. I meant to remind you last week and I forgot.' A sudden thought struck her. '*She* isn't coming, is she?'

'Who, Ivy? No, of course she's not. She sent a parcel home with me for Jackie to open today, but she's not coming to her party. Why would I even ask her, Dora? She's my babysitter, colleague and a good pal. She means nothing else to me; like I keep telling you.' He shook his head and poured mugs of tea and carried one through to Mam on his way out to Dolly's.

Dora finished making the potted beef sandwiches and covered the plate with greaseproof paper to keep them fresh. She checked the eggs on the stove and ran cold water over them in the sink before shelling them and mashing the insides in a bowl with a knob of marge and a drop of milk. Frank came in and wrinkled his nose.

'Good job egg sarnies taste better than they smell,' he said with a grin. 'They don't half pong.'

Dora gave him a friendly push. 'Go and see if Mam's okay. Joe took her some tea through and she might have finished it and can't reach to put her mug on the coffee table.' Since the accident, Mam seemed to be getting stiffer and slower. The doctor said it was arthritis and had prescribed painkillers, giving instructions that she should massage her joints with warm olive oil each day, but it didn't seem to be doing much good. She'd lost her confidence and her lack of mobility left a lot to be desired. She needed help getting upstairs to bed, going outside to use the lavatory, and didn't like being left in the house on her own. With both of them back at work during the day, they had to rely on neighbours popping in. How much longer that could go on for, Dora didn't know. It was certainly a worry for the future. If only she didn't need to work, she could look after Mam like she'd looked after Dora, in her time of need. It was a pity Frank didn't work for the ROF; then they might qualify for a bungalow like Joe's with everything on one level, no stairs to worry about.

After a noisy birthday tea, Frank organised the games. He stopped the music as the circle of excited little girls sitting on the floor gasped. Dolly's Alice had got the parcel and chucked the last piece of paper into the centre of the group. She held aloft a crayoning book as everyone clapped. 'One more game of pass the parcel and then we'll play musical bumps,' Frank shouted above the loud chattering. 'Ready, ladies,' he said, making them all smile.

Musical bumps proved popular but there wasn't much bumping done as the girls all joined in singing along to 'How Much Is That Doggy in the Window?' with Uncle Frank doing the 'Woof, Woofs', making them all collapse with the giggles.

'They're having a great time,' Dora said as she and Agnes washed up in the kitchen. 'I'm so glad you came. It's lovely to see you again.'

'And you. Not long now to Patsy's birthday. I hope you and Joe and the girls will come.'

'Oh, of course we will. We'll look forward to it.' Dora didn't see the look of satisfaction on Agnes's face as she accepted the invite for them all. She looked up as Joe brought a few more pots in and put them in the sink, stroking her arm affectionately as he passed. She smiled. It was a nice feeling to know he still cared for her. She enjoyed them being together as a family and Carol was certainly happier here than she ever was at Wright Street.

Frank popped his head around the door. 'Jackie's opening her pressies and then we need to do the candles on the cake. Mam's struggling to keep her eyes open. I'll take her home after we've sung "Happy Birthday", then I'll come back for you and Jackie, Sis.'

'I'll run Dora and Jackie home,' Joe said. 'No need to dash back, Frank. I'll pop Carol into Dolly's for a bit.'

'Thanks, mate.' Frank went back into the sitting room, carrying the birthday cake.

'Are you sure you don't mind?' Dora frowned.

'Not at all. Right, let's go and sing, they're all squealing in there. That'll wake your mam up for a few minutes.'

'I think the painkillers she's taking make her extra tired. She's not right though, and I'm worried about her.'

Frank held his hands up for quiet. Jackie was sitting on the rug surrounded by coloured wrapping paper. Dora got down beside her and gathered up the torn pieces. 'Did you keep the labels that your name was written on?' she asked. 'Then we know who to thank.'

Jackie thrust several small pieces of card at her and smiled happily. 'Look.' She held up a dolly's tea set. 'It's got a tea pot. We can play parties. And clothes for my dolly too. Carol said Granny knitted them.'

Dora smiled and gave her daughter a hug. 'Oh, you've got one parcel left.' She picked it up and saw 'To Jackie, love from Ivy and Roly' written on the label. It wouldn't do to tear the label up in front of everyone, so she gritted her teeth, smiled and handed the parcel to Jackie. 'From Roly,' she said, staring up at Joe, who raised an eyebrow.

Jackie tore off the wrapping and pulled out a pink, hand-knitted cardigan with white heart-shaped buttons down the front. 'Ooh, look, it's luverley,' she said. 'Did Roly really make it, Mammy? Isn't he a clever doggy?'

'Yes, he is, very clever,' Dora said, swallowing the bile that had risen in her throat. It was indeed a lovely cardigan, but the fact that Ivy had actually sat and made it for Jackie made her feel sick. She got to her feet and excused herself. In the bathroom she leaned against the sink and took a few deep breaths. As soon as she felt calmer she made her way back into the sitting room where Frank was bringing in the cake with the candles lit. .

Jackie stood by the table, her eyes aglow, as everyone sang loudly and wished her a happy birthday. She blew out the candles and clapped her hands. Dora took the cake into the kitchen and cut it into slices.

Dolly came and stood beside her. 'Shall I wrap 'em for you, gel?'

'Please, Dolly. There are some paper serviettes in that box next to you.' It was good to see her old pal again. Dolly never changed. Her red hair had faded slightly but still stood out around her head like a fuzzy halo. 'Thanks for all the help you give Joe with our Carol. He really appreciates it, you know.'

'Ah, she's no trouble. Like one of me own now, is Carol. How's life on Wright Street these days? Joe said you've lost your neighbour. Are you managing to get Jackie minded okay while you work?' Dolly licked the buttercream from her fingers as she wrapped the last piece of cake.

'I take her into work with me. They're very good about it. She sits with Esther, my boss's wife, while I'm up in the workroom and then she comes to the theatres with me. She loves that. Keeps Esther entertained with her song and dance routines as well. And as for Wright Street, to be honest, it's a dump, but it's better than nothing, I suppose.'

Dolly raised both eyebrows. 'You're mad, Dora!' She gestured with her hands. 'You've swapped this lovely house for living down there. Joe would have you back today; you know that, don't you? You'd soon sort yourselves out.'

'We're nearly divorced now. It's much too late to start changing my mind. Anyway, I can't do that.'

'It's never too late.' Dolly stopped as Alice ran into the kitchen followed by Carol and the other little girls, all demanding cake. She handed out the wrapped slices. 'Take them in the garden and put your paper in the bin.' She turned her attention back to Dora. 'Think on what I've said. You *can* do it. Don't lose him to *her*.'

As Dora waved goodbye to her mam and Frank, Alan pulled up at the front. 'Agnes,' Dora called, 'Alan's here.'

'Phone me in the week from work,' Agnes said as she left with Patsy.

'I will. We'll catch up soon. Thank you for Jackie's tea set. She's been dying for one for ages.'

'Patsy plays with hers for hours. You'll get a bit of peace and quiet while you do some sewing. See you soon.' Agnes gave Dora a hug. 'Joe has hardly taken his eyes off you this afternoon. I do wish you'd sort yourselves out,' she whispered, almost echoing Dolly's parting words.

She dashed down the path and hurried Patsy into the waiting car, leaving Dora staring open-mouthed as Alan pulled away down the road.

Chapter Eighteen

'Can Mammy and Jackie sleep here tonight?' Carol was asking Joe as Dora went back into the sitting room.

'That's up to Mammy,' Joe said, looking at Dora, who could feel her cheeks heating. She suppressed a smile as her stomach lurched with anticipation. Were they all in on this, the kids, and Agnes and Dolly too?

'Please, Mammy, please,' Carol begged and Jackie joined in with her pleas. The pair of them were on their knees in front of her with their hands clasped together.

'Go on outside for a quick play before it gets too dark,' Joe said. 'Let Mammy and me have a talk and a cuppa in peace.'

He followed the girls to the back door and Dora sat down on the sofa, her heart beating nineteen to the dozen. She took a deep breath as Joe brought two cups of tea through. They sat side by side, an awkward silence between them. Joe spoke first.

'It does seem a shame that they can't spend the time together when they're getting on so well. Why don't you stay? No strings, honestly. They can share my bed, you can have Carol's room and I'll sleep on the sofa.'

Dora chewed her lip. 'Are you sure?' It would be lovely to have some company tonight instead of sitting alone in her own house sewing and listening to the noisy neighbours. And no strings sounded just fine to her. It was good for Jackie to be getting along so well with her sister for a change. It *did* seem a shame to drag her away.

'I'm positive,' Joe replied. 'I've no show to play tonight. And then tomorrow we can all go to New Brighton for the day on the ferry. A nice way to finish celebrating Jackie's birthday weekend. What do you say?'

Dora smiled. 'That would be lovely. It'll be a bit windy though. We'll have to call at my house to get our jackets.'

Joe nodded and got to his feet. 'We'll sort all that out tomorrow. Shall *I* tell them you're staying or will we do it together?'

Dora kicked off her shoes and with a sigh of relief flopped down on the sofa. Their giddy daughters had taken ages to settle down after a mad splashy bath time and four stories that Joe had read them. At least they were quiet now, snuggled up together like they'd never had a scrap in their lives.

'I'm going to pop out to the off-licence to get a jug of ale. I'll get some sherry too. I've nothing in that's suitable for ladies to drink.'

'Lady, eh?' Dora laughed. 'That would be lovely. I haven't had a glass of sherry for ages. Switch the telly on for me, please, Joe. *Fabian of the Yard*'s on in a bit.'

In Joe's absence Dora lay stretched out on the comfy sofa, her stockinged feet up on the coffee table, relishing the peace and quiet. It had been a lovely day and she felt so relaxed, calmer than she'd felt for weeks in fact. Maybe now that Carol had enjoyed her time with Jackie she might be persuaded to stay overnight at Wright Street. She still felt annoyed by Ivy's present, but had to admit that the cardigan looked lovely on Jackie, and was much nicer than anything *she'd e*ver knitted for her, so she'd try not to hold too much of a grudge when she wore it. She hoped Sadie would realise that she'd stayed over this side tonight and keep her eye on the house. Joe came back and poured them both a drink. They sat side by side, chatting comfortably.

'Have you had any more thoughts on changing your job yet?' she asked.

He shook his head. 'Can't do it at the moment. We'd have to move nearer to Crewe and that would mean uprooting Carol and her being further away from you, and I'd have to find someone who does as good a job as Dolly looking after her and that won't be easy. It can wait. The motor trade will become established in Liverpool at some point in the not-too-distant future. How's work with you? Are you managing okay now Vi's moved away?'

'Not bad.' Dora took a sip of sherry. 'Sammy and Esther are very good with me and Jackie loves them too.'

'She likes the theatres, doesn't she? Little madam.' Joe laughed. 'Mind you, she was good in that Christmas panto. I felt dead proud seeing her up on stage.'

Dora smiled. The choreographer at the Empire had been as good as his word and Jackie had been chosen from all the other little girls at Marjorie Barker's dancing school to join the dancing troupe for *Babes in the Wood*. Hopefully there'd be more to come.

Joe got up and put a record on the gramophone. As Jo Stafford's voice filled the room, he held out his hand. 'Old times' sake. Come on.'

She got to her feet and took his outstretched hand. He pulled her closer but not so close that she felt uncomfortable. He sang along to the chorus of 'You Belong to Me'. Dora loved the song. It was being played time and again on the wireless at the moment. A number one hit record, as the announcer had said the other day. She loved the words and lost herself in them as Joe sang softly and they swayed in time to the music. Being in Joe's arms felt good. But as soon as the song ended she sat down again, feeling self-conscious. They shouldn't be doing this. They were almost divorced. It was one thing being friendly for the sake of their girls, but dancing in close proximity to his body had aroused desires she'd long buried. Desires that were dangerous, and she couldn't allow them to take over common sense. She moved as far away from him as she could when he sat down again.

He smiled and patted her hand. 'I'm sorry. It felt so good to hold you again though. I'm not going to deny that. But I'm not about to spoil the nice day we've had by making you feel uncomfortable.'

'Thank you.' She drew a deep breath, glad of his understanding. 'I'll go to bed in a minute. I'm sure the girls will be up at the crack of dawn, so we both need an early night.'

'Daddy's not here but Mammy is,' Dora heard Carol say as she emerged from the bathroom. Carol thrust the phone at her and ran back into the sitting room to Jackie. Dora hadn't even heard the phone ringing as she'd been running water and cleaning her teeth. Joe had popped out to get a newspaper and cigarettes. She frowned and put the receiver to her ear. 'Hello.' She heard a sharp intake of breath and then a woman spoke. 'Is Joe there please?' Dora recognised Ivy's voice and her stomach turned over. 'Sorry, no. He's popped out. Can I take a message?'

'Tell him I'll be near the boating lake in Sefton Park at two thirty.'

Dora raised an eyebrow. That sounded more like a summons than an invite. 'Actually, Joe and I are taking the girls to New Brighton today.' She couldn't resist adding, 'We're finishing Jackie's birthday weekend in style. I suggest you call him later, or wait until tomorrow and speak to him in work.' She hung up before Ivy had the chance to say anything else. It was still fairly early in the morning and the woman wasn't daft. She'd know there were no trams and buses running at this time of day, so would no doubt guess that Dora had stayed over last night. Let her stew on it, Dora thought, and went to see to her daughters, who were waiting to have their hair brushed and plaited. She wasn't passing any messages on; she was just wanting to sound polite. Ivy didn't pass on *her* message to Joe the day Carol was born.

*

Ivy stared at the receiver in her hands. She dropped it back into the cradle and made her way upstairs to her flat. What the hell was Dora doing at Joe's so early in the morning? She'd sounded all bright and breezy too. *And* they were going for a family day out. *That* hadn't been on the cards when she'd spoken to Joe on leaving work last Friday. He'd told her he was doing a birthday party for Jackie with the family on Saturday and then taking Carol to Dora's on Sunday, so he would have a couple of free hours to meet her and Roly at Sefton Park in the afternoon. He'd been blowing hot and cold again since the ROF Christmas dance mid-December when he'd done the same as the first time he'd invited her and spent the night with her. It was hardly a relationship – or even an affair for that matter, as the last time they'd slept together before then was in the caravan in August.

She couldn't fathom Joe at all. When he was with her he seemed keen enough, but it was fleeting and she was getting fed up of playing second fiddle to a marriage that was over. Or was it? Had Dora spent the night there? It seemed that way. So what was going on between them? Ivy knew their divorce was on the horizon. Not that Joe had told her. For some reason he was keeping it to himself. But she'd seen the papers a few months ago when she'd babysat Carol and had a snoop around while he was out. It was only a matter of weeks now before he became a free man. She'd need to act fast if she was going to pin him down. She had a plan up her sleeve and wasn't worried about putting it into action as soon as possible now. Sod what anybody thought of her, and there'd be plenty with a lot to say, she'd no doubts about that. But with her long-awaited goal almost in sight, she was not about to let it get away in a hurry.

Dora hung onto Jackie's hand as the ferry pulled into the New Brighton landing point by the pier. Joe had hold of Carol and the shopping bag containing their picnic and a flask. The girls were excited, eager to be off to play on the sands and have a promised donkey ride. They ran on ahead down the pier, giggling, Carol pulling Jackie along. Dora smiled. They'd had no holidays together as a family. The last time she'd been away with Joe was to Blackpool when Carol was a toddler. Jackie had been conceived on that holiday, and after her birth and the long months of depression that followed, their marriage had broken down under the strain and they'd parted. She glanced sideways at Joe as he kept his eyes on their daughters. He was still a good-looking man, tall and slim but not scrawny, his light brown hair blowing in the breeze, the carefully styled quiff now dangling down. He swept it back and smiled at her, his lovely hazel eyes twinkling.

'Girls,' Joe called. 'Wait by the entrance for us. Don't run on the road.'

They caught up with the girls and stopped at a kiosk on the promenade. Joe bought buckets and spades and some small paper flags for the top of the castle that he'd promised to help them build. He handed the picnic bag to Dora and picked up two deckchairs from the seller on the promenade. 'Right, let's go and find ourselves a nice spot to relax and unpack the picnic,' he said as the girls led the way.

Dora had tucked her latest copy of *Woman* magazine in the bag when they'd stopped off at Wright Street for the jackets. She laid out the picnic, mostly food left over from Jackie's birthday tea, which was eaten in record time, and then settled down in her deckchair to read while Joe chased their daughters up and down the beach and built the promised sandcastle. There was a strong breeze and as the afternoon wore on it got colder. Dora shivered and pulled her jacket around her shoulders. She repacked the flask and gathered up the empty paper bags. 'Joe, shall we take them on the fair? The sun keeps going in and I'm cold sitting here. Girls, come and put your socks and shoes back on.'

Carol pulled a face but Jackie, whose nose was streaming, came willingly to her side. Joe got the buckets and spades together and told Carol to do as she was told.

'Can we come again?' she said, sitting down by Jackie and pulling her socks on. 'Ugh, my toes feel all funny.'

Dora bent to take Carol's socks back off and gave her feet a rub with a towel she'd packed in the bag. It was too cold for a paddle to rinse off, but there was nothing worse than sand between toes when you put your socks on.

'Can we, Mammy, can we come again next week?'

'We'll see. If you're a good girl, perhaps we might do.'

'Goody. Come on, Jackie, I'll race you to the steps.' Carol grabbed her sister by the hand and dragged her along.

Joe pulled Dora up and held onto her hand. 'Can we, Mammy?' he teased. 'Please!'

She laughed. 'If you're a good boy, maybe. Now grab those deckchairs and carry them back up to the prom and I'll bring everything else.'

After rides on the carousel, the ghost train and the bumper cars, Joe bought ice-creams and he and Dora sat on a bench seat to enjoy them while the girls played on the grass nearby. 'It's been a lovely weekend,' he said. 'It's a long time since I enjoyed myself so much. I keep thinking about the day we came over here just before we got married.' He sighed. 'A lot of things have happened since then, eh, gel?'

Dora nodded. 'I remember it well. We had everything to look forward to in those days.'

Joe leaned across and stroked the hair from her face. 'We could still have something to look forward to, a future. The divorce can be cancelled, or if it's too late to stop it going through now, we can always remarry. The girls are so much happier when we're all together. All I want is for us to be a family again and doing the best for *them* as well as us two.'

Dora chewed her lip. 'Oh, Joe, I don't know. There's the issue of trust… and I'm terrified of getting pregnant again. And us not being together is the only way I can guarantee it won't happen.'

He nodded and took her hand. 'I understand that. But what if we agree to a celibate marriage, for now anyway? Nobody needs to know what we do and don't do, it's *our* business. And then maybe in time you can have the operation. Last night was lovely, wasn't it? We can live like that for a while. It's better than nothing, Dora. We can work something out to suit us both. I'm not pushing you; I want you to take your time. But will you have a think about it, please? I know I've made mistakes, and you've no idea how sorry I am, but you're the only girl I've ever wanted and I'm sure you know that.'

Chapter Nineteen

With Jackie skipping along beside her, singing as usual, Dora set off for work on Monday morning with a spring in her step, but her mind full of what-ifs. The weekend had bucked her up no end. She'd enjoyed them all spending time as a family with no arguments between the girls, or her and Joe either. Last night, after Jackie had gone to bed, she'd thought over what Joe had said, and Dolly and Agnes too. Could she and Joe *really* make a go of it again? But how could a celibate marriage work? He'd said 'for a while', which meant that he'd only put up with it for a few months and then – what? If she still refused to have the sterilisation operation, would he go elsewhere? And if he did, then she'd be back to square one. It needed a lot of thinking about. She was halfway there. Maybe she'd call Agnes on her dinner break. See what she thought about it once she knew what Joe had in mind.

'Good morning,' Sammy's voice boomed as they stepped into the shop, Jackie swinging the door once more for good measure as she loved to make the bell jangle. 'How did the birthday party go?'

'It was fun. We had cake and balloons.' Jackie jiggled from foot to foot and held out her little bag complete with tea set.

'She's in charge of brewing up today,' Dora said, laughing.

'We have a young lady coming in later for a wedding dress measurement,' Esther announced. 'She wants one exactly like your window display and three bridesmaids' dresses, one adult, two children. We've asked her to come in and discuss the matter with our consultant. How does that sound?'

Dora laughed. 'Sounds posh. Is that me? The consultant, I mean?'

'It is.' Sammy nodded. 'Now the lady can't get here until after two, so I'll do the theatre run this morning and take Jackie with me. Is that okay? Then at least we'll both be here when she arrives. You can arrange some samples of fabric for her to look at.'

Dora smiled. This was the first bit of interest in the wedding outfits since she did the window display a few weeks ago, although there'd been a lot of people stopping to admire the white satin and lace dress and pale pink Bo-Peep-style bridesmaid's dress. But spring was in the air and weddings were being planned, no doubt. 'That's lovely. Jackie would be disappointed if she thought she was missing out. Right, I'll go up and finish the final repair on the theatre costumes and then they're ready for the off. You be a good girl now for Esther,' she said to Jackie, and to Esther: 'She's got crayons and a book in that bag too, so those should keep her quiet until Sammy's ready to take her to the theatre.'

When Sammy and Jackie left for the Empire, Esther made a pot of tea for her and Dora.

'A bit of peace and quiet,' Dora said. 'I bet she's not stopped all morning.'

'She hasn't, but I love to hear her chattering away. I wish we had grandchildren. But Sonny shows no signs of wanting any and nor does his wife. That's why I enjoy having Jackie here so much.'

'Maybe he doesn't feel ready,' Dora said. 'They *are* quite a responsibility.'

Esther snorted. 'Huh! I don't think he'll ever be ready. He's too selfish to share his life with children.' She finished her tea and put on her jacket as Dora stared at her unfathomable expression.

'Would you mind holding the fort while I pop out to the bank and get a few bits of shopping in?' Esther asked, picking up her basket from the floor.

'My pleasure,' Dora said. 'I'll cut a few samples for the wedding orders, and is it okay if I just make a quick phone call?'

'Help yourself. It's quiet this morning. Mind you, Monday always is. Gives us time to catch up a bit.' She left, with a little wave as she passed the window. Dora frowned and wondered why Esther seemed to have such a low opinion of her son, but she didn't like to pry.

She put Sonny out of her mind and called Agnes, bringing her up to date with Sunday's news. 'So what do you think?' Dora said.

'You *know* what I think.' Agnes's voice held a hint of excitement. 'You and Joe should never have been apart. Tell him yes, as soon as you can.'

Dora smiled. 'I'm not seeing him until next Saturday when he brings Carol over. That gives me a few days to think it through. He said there was no rush.'

'There's nothing to think about. I know you still love him and he's so bloody crazy about *you*, he can't hide it. It's in his eyes, on his face when he looks at you. Ring him at work and tell him yes you'll go back.'

'I don't want to do that. If his mates are listening in he'll get embarrassed. It's too private. And I need a bit of time to think it through properly. It can wait until Saturday.' The doorbell jangled. 'I've got a customer, I'd better go. I'll be in touch. 'Bye.'

'You'd better be. 'Bye,' Agnes said.

Dora looked up and smiled at the young man and his friend, who were carrying paper bags and wearing sheepish expressions. 'Can I help you?'

'Er, yeah,' the taller youth replied. He wore his black hair styled into a quiff like the ones Joe and Frank wore, but more elaborate, and she could smell the Brylcreem he'd plastered on to keep it in place. His pal had a similar quiff in his blond hair, but not quite as big. It flopped into his eyes, like Joe's did. 'Do you take trousers in, you know like, make the legs narrower.' He pulled a pair of plain black trousers from the bag and laid them on the counter. 'See, they're too wide and flappy and dead old-fashioned. I want 'em doing like the ones the Cunard Yanks wear.'

Dora frowned. 'Cunard Yanks?'

The other youth nodded. 'Yeah, the Yanks from the ships. They wear their trousers tighter than we do, and nobody sells 'em like that over here. We thought you might be able to help us.'

'I don't see why not,' Dora said, taking a tape measure to the width. 'So how much narrower would you like them, bearing in mind you've got to get them over your feet? Is this a new fashion, then?'

The taller lad shrugged. 'It's like what they wear in the films, you know, like Roy Rogers and the Lone Ranger. Except they wear denim jeans but we haven't got any yet. They call 'em drainies, you know, like drainpipes.'

'Okay. But just one thing. I'm not about to start chopping up your school trousers, am I? Don't want your mams coming in here giving me what for.'

'No, Missus, these are my going-out trousers. I've left school anyway. So has Jim. We both work at Blacklers. It's our dinner break.'

Dora nodded. She took both young lads' measurements, around their ankles, calves and knees. 'Right, leave them with me. Are yours the same, Jim? Black, like your pal's?'

Jim nodded. 'Any chance they could be ready for picking up on Saturday? We're meeting a couple of girls at the Grafton ballroom.'

Dora chewed her lip. 'We're closed on a Saturday, but I'll have them ready for Friday if you can nip in then. We'll be here until just gone six if you come straight from work. Now what's your name, and I'll give you a ticket for collection.' She handed one to Jim and pinned a copy onto his bag with his measurements.

'I'm Colin,' the other lad said. 'Do you know how much they'll be?'

'Not until my boss comes back, but don't worry, it won't break the bank. We'll see you on Friday.' She smiled as they said their goodbyes. Nice boys and they might as well as enjoy themselves before they were conscripted for their two-year stint in the army. National Service was still in force, but hopefully they wouldn't be fighting any wars. Pity that flipping Lenny Smyth hadn't been called up yet. He must be almost old enough. With a bit of luck it shouldn't be too long now.

Esther arrived back with a bag of assorted goodies from the market. 'They've got a lot of fruit down there on one of the stalls; I got a couple of bananas for Jackie. A nice treat to see them properly on sale again.'

When Sammy came back with an excited Jackie he looked at the order Dora had taken for the drainies. 'Might catch on,' he said, laughing. 'What next, I wonder?'

'That's what I thought,' Dora said. 'If it's the latest craze, they'll tell all their mates and we should get a bit more work out of it.'

Dora's bridal appointment arrived just after two and was taken upstairs to where Dora had laid out sketches on the long table along with samples she'd taken from the shop's stock. The bride-to-be, who introduced herself as Sandra, looked very young, but then anybody under twenty looked young these days, Dora thought. Her sister Anne, the chief bridesmaid, had accompanied her. The wedding was booked for the last week of July, so there was plenty of time to make the dresses.

'I'm Dora,' she introduced herself and pulled out two chairs for them. 'Take a seat. Would you like some tea?' Esther had told her to offer and she'd bring it up with the best china.

'We're okay, thank you,' Sandra said. 'We've just had a drink in the Kardomah.'

They pored over the sketches and Sandra held up the one like the dress in the window. 'I like this, but I also like this one.' She pointed to the pad.

Dora swallowed the lump in her throat. 'That's the style I wore for my wedding a few years ago. It *does* look lovely on.'

Sandra smiled. 'Then I'll go for that one. It must be a lucky dress if you chose it. You still look dead happy, sort of glowing.'

Dora did her best to look *dead happy*. 'Do I? Well there you go then.' If only she knew. But Dora wasn't about to burst the young girl's bubble. Things might work out for her just fine, like they had with everyone else she knew. She hadn't brought the sketch of Joanie's dress along. It was the one thing she couldn't face, seeing someone else in that style.

Dora took their measurements and Anne decided on a pale green satin for her princess-line dress. Her dark hair would complement a headdress with matching trim. Sandra's dress was to be traditional white satin with a lace bodice and sleeves and a neat white veil. 'Okay, two weeks and we'll be ready for a first fitting.' Dora gave them a card with the time and date. She took a two-pound deposit on each dress and led the way back downstairs. 'What about the younger bridesmaids – I believe there are two?' Dora asked.

'Yes, our little cousins. We'll need to bring them in after school, if that's okay. I like the Bo Peep dress in the window and my aunty has seen it too and she loves it. So it will be two like that.'

'Well if you bring them in as soon as you can, we'll get them measured up, and then we can order the fabric.' Dora smiled as they waved goodbye.

'Lovely young ladies,' Esther said. 'I'll make us a brew. Jackie's doing a jigsaw puzzle with Sammy in the back.'

Dora frowned. 'We didn't bring a puzzle with us.'

Esther laughed. 'He's a sucker for a pretty face. They passed a toy shop and spotted it in the window. Teddy Bears' Picnic. He's a softie when it comes to Jackie. We both are.'

Dora shook her head. 'What's he like? You both spoil us something rotten.'

'You're like a daughter to us and Jackie's the nearest we've got to a grandchild. Allow us a bit of indulgence now and again.'

Dora gave Esther a hug. 'Thank you. I really don't know what I'd do without you. I feel so blessed.'

On the way home, dragging a tired Jackie along with her, Dora wished she'd called Joe like Agnes had suggested. She was pretty sure she knew what her answer would be. It was a bit pointless to make him wait until the weekend. She'd do it tomorrow; invite him and Carol over for tea and tell him then. She'd still be able to work and keep the bit of independence she enjoyed and the money she earned would give them a better standard of living. They'd be able to buy a house sooner so that they'd be settled for when Joe decided to change his job. She'd love a house like Agnes and Alan's on The Avenues in Fazakerley. Maybe Esther and Sammy would agree to her bringing more work home and then she could also see to her mam and have her over at the house during the day while Frank was at the docks. It would work out just fine for them all and the girls would both be so thrilled. But she'd make one firm concession: that Joe change his job and have nothing more to do with Ivy, as either a friend or a colleague. With that decision, Dora felt happier and more settled in her mind than she'd felt for a very long time.

Chapter Twenty

During Monday afternoon tea break, Joe looked up as Ivy called out to him. Damn, he'd done his best to avoid her all day, bringing sarnies and a flask from home. But now his flask was empty and he was spitting feathers for a brew. He'd got Eric to bring the mugs across to the table while he'd nipped out for a quick pee. Last night, as he was tucking Carol into bed, he'd remembered that he'd promised to see Ivy on Sunday afternoon. She'd be giving him earache for forgetting now. He should have rung her to tell her he was busy with the kids and couldn't meet her. He'd just been so happy to have Dora staying that meeting Ivy had gone clean out of his mind.

'Here's your mate,' Eric whispered as Ivy marched across the canteen towards him.

'I need a word,' she said, lips pursed. 'I'll be over there at our usual table.'

'Go on, you've been summonsed,' Eric teased. 'Look at the face on it, though. Wouldn't like to be in your shoes, matey.'

Joe sighed and got to his feet. He carried his mug of tea to the table under the window that was in a more private position. He sat down opposite Ivy and lit a cigarette. 'What's up?' he asked and blew a cloud of smoke into the air above his head.

'Did you enjoy your day in New Brighton?' she began, a sarcastic edge to her voice.

'Er, yeah. How did you know I went there?' He frowned and flicked ash into the ashtray.

'Dora told me.' Ivy folded her arms.

'Really? Well, when did *you* see Dora?'

'I didn't. She told me you were all going when I phoned you yesterday morning.'

Joe shrugged. 'Ah, right. She didn't tell me you called.'

'I needed to see you on Sunday, Joe. You were supposed to be meeting me at Sefton Park.'

'Yeah, right, sorry about that. Going to New Brighton was a last-minute decision for Jackie's birthday.'

'Dora was at yours very early. Did she stay over on Saturday night?'

Joe sat back on his chair, his ciggie dangling from his lips. He took another long drag and stubbed the butt end out. 'That's got nothing to do with you. As it happens, yes, she did stay. But that's *our* business.'

'I thought you were getting divorced?'

'Look what is this; the bloody Spanish inquisition? What me and my wife do is our own business.'

Ivy took a deep breath and continued. 'Don't be so bloody horrible, Joe. I do a lot for you, supporting you, babysitting, arranging a holiday and always being there when you need me. You could have at least let me know you had no intention of coming to the park. I waited all day for you to get in touch.'

Joe shook his head. 'Well you knew you'd see me today. So, come on, I'm here now, what do you need to talk about?'

Ivy took a quick look around to make sure no one was watching. 'I've got a problem.'

Joe nodded. 'Right, so what's it got to do with me?'

'Everything. I'm expecting your baby, Joe!'

Joe's eyes widened, his jaw dropped and he spluttered out his response. 'What? You can't be,' he shouted, and then, remembering where he was, lowered his voice. 'How the hell?' He shook his head. 'I haven't been with you since before Christmas.'

Ivy raised an eyebrow. 'That's when it happened. I'm just over three months gone.'

'Shit!' Joe sat back on his chair, his heart racing. What on earth? 'It can't be mine,' he muttered. 'You'd have told me sooner if it was. And I was careful. You know I was.'

'Not careful enough,' Ivy whispered. 'It *is* yours. I don't sleep around.'

Joe held up his hands. She didn't and it was unfair of him to imply it. 'Okay, I'm sorry, I know you don't. But what the hell are you gonna do?'

Ivy stared at him, her cheeks flushing bright pink. 'What am *I* going to do? Don't you mean, what are *we* going to do? This is *your* problem too, Joe.'

Joe shook his head. 'I don't want anything to do with it.'

'Really?' Ivy got to her feet. 'Well whether you want to or not, you don't have much choice.'

'What do you mean? *I* can't do anything about it. Dora and I, well, we're probably getting back together. I can't tell her this. It will send her over the edge again.' He sat with his head in his hands as Ivy walked away without another word. He looked up as someone tapped him on the shoulder.

'Come on, Joe, we're late back. Be getting our wages docked if we don't shape up,' Eric said. 'You okay? You look a bit on the pale side. Has that miserable bugger upset you or summat?'

Joe got to his feet. He felt sick, as though he would chuck his sarnies back up at any minute. He couldn't go back on the factory floor just yet. 'I feel a bit rough, Eric. Tell the foreman I'll be up soon. I'm going to have to go to the carsey.'

Eric nodded and hurried away.

The canteen was empty now except for Ivy and Flo, who was busy clearing tables. Joe beckoned to Ivy, who re-joined him at the table. 'Have you seen a doctor then?'

'Not yet,' Ivy muttered. 'I've felt so ill and sickly too, but I'm so embarrassed, you know, with not being married and all that. I wanted to speak to *you* first. It's taken me ages to pluck up the courage. But I'm absolutely sure, it's been weeks. Remember, Joe, I've been pregnant before, so I know what's what.' She dabbed at her eyes with a hanky. 'I just feel grateful that God has given me a second chance to be a mother.' Ivy had been widowed during the war and lost her expected baby within weeks of her young husband's death.

Joe stared at her. Since when did God feature in her life? She never went to church, to his knowledge. 'It's got nowt to bloody do with God,' he snapped. 'Don't be giving me all that religious rubbish, making me feel guilty. You'll have to do something about it.'

Ivy's lips quivered. 'I thought you'd be happy for me. That you'd want to stand by me. After everything I've done for *you*, helping you with Carol and always being there for you when you were having a bad day.'

'How can I stand by you? What about Dora and my kids? They're my family and they need me – and I need them,' he finished.

'You should have thought about that before you jumped into bed with me then,' she snapped. 'You used me and now you don't want to know. What sort of a man does that?'

Joe could think of plenty, but that wouldn't help, so he lit another cigarette and stared into space.

'You'll have to tell Dora,' Ivy said quietly. 'Because if *you* don't, *I* will. I'm going to be showing soon and people will guess. She might not *want* you back once she knows about this.' And from next week she'd make sure she *was* showing. It would mean holding her stockings up with garters rather than the girdle that controlled her very rounded stomach. But if it did the trick of making her look pregnant that was fine.

Joe gritted his teeth. 'I don't think there's any *might* about it, do you?' he growled. Bloody hell, just when he was getting his family back under one roof, she goes and ruins everything. He ran his hands through his hair as Flo called over for Ivy to come and help her. 'Right, let me get my head together. Don't say a word about this to anyone, especially Flo.' He got to his feet. He'd need to go and tell his boss that he felt unwell and hopefully he'd let him leave early. He didn't trust Ivy to keep this to herself. He had to see Dora as soon as possible and tell her before anyone else did.

Ivy stared after Joe as he slammed the canteen door shut on his way out. She let out a long breath and smiled. That was the first part of her plan over with. And when Dora found out, she would tell him where to go again. His divorce would be through in the next few weeks by Ivy's calculations and then he'd be free to marry her, which she was certain he *would* do, when all the mess was sorted out.

Once he was hers, there'd be a convenient miscarriage after a few weeks. She could remember well enough how that felt, enough to act it out convincingly. It was a dramatic step to take, and Ivy felt a pang when she remembered how traumatic her miscarriage had been, but she could feel Joe slipping away from her, and she couldn't bear the thought of him going back to Dora. The next thing to think about was to make sure Joe handed Carol over to her mother as soon as possible. She didn't want to be lumbered with his kids. She'd play the sickly pregnant wife to the best of her abilities, incapable of doing anything for herself for a while, until she 'lost' the baby.

From the first day she'd set eyes on him, she'd been determined that one day he'd be hers. And they got on well enough when Dora wasn't around. He made her laugh and feel good about herself. He was a good-looking man and she always felt proud to be seen with him. She was absolutely certain that once they were together, hopefully as husband and wife, she could make him happy.

*

Joe drove back to the Belle Vale estate before going to see Dora. Dolly would still be out picking up the kids from school, so he wasted a bit of time by getting changed out of his working clothes and into something smarter. He was hoping Dolly would hang onto Carol until he got back from Dora's. He sat down on the sofa, his head in a whirl. Christ, he didn't even know how to *start* telling Dora. One half of him hoped that with their new-found solidarity she might understand and would forgive him and they could help support Ivy and the baby, but the other half knew that was just a pipedream; she'd go absolutely crazy and want nothing more to do with him. He'd never felt so helpless in his life. Everything he wanted and was so close to having again was about to slip through his hands and this time he knew he would never get them back. He heard the sound of childish voices outside and then Dolly's foghorn voice telling them not to run on the road. He looked through the window. She came to a halt when she spotted his car.

He went to the door as Dolly walked up the garden path, a puzzled expression on her face. 'Can you hang onto Carol for me? I've finished a bit early and I've got an important errand to run.'

Dolly nodded. 'Course I can. You okay, Joe? You look a bit peaky.'

'Yeah, I'm fine. A bit tired from the busy weekend, you know, and then having to be up at sparrow fart this morning.' He tried to make light of things, but he knew Dolly wasn't easily fooled.

She looked at him through narrowed eyes. 'Were things all right with you and Dora yesterday? I didn't get chance to ask you this morning, but Carol said you held her mammy's hand at the fair.' She raised an eyebrow. 'I'm hoping for some good news soon. Right, kids, come on. Let's go inside and have a snack.'

'Jam butties please,' Carol shouted. 'I love jam butties.'

Joe half-smiled as Dolly shepherded the kids indoors. She would be furious with him. Everything she'd warned him about Ivy was true. He couldn't understand how he'd got her pregnant. He'd been careful; they'd used Durex and there'd been no leaks, he'd made sure of that. He walked to the car, his feet feeling like lead. He could do with a drink, but the pubs weren't open yet and he'd got nothing in.

He drove slowly across Liverpool and down to Wright Street. It was still too early for Dora to be home from work. He could have met her at the shop, he supposed, but he couldn't face her just yet. Parking the car outside her house, he grabbed his jacket from the passenger seat and decided to walk to the pier head to get a breath of fresh air.

Sitting down on a vacant bench, he lit a cigarette. A passenger ship was about to set sail to far-off lands and a small crowd of people were gathered on the quayside to wave off their friends and relatives. He wished he was on board, about to vanish for ever to the other side of the Atlantic. He felt like crying. Life was so bloody unfair. All he wanted was the best for his little family and he'd been working towards it for weeks now, winning Dora's love back slowly but surely. What sort of a God would favour Ivy over Dora? Not his sort and that was for certain.

He sat for a while with a ciggie and watched the tug boats tooting and pulling the big liner out to sea, the three red funnels belching steam up to the blue sky, seagulls swooping and diving into the water as fish and titbits were churned up to the surface in the foaming water. He finished his ciggie, stubbed the end out under his heel and set off back to Dora's house, his head down, watching where he was walking. He didn't see Dora on the opposite side of Scotland Road until he heard his name being called.

She ran towards him, pulling Jackie along with her. 'Hiya, Joe, I didn't expect to see *you* until later in the week,' she greeted him, with a beaming smile. 'What a lovely surprise. Is Carol okay? Where is she?'

'She's fine,' he said, swinging Jackie up into his arms. 'She's at Dolly's having her tea. I got off work early. I, er, wanted to come and talk to you.'

'Oh, okay. I was going to call you tomorrow and invite you and Carol to tea. Well, you can still come anyway.' She laughed and slipped her arm through his. 'I've made a decision. Shall I tell you now?'

His heart almost stopped beating as he looked into her sparkling blue eyes. She was going to say yes. And bastard that he was, he was about to turn her world upside down, again.

Chapter Twenty-One

Dora hurried back to her house. Joe had asked her to take Jackie down to Sadie's for half an hour as they needed to be on their own. He wouldn't elaborate further than that. She felt a bit guilty as Sadie was looking harassed, trying to see to the new baby and giving the kids their tea. She told Dora that Stan was working overtime and was being dropped off later by Frank. Sadie sat Jackie next to Belinda and dished her up a plate of blind scouse.

'Thank you so much. I'll be as quick as I can.' No doubt when he dropped Stan off, Frank would pop in with a quick update on Mam, Dora thought as she dashed back inside to find Joe pacing up and down the front room carpet and puffing frantically on a cigarette. He looked a bit pale. Maybe he was feeling nervous and, like her, had been thinking things over as the day wore on. He probably didn't want to wait until next Saturday for her answer. 'Would you like a cuppa?' she asked, taking off her jacket and dropping it over the arm of the sofa.

Joe shook his head. 'Not right now, love. Sit down, and please hear me out before you say anything.' He threw the remains of his ciggie into the fireplace and joined her on the sofa. He took her hands in his. 'I've got something to tell you, and I'm afraid it's not very nice. And at the moment I absolutely hate myself for having to do this.'

She frowned as he continued. 'I love you and the girls more than anything; you know that, don't you? I want nothing more than for us to be together again. But something has happened today that might change the way you feel about me and the future, for all of us.'

'Joe, what is it? Have you lost your job? We'll manage, I'm working, and we could move so that you can get a new job in Crewe like you wanted to.'

Joe closed his eyes. When he opened them again she could see tears welling. A cold fear clutched at her heart. 'Are you ill? Is that what you're trying to tell me? You look so pale. Don't worry; I'll be there to help you through it.'

'Oh God, Dora, if only it was something like that and we could deal with it together.' Tears were running down his cheeks now. 'I'm so sorry, love, but it seems Ivy's pregnant and she says I'm the father.'

Dora sat back, shock running through her like a bolt of lightning. She stared at him as his face crumpled. Had she heard him right? 'Ivy? Pregnant?' she whispered. 'No.' She snatched her hands away from his. 'Are you sure?'

He nodded. 'She told me this afternoon. I can't believe it either.'

'But you said you were just good friends.'

He shrugged. 'We are. It was one of those things. She means nothing to me. I don't love her or anything. She knows that. I also told her that me and you, well, that we're getting back together.'

She shook her head. 'I don't believe this. Are you sure she's not lying because she knows about us? She phoned you on Sunday while you were at the paper shop. I didn't tell you because I didn't want to spoil our nice day out.'

Joe shrugged. 'I know. She told me. But I don't think she's lying. She's three months gone. It happened after the Christmas do. And that's it, honestly, I haven't been near her since and nor do I want to.'

'And she leaves it until now to tell you? When she knows I stayed over on Saturday?'

He nodded. 'She said she'd make sure you found out if I didn't tell you right away.'

Dora burst into tears. She could hardly breathe, feeling nothing other than disbelief. She gagged on bile that rose in her throat and dashed into the kitchen, where she vomited into the sink. She turned the tap on full and ran water, leaning over until she was certain there was nothing more to come up. Joe had followed her and reached to touch her arm but she batted him away. 'No, just leave me alone. Go away, Joe. Go back to Ivy. It would never have worked anyway with her always in the background. We should just be glad I hadn't moved back in with you already. God, I would have lost my home.'

'Dora, I can't leave you here on your own. Please, love, come and sit down and let's talk about how we're going to deal with this.'

'We? How *we're* going to deal with it? It's nothing to do with me. It's your horrible mess, yours and that bloody Ivy's.'

'We could still make it work. Me, you, the girls.'

'No, we couldn't. How can you think that? She'd never leave you alone. She'll always have a reason to be contacting you. She'd want money from you. We'd never be rid of her, Joe, her *or* her bloody kid. You'd better go. I need you out of here now before you make me sick again.' As she spoke the front door-knocker rattled and Frank popped his head in.

'Only me,' he called, walking into the front room. 'Just dropping Stan off so I thought I'd cadge a brew. I see Joe's here—' He stopped as the pair turned to look at him. 'Oops, have I come at a bad moment? Sorry.'

'No you haven't, Frank. Joe's just leaving,' Dora said, pushing Joe towards the door.

'Dora, I'm going nowhere until we sort this out.'

'There's nothing *to* sort out,' Dora snapped. 'Now if you don't mind, I want to talk privately with my brother.'

Joe shook his head and looked at Frank. 'Tell him, tell Frank what I've told you. See what he thinks we should do.'

Frank frowned. 'What's going on, Sis?'

'*He*,' she jabbed a finger in Joe's chest, 'he has only got bloody Ivy Bennett pregnant! Just at a time when we were planning to get back together. And he wants *me* to help him sort it out.'

'Dora, *no*, we weren't planning on getting back together until recently. I didn't know she was up the spout,' Joe said to Frank. 'She decided to tell me today.'

'Oh shit!' Frank said. 'You sure it's yours, mate?'

'Apparently so.' Joe held up his hands. 'I can't believe it and I'm so sorry to hurt Dora. It was never meant to be like this.'

Dora took a deep breath. 'You should have kept it zipped up then, shouldn't you? Just get out of my house and don't come back. Frank, *you* can bring our Carol to me on Saturdays please. And tomorrow I'll be on the phone to the Children's Welfare to get her back permanently. I don't care what Mr-bloody-Oliver says, you're not fit to be a father and I don't want *her* anywhere near my child either. Now go. I don't ever want to set eyes on you again.' She pushed him down the hall, Frank following her.

'But what about Jackie? She's my daughter. I want to see her. You can't stop me.'

'Frank will bring her to you.'

Frank gave him a gentle push out onto the street. He pulled the door to behind him. 'Just go, mate. You've done enough damage for one day. I'll see to Dora. Get yourself sorted out with that bitch Ivy. God help you. But no matter what happens, don't you ever upset my sister again, just stay away from her, or you'll have me to answer to.'

Dora looked up as Frank brought a mug of tea through to her. She'd been sitting on the sofa, feeling like the stuffing had been knocked out of her, just staring at the photo of Joanie on the mantelpiece. Frank put the mug down on the side table.

'I put extra sugar in. Do you want me to go and bring Jackie back from Sadie's? I'll get her ready for bed for you. Then I need to get off home to Mam. She'll wonder where I am if I'm much later. I don't want to worry her.'

Dora nodded. 'Thanks for staying with me, Frank.'

'Well I wasn't leaving you on your own, Sis. You look shell-shocked.'

She raised an eyebrow. 'I feel it. I just don't believe this has happened. Oh God, I hate that woman with all my heart. I hope she loses that bloody baby before he gets the chance to marry her.'

'Dora! That's not very nice.'

'I don't care. Neither is Ivy.'

Frank shook his head. 'Drink your tea. I'll go and get our Jackie. Do you want me to tell Sadie?'

She chewed her lip. 'No, she'll be busy getting all the kids to bed, but if she has a spare minute later, ask her to pop down for a bit. I'll tell her myself.'

'Okay, see you in a few minutes then.'

Dora sat in silence after Frank had got Jackie settled and he'd gone home. She just wanted to cry until she could cry no more. But she didn't want Jackie to see her upset. It would frighten her. She was still awake; Dora could hear her singing. She'd hold onto her tears until later. There'd be no sleep for her tonight, even though she felt drained.

She got up to answer the door. Sadie hurried in, looking worried.

'What's wrong? Frank told me something had happened but he said you'd tell me.'

'Sit down,' Dora said. 'I'll make us a drink.'

'I'm okay, thanks,' Sadie said, 'unless you've got a drop of sherry. I could do with something to calm my nerves. Those kids are getting to be hard work as the days go by. I've got three in one bed now. Roll on moving to somewhere bigger.'

Dora nodded. 'There's a drop left in the kitchen cupboard. I'll split it between us.'

Ten minutes later, her sherry glass drained, Sadie sat and stared at Dora, her mouth a silent O. She shook her head. 'I don't know what to say. I'm so sorry, Dora.'

Dora sighed. 'I'm so angry with him, but at the same time I can't help feeling a little bit sorry for him. He's stuck with Ivy now for the rest of his life.'

'Why do you feel sorry for him? I wouldn't. They bloody well deserve each other. *She* knew Joe was still a married man, even though you weren't living together. It would serve her right if Joe dumps her and denies it's his baby.'

'It would. But Joe wouldn't do that. People will talk, and there are those who've seen them at the dances and will put two and two together. I'm just glad no one knew that I'd decided to go back to him this week. There's only Agnes and you know that I was thinking about it. God, Dolly will go mad with him when he tells her and Agnes won't be best pleased either. I've only got her and Dolly's sympathy to deal with, no one else's. I'm determined now to get Carol back. I will *not* have Ivy bringing up my daughter.'

Chapter Twenty-Two

On Wednesday morning Joe stared in dismay at Dolly as she practically slammed the door in his face. Only by putting his foot out to stop it happening was he able to talk to her. She'd pulled Carol inside but seemed keen to send him off with a flea in his ear. 'Dolly, look, I'm sorry if you're upset by what's going on, I'm trying to do the best I can for all concerned—' he began.

'Hmm,' she snorted. 'If that was the case you'd have told that Ivy one where to go ages ago. Making accusations and breaking families up. She wants bloody horse-whipping, she does.'

'Yes, well, too late for that now,' Joe said wishing he'd listened to Dolly's warnings and kept Ivy away from his home and family. 'And she didn't actually break my family up. Me and Dora are almost divorced. Okay, things were starting to look up for us again, but Dora doesn't want to know now.'

'And who can blame her?' Dolly folded her arms under her ample bosom. 'I'll tell you this, Joe. I'll help you for now with Carol, but if you move *that* one in, I won't be helping you no more. You'll have to get *her* to pull her weight.'

Joe nodded and walked away down the path. This was not going to be easy. Yesterday had been a nightmare at work. A call from the welfare department's Mr Oliver during the morning break, when he'd been trying to speak privately to Ivy, had alerted him to the fact that Dora had told them he was moving an irresponsible woman in who Carol didn't really know. Joe had told the man that Carol had been looked after by Ivy many times and she knew her very well, that she was far from irresponsible and he had no immediate plans to move anyone in. Mr Oliver asked him was it true that Ivy was expecting a baby and he'd admitted that it was. He was told that Mr Oliver would now be reviewing the case with the new information he'd been given and would be in touch soon. When he'd gone back to talk to Ivy, to tell her that he'd spoken to Dora and she'd told him where to go, she'd sat there with a stony-faced expression.

'So, what did the man from the welfare want?' she asked.

'Dora has applied for custody of Carol, in view of all this mess,' he said. 'I'll fight it. Carol's settled with me. I'm not having her moved from pillar to post. Nothing needs to change there.'

Ivy took a sip of her drink and stared at him over the rim of her mug. 'She needs to be with her mother. *All* children do. Dora hasn't done anything wrong. That Myrtle Carter's case was in the papers last week. She won't be roaming the streets again for a long time.'

'All that was taken into consideration,' Joe said. 'Carol would have to change schools twice if she went to Dora's. Mr Oliver said the other week he would review things once Dora had moved to a new place. Now it's all been stirred up again because of this bloody mess we're in.'

Ivy slammed her mug down on the table. 'Will you *stop* calling my baby *this mess*?' She got to her feet. 'I'm not asking you for anything, Joe. I'll manage on my own, thank you. All I want is for you to show some responsibility towards me and…' She rubbed her hand over her stomach.

Joe looked around to make sure no one was watching. Eric knew, of course, but he and Dolly had been sworn to secrecy for now. 'Stop drawing attention to it then,' he hissed. 'It'll be bloody obvious soon enough. But the dust will have settled a bit by then. I've got enough to worry about at the moment without the gossips having a field day. Anyway, I'll see you later. I need to get back upstairs. And remember; just keep your trap shut for now.'

Ivy watched Joe walk away, her heart sinking a little. It was obvious he wasn't over the moon. She hadn't really expected him to be, especially now his plans for a happy family future had been snatched from his grasp. But a little bit of consideration and reassurance from him wouldn't have gone amiss. God help her if she really had been in the family way. And there was Carol to consider. That was going to be a tricky one to resolve. There was no way she wanted her living with them. She was a nice enough little girl and so was the other one, but when she finally got him to propose, she wanted him all to herself.

They would never have kids of their own as something had been damaged when she'd miscarried years ago, and her womb had been removed to stop her bleeding to death. But of course Joe didn't know that and he never would. She'd just have to fake her monthlies if they *did* get married. Whatever happened in the next few weeks, she was now closer to her goal than she'd ever been and Joe was closer to being a divorced man than *he'd* ever been. She allowed herself a little daydream about wedding dresses and honeymoons as she cleared the tables and joined Flo in the kitchen.

That week Dora had to force herself to concentrate on her work and put the last few days behind her. She'd already cut two left sleeves for the wedding dress order in error. Luckily there was more white lace on the roll and she could use the wasted pieces for trim on another garment, but mistakes like that cost money. The trousers for the young lads were ready and waiting to be collected tomorrow. She just hoped they could get their feet through the narrow bottoms. She was pleased with them though. They looked quite nice and an improvement on their previous wide-legged style. She wondered if they could make a line of tapered trousers to sell if the style caught on. When she'd discussed it with Sammy he'd nodded.

'Let's wait and see what happens. Fashions are changing all the time. If we see a demand for more alterations we'll have a word with the young lads and ask their opinion. We can only do so much between the two of us and we may well be busy with wedding dresses this year.' He stopped and looked at her. 'How are you feeling now, sweetheart?'

Dora blinked rapidly, his kind words making her want to cry. She'd been in such a state on Tuesday morning that they'd sat her down and closed the shop for an hour while she told them the events of the previous evening. Sammy had been lost for words but had administered comforting hugs, while Esther had made many cups of tea and forced her to eat biscuits to keep her strength up. She hadn't spoken to Agnes yet; when she'd called yesterday, Dora had shaken her head at Esther, who'd told Agnes she'd gone out on theatre deliveries and she'd pass on a message. She would catch up with her on Saturday morning at their daughters' dancing school.

On the way home that evening Dora popped into the market for a bit of shopping, Jackie pulling a face and dragging her feet as she'd wanted to stay with Esther for a bit longer. 'Uncle Frank's calling on his way home, so we need to get back,' Dora told her. 'I'll get you a slab of chocolate if you're a good girl.' Jackie perked up and stopped moaning while Dora concentrated on her purchases. She wasn't looking forward to going back to an empty house, even though it was no different to the empty house she'd been going back to for weeks now. It shouldn't feel any different really, but somehow it did. She felt hollow, empty and lost and so did the house. There was nothing to look forward to any more. Weekends with Joe were over and done with for ever and that thought filled her with despair, even though at the same time she was raging with anger towards him and hatred for Ivy. She'd been robbed of the future she'd just allowed herself to admit she wanted.

Sadie waved to her from the front door and beckoned her to come inside.

'You look worn out,' she said, giving Dora a hug. 'Aren't you sleeping?'

Dora shook her head. 'Only for about an hour each night since Monday.'

'Oh, you poor thing. Sit down. I'll pour you a cuppa. The kids have had an early tea. The older three are in the backyard, Jackie, if you want to go out and play with them for a while. The other two are actually in bed early. Peace and quiet. Stan's coming home with Frank when he comes to see you.' She opened the back door to let Jackie out. 'Look after Jackie, Heidi, and make sure she doesn't get tar on her dress.'

Sadie came back into the room with two mugs of tea and sat down. She picked up an envelope that was lying on the table and took out a letter. 'I hate dropping this on you now when you're feeling so sad, but we've been offered the keys to a new house in Allerton. The letter came this morning. Trouble is, it's only three bedrooms. I rang the council to tell them we'd been promised a four-bedder. The lady was very nice and told me there are none available. She said the bedrooms are quite big, so we'd have a lot more space than here. And she also said that when the kids get older we can put in for an exchange. We can get some bunk beds I suppose. I'll see what Stan says. I need to get out of here as soon as possible though, Dora. We're bursting at the seams. We need a bathroom and a proper garden.'

Dora forced a smile. 'I'd go for it. You'll be fine. I hope I get offered something soon too. I'm ready for a fresh start.'

'It won't be long. Gloria Smyth's going too. I saw her out on the front earlier when I was going to the phone box. They've been given a two-bed flat in Childwall. So the offer letters are coming out, gradually.'

Dora chewed her lip. She'd miss Sadie and dreaded her going. But her friend had struggled for long enough. It was difficult enough with one child and no bathroom; God knew how hard it must be with five. She finished her tea and got to her feet. 'I'd better go and get the tea started. I'll leave our Jackie out there and call her in when it's ready. See you tomorrow – and good luck.' She gave Sadie a hug and went on her way.

Frank was just pulling up as she put the key in the door. Stan got out and greeted her before going into his own house. Frank carried a bag inside and put it down in the hall.

'What you got?' Dora asked.

'Records,' he replied. 'I'm going to try and sell them on. The Yanks brought them over. Big hits that we haven't got here yet. Don't wanna chance leaving them in the car with that lot across the way.'

Dora nodded. 'They'll be going soon, well, Gloria will,' she muttered. 'So will Sadie and Stan—' She burst into tears. Frank wrapped his arms around her as she sobbed on his shoulder. He led her to the sofa in the front room.

'Have they been offered a place? Sadie and Stan, I mean.'

'Yes,' she sniffed. 'The letter came today.'

'You'll probably get something yourself very soon,' he said. 'It can't be much longer now. Apart from you and the girl at the end with all the kids and Gloria's sister, there'll be no one left.'

'I know. And that's what scares me. I don't want to be here on my own when they've all gone.'

Frank sighed. 'I wish I could help. Buy a place big enough for us all to live in, Mam as well. But I just don't earn enough.'

'Frank, I've got to stand on my own two feet. I'll be fine. It's just been a right draining week, that's all. Anyway, how's Mam?'

He shook his head. 'Not great. Apart from her aches and pains, she's doing weird stuff. Her glasses went missing last night. I found them in the fridge. And she put salt in our tea this morning. She's been getting worse memory-wise since that bump on the head.

One of us could do with taking her to the doctor's really. But with us both working all day, it's a bit difficult. Anyway, see what you think on Sunday. Or do you want me to come and get you on Saturday for Jackie's dance class? Save you getting the bus, and then you might as well stay for the weekend and I'll go and get Carol from Joe's.'

'That sounds great. Better than staying down here now that family weekends with Joe are no more. I'll shout Jackie in before you go. Are you having your tea with Mam or do you want something with us? It's only egg and chips I'm afraid.'

'It's okay, Sis, I'd better get back and make sure Mam's okay.'

Dora opened the back door. She beckoned to Frank to come and look, putting her finger to her lips. The kids from the top house, alongside Sadie's lot, were sitting on the floor in a semi-circle and her daughter had centre stage, strutting up and down, performing Shirley Temple's 'Animal Crackers in My Soup' to her captive audience.

Dora grinned as Frank whispered, 'If that one doesn't end up with a career on stage I'll eat my hat.'

'She's a right little diva,' Dora said. 'And though I say it myself, she's pretty good, isn't she?'

Chapter Twenty-Three

Joe picked up the post from behind the front door: two envelopes, a large buff one and the other bearing the welfare department's stamp across the top. He threw them onto the table and went into the bedroom to get changed out of his work clothes. The last two weeks had been nothing short of a nightmare. Dora was still refusing to speak to him and the weekends had been difficult with Frank doing the go-betweens with the girls, collecting them and dropping them off. Carol had been taken to Dora's mam's house for the weekend visit with her mother and Jackie had been here with him after her dance classes. It had put Ivy in a bad mood as she'd wanted to talk to him alone about his plans. When he told her he needed to spend some time with his daughter and he didn't have any plans yet she'd hit the roof. People were pointing fingers at work and she said she was struggling to hide her rounded belly from them. She was constantly going on about how embarrassed she felt. She'd hinted at needing a ring on her finger to show his intentions. He knew he couldn't avoid it for much longer, and his still clinging onto the hope that Dora would agree to speak to him and they'd sort things out was just plain stupid; it wasn't going to happen. He knew it was time to acknowledge that and make an honest woman of Ivy as soon as he could.

The buff envelope contained what he expected it to contain; the papers for his decree nisi. The courts had decided his marriage was no longer viable. In just over six weeks' time he could apply for his decree absolute and would be a free man – and he really didn't want to be. There was a very slight hope that Dora wouldn't accept it, but that was unlikely. He sighed and opened the second envelope. He breathed a sigh of relief. Mr Oliver, as previously stated, said that Carol was to remain in his care until Mrs Rodgers was rehoused, at which point the situation would be looked at again. He was to inform the authorities if his marital position changed before that time. He pushed the letter back into the envelope, wondering if Dora had received similar mail today. No doubt he'd hear something from Frank if that was the case. It was time to collect Carol from Dolly's and, once she was in bed, to sit and contemplate the future.

Ivy smiled as she put the phone down. Joe had just called her to let her know his decree nisi was through. She was almost there, although what he'd said afterwards didn't fill her with joy. Carol was to remain with him for the foreseeable future.

Ivy sighed and went back upstairs to her flat, Roly on her heels. He spent more time with her than he did her landlord and never missed an opportunity to follow her. She picked up the sewing project she was working on, an underskirt with a bodice that she'd pinned a panel on inside at the front. She'd unpicked an old cushion that was stuffed with cotton flock and planned to stuff the panel with half, saving the rest for later to pad it out a bit more. Joe wouldn't realise it wasn't her body filling out as he hadn't been near her since she'd told him her news. He'd not even given her a hug. He just looked at her with contempt in his eyes most of the time but it didn't stop her living in hope. Deep down he was a good man and she knew they'd be really happy one day.

She was still in touch with an old school friend who lived in Manchester. They hadn't met up for ages but they wrote to each other every few months. Ivy was going to visit her friend in a few weeks, which would have to be before the wedding, *if* there was to be one. The timing would all need careful planning, and if Joe bought her a ring soon, she knew it wasn't in him to be so cruel as to dump her right after a miscarriage, which would happen while she was in Manchester. He'd be sure to want to look after her when she got back and not cause her further upset by calling it all off. And Carol would hopefully be back at her mother's by then, once he'd let the authorities know of his impending wedding. Her plan was falling into place. The next few weeks would be crucial, but Ivy was quite certain it would all come right in the end.

'And have you any idea how much longer it's going to be?' Dora asked. 'There's only me and one other neighbour left in the street. It's dangerous. There's all sorts of unsavoury strangers hanging around and there are rats in the yard. I've got a little girl who likes to play outside. I have to keep her indoors all the time now.' She listened as the man on the other end of the line said he had no idea when she would be rehoused. She hadn't been on the list very long; her needs were lower than others in that area and she only had the one child. Bigger families than hers were still waiting, he told her. Dora slammed the phone down and shook her head in despair.

'No joy?' Esther said, handing her a cup of tea. She raised an eyebrow in Sammy's direction and inclined her head towards the stairs behind them. He nodded and disappeared, leaving them chatting.

'No. It's ridiculous.' Dora helped herself to a biscuit from the tin Esther held in front of her. 'I can't get Carol back until I move and yet if I had her with me we'd be moving sooner because we'd be a bigger family. It's one of those stupid situations where you go round in circles all the time.' Dora felt like her nerves were on a knife edge lately. The thought of going back to Wright Street after work filled her with despair. The only bit of light was Frank popping in whenever he could on his way home from work. But that was becoming less frequent as the days went by. He didn't like to get back to Knowsley too late. Mam's neighbours were very good at sitting with her for a few hours each day, but most of them had homes and families to see to.

Frank had recently taken a day off work and had brought the doctor out as Mam was refusing to leave the house. The doctor said her confusion and memory loss were down to old age and not just the bump on her head. It was his opinion that she needed to be looked after full-time in a local authority old people's home, of which he said there were several in Liverpool centre and the surrounding areas. If they were in agreement, someone would be brought in to assess Mam's needs before she would be accepted.

Dora wished she could look after her but Mam was struggling with stairs and needed to be living on one level. She and Frank were still considering what they should do for the best. Maisie opposite had thrown up her hands in horror and told them they couldn't put Mary in the workhouse. She'd gone home in tears and Dora had run after her to tell her the homes were nothing like the workhouse and that if they did choose to get her looked after properly, then maybe she could come with them to look around and to put her mind at rest.

Dora went back upstairs to the workroom and carried on with the wedding orders. The bridal gown was draped over a mannequin in readiness for a fitting later in the week and she began to pin the pattern pieces onto pink silk fabric for the little bridesmaids' dresses. The wireless was playing softly in the background and she hummed along to Doris Day's 'Secret Love'. Jackie was downstairs with Esther, drawing as usual. Esther had taught her the numbers up to ten and the alphabet. Jackie could not only recite them perfectly, but could also write each number and letter and something that resembled her name. Dora felt proud that her youngest would have a head start for starting school in September.

Sammy was on the top floor of the building, banging around and moving what sounded like heavy boxes about. They never used the top floor and Dora had only been up there once since she'd worked here. She heard footsteps on the uncarpeted stairs and he appeared, cobwebs in his hair and beard, but with a big smile on his face.

'Just popping down to have a word with Esther and to wash my hands,' he said.

Dora nodded and wondered why he couldn't have washed his hands in the small cloakroom up here where they had a sink and a hot water geyser as well as a lavatory. Doris Day finished and Patti Page's 'Tennessee Waltz' began. Dora drew a deep breath. She and Joe had danced to this song so many times. It had been one of their favourites. She could feel tears welling and blinked them away.

Chapter Twenty-Four

Joe picked up a bunch of colourful flowers from the passenger seat. He felt in his pocket for the small box, gritted his teeth and got out of the car. He'd phoned Ivy earlier to tell her he would come over later as both girls were with Dora for the night and he wanted to ask her something; Ivy had said she would cook them something nice. He walked up the path of the large detached house, rang the doorbell and rocked on his heels while he waited for her to let him in. He could hear Roly barking somewhere in the house and hoped her landlord wouldn't come to the door and have a go at him for getting Ivy in a mess.

The door swung open and Ivy greeted him with a peck on the cheek. He made to take her in his arms but she pulled back and led the way upstairs to her first-floor flat. He shrugged and followed her. She was probably playing hard to get. He didn't blame her; she'd know his heart wasn't in what he was about to do. But he also knew she wouldn't turn him down. His stomach growled at the appetising aroma of whatever it was she'd made for their tea. 'Smells good,' he ventured.

'Steak and onions,' she said with a smile. 'Have a seat Joe.' She gestured to the sofa. 'I won't be a minute. Just finishing off in the kitchen. Can I get you a glass of something? I've got some pale ale in, or sherry.'

'Ale, thanks.' He sat down and looked around the neat and tidy sitting room. There was nothing out of place, but the one thing Ivy wasn't good at, unlike Dora, was putting colours together. Nothing matched; the orange and brown carpet square clashed with the pink floral curtains and the blue and gold patterned cushions looked out of place on the green tweed sofa and chair. He shook his head. Living with Ivy would be worse than living in a kaleidoscope. But that was the least of his worries, he thought as she handed him a glass of ale. At least she could cook. She sat down in the chair opposite him with a small glass of sherry.

'Are you not sitting with me?'

'Er, no I'm fine here, Joe.' She wafted a hand in front of her face. 'I like the breeze coming in from the open window. I get really hot at the moment, you know…' She tailed off and looked away from his gaze.

'Fair enough.' He pointed at the flowers that he'd laid on the small coffee table. 'I brought those for you.'

'Thank you. It's a long time since anyone bought me flowers. I'll put them in a vase.' She got up, making a grunting noise as she did so, and went back into the kitchen.

Joe stared after her. The navy dress she had on was one of those smock styles like Dora had worn when she'd been pregnant. It was hard to gauge exactly how big Ivy's baby bump was as the dress draped like a tent around her, but he could tell she was nowhere near as big as Dora had been at this stage, even when she'd been carrying only Jackie and not the twins. Ivy came back into the room with the flowers and put the vase in the centre of the table that was set for two. She lowered herself back into the chair and picked up her glass of sherry.

'So, how are you keeping?' he began. She didn't look pale or tired or anything like he'd expected she would. 'You said you'd been sickly and what have you.'

'I'm all right. It seems to have passed now,' she said, looking down at her glass. 'Tea won't be long. Just waiting for the carrots to cook.'

'Okay, well while we're waiting, I think you know why I'm here tonight.' He winked and rooted in his pocket. Her cheeks flushed pink and she gasped.

'Oh, I don't think we should, Joe, you know, not until I've seen the doctor, I mean. With me already having lost a baby, it might be dangerous. We need to make sure everything is okay, er, down there, before we do anything again.'

Joe stared at her, the black velvet ring box in his hand. 'What are you on about?' Then it dawned. 'No, no, Ivy, you've got it all wrong. I'm not trying to drag you off to bed, gel. And yes, I agree, we'll wait until the doc says it's okay. We don't want to do any harm, do we?' Joe sighed with relief. He was in no hurry to make love to her again, at least not tonight. There were still a couple of weeks to go before his decree absolute came through and he always lived in hope. He shook his head to clear it. Why on earth was he thinking that? Here he was, about to propose to his pregnant bit-on-the-side, and he was still hoping his ex-wife would come back. 'Get a grip, Joe,' he thought as he got to his feet. 'Ivy,' he said, dropping down on one knee, just like he'd done with Dora eight years ago when he came back from the war. 'Will you marry me, please?' He nearly choked on the words but managed a smile as her hands flew to her mouth.

She nodded, her eyes bright with tears. 'Oh yes, Joe, of course I will.' She stayed seated while he slid the ring onto her finger and then leaned over to plant a gentle kiss on her lips.

He hurriedly got to his feet as she stared at the little diamond solitaire ring that had taken a chunk of the money he'd been saving towards a house deposit. He'd have to start again now; he was determined to leave the ROF at some point and with that move he'd lose the bungalow. Still, with Ivy to look after Carol soon enough, there was nothing to stop him working further afield.

'It's beautiful. Thank you.' She smiled at him, her eyes sparkling.

'You're welcome,' he said, sitting back down again and wondering how he could conjure up a bit of *something* for her so that he could make her feel a bit special.

'I'll go and serve up our meal,' she said. 'Why don't you sit at the table? I won't be a minute.'

As she vanished into the kitchen he breathed a sigh of relief. All being well now she wouldn't expect him to stay the night.

Dora tucked Carol and Jackie up in the double bed and told them to stop giggling as Granny was trying to go to sleep in the other bedroom. They'd had a nice afternoon out with Frank and her mam at Sefton Park. Mam had said she'd stay at home but both she and Frank had insisted she join them and she'd enjoyed herself. Frank had taken the girls out on the boating lake and to see the Peter Pan statue that they loved so much, while Dora took Mam into the Palm House café for tea and cake. It was good to see her taking an interest in her surroundings again instead of sitting in her chair by the fire and twiddling her thumbs. When she'd said in a loud voice that a nearby woman's hat, a mass of colourful feathers, looked ridiculous and she'd probably been poaching pheasants on Lord Derby's land, Dora knew something of her old mam was still in there somewhere.

They'd still not made a decision on Mam's future. Dora kept hoping she'd regain a bit of confidence and be able to live independently for a while longer. But it was the memory loss that seemed to be getting worse and that could prove dangerous if Mam turned the gas stove on and forgot to light it, or something. Maybe the company of other elderly ladies in a home would be good for her, someone to gossip with. She and Frank needed to have a chat soon and get things moving.

*

Joe set off to collect his daughters. He was looking forward to spending a nice day with them and was taking them swimming and then back to the bungalow for a bit of dinner. Ivy had told him last night that she wouldn't be in work for three days from Monday as she was visiting an old school friend in Manchester. She was leaving this afternoon on the train from Lime Street. He'd offered her a lift to the station, but she'd told him it was all in hand as her landlord was taking her. Joe was secretly relieved she was having time off; it meant she wouldn't be flashing her ring around the canteen for a while, and they could keep the baby news to themselves for a bit longer.

He pulled up outside Dora's mam's place, ready to face Frank's wrath about how irresponsible he'd been, as had happened each time they met lately, and was shocked when Dora opened the door to him. He took a step backwards as she half-smiled and ushered their daughters outside.

'Dora, I, I, er, wasn't expecting you,' he stuttered, taking the bag with swimming costumes and towels from her.

'Frank's out with his mates,' she told him. 'He's joining me later at my place. Mam's across the lane at Maisie's for the afternoon. It's a nice change for her. I'm going to call home and then go and see Esther and Sammy while I've got a bit of spare time. They have a lovely garden and it's a pleasure to sit in it. Jackie loves going there and they treat her like she's their own grandchild. They'll be the same with Carol once they get to know her; which is more than I can say for *your* mother. She's only ever seen them a handful of times since they were born.'

Joe wasn't about to get into a slanging match about his mother. He agreed with Dora. His mum had hardly been supportive. Apart from buying a pram for Carol and giving him money to put towards a car when she sold her house, she'd always kept her distance. Since her move to Cheadle in Cheshire a few years ago there'd been no commitment from her and the last time he'd called her to tell her he was getting a divorce from Dora she'd been more than displeased, telling him he should never have married the girl in the first place. He dreaded introducing her to Ivy.

'Yes, I know she has,' he muttered. 'Right, come on, girls, let's get going.'

'Are we seeing Ivy and Roly today, Daddy?' Carol asked, not even waving goodbye to her mother, who was hugging Jackie on the garden path.

'Er, no. Not today.' Ivy's away for a few days. It's just me, I'm afraid. Say goodbye to Mammy in case you don't come back with me when I bring Jackie home.'

'Bye, Mammy,' Carol called and clambered into the car.

'What time will you be home?' Joe asked, ushering Jackie into the car alongside Carol.

'Teatime, I expect. Mam'll be tired by then.'

'Okay.' He walked around to the driver's door and stopped. 'Look, Dora, can I give you a lift into town? Save you waiting around for buses that are rubbish on a Sunday. Seems a bit daft when I'm taking these two swimming down that way.' He looked at her as a hopeful expression crossed her face, closely followed by a guarded one.

'Well, if you don't mind. Thank you. It will certainly save me some time. Just let me nip over to Maisie's to tell Mam I'm going now. Wait in the car while I get myself organised.'

Joe did as he was told. At least she hadn't bitten his head off and sent him away with a flea in his ear. He'd need to tell her about his proposal to Ivy, sooner rather than later. But not today; it was unexpected but nice to see her again, and there'd be time enough for the final nail in his coffin another time.

Chapter Twenty-Five

'You can drop me off on Scottie Road, Joe. I'll walk the rest of the way. Save you messing about having to turn the car around on Wright Street. I've got plenty of time now. I might even get a bit of work done before I go on my visit.'

'Okay, if you're sure. I'll bring Jackie back later to your mam's.'

'Thanks. Have a lovely time with Daddy, girls.' She blew them both a kiss and got out of the car, waving as Joe pulled away. She hurried down the street and rummaged for the front door key in her handbag, then noticed the door was already standing ajar. Her heart thudded as she called out, 'Hello. Who's there?' She hoped it might be Frank arrived early. He had a spare key for emergencies. No reply. Dora pushed the door open further and warily stepped inside. The house felt cold, as though it had been open to the elements all night. A shiver ran through her as she opened the door to the front room and looked around. There was no mess, but her wireless was gone from the shelf in the chimney breast alcove and her Singer electric sewing machine, a present from Frank a few years ago, wasn't on the table where she'd left it after finishing a job the other night. Nor was the machine's case on the floor next to the chair under the window.

Heart pounding, she hurried into the back room, but it all seemed to be in order as she glanced quickly around. There was nothing in here that a burglar would be interested in anyway. She had little of value to steal. She strained her ears at the bottom of the stairs before willing herself to go up there. It was just as she'd left it; tidy with the bed made. Her wardrobe door was closed but she looked inside anyway. The few clothes she had were still hanging there. She glanced around and frowned as she saw something white spilling out of one of the drawers of the dressing table.

Her stomach lurched as she realised it was the drawer where she kept her underwear and the small, carved wooden jewellery box that Joe had brought her back from his war travels. She kept her diamond engagement ring and the wedding ring she no longer wore in it. She snatched the drawer open and pushed back the stray slip that had got caught up. She rummaged amongst her underwear, and sure enough, the box had gone. With a sick feeling she pulled everything out, looking for the big white envelope in which she kept all the smaller envelopes that Joe gave her each week, containing money for Jackie that she'd been saving for her daughter's future and the possibility of sending her to drama school when she was old enough. The envelope was missing too. All the money and anything of value that she had in the world had gone, stolen by someone who knew she wasn't home, even though the curtains had been drawn and lamps left on while she was in Knowsley. She sank to the floor and burst into loud sobs.

By the time Frank arrived with his mate, who had given him a lift on the back of a motorbike, Dora was in such a state she could hardly speak without crying. She'd called the police from the phone box on Scotland Road and they'd been round to check for fingerprints and to take a statement from her. They suggested she get a new lock and bolt for the front door and Frank said he'd see to that. She told them about the Smyths from across, who'd recently moved and knew that she occasionally spent the weekend away from the house. One of the officers told her they'd check that out as the Smyths were known to them.

Frank and his mate went off to Knowsley so that Frank could pick up his car to take Dora back to their mam's. Dora waited anxiously for him to return, with a chair wedged behind the front door and under the back door handle.

'I can't stay here tonight,' she sobbed as he arrived back. 'I'd be too scared, and you need to stay with Mam, Frank, so you can't be here with me and Jackie.'

Frank had found a couple of old bolts and a lock in his dad's shed and fixed them to Dora's front door, making it secure, before they left by the back door.

'Don't forget you'll have to come in by the back door,' he reminded her as she slipped the key into her pocket.

'Thanks, Frank,' Dora said, giving him a hug. 'I haven't got much, but I can't afford to lose anything else.'

'If I ever get my hands on the bastard that robbed you he'll be sorry he was ever born,' Frank growled, placing a protective arm around her shoulders. 'The rest of your things should be safe enough for now. But we need to get you moved out of there as soon as possible, Sis. I'll start asking around my mates to see if they know of anything going and tomorrow you get on to the bloody council again and give them what for.'

Ivy's friend, Vera, was meeting her at Piccadilly station when she got off the train in Manchester. Ivy, wearing her padded underskirt for effect, adopted her best pregnant waddle and made her way across the platform to where Vera was sitting on a bench with a look on her face that told Ivy she was miles away. She'd always been *away with the fairies*, as Vera's mother used to say, even at school. She reminded Ivy of Flo: old-fashioned dress sense, and her mousey brown hair fluffed out around her face in no particular style, but a nice enough person. Vera jumped as Ivy approached and bellowed her name above the noise of the engine, which was announcing with a belch of steam and a loud toot that it was leaving the platform behind her.

'Ivy,' Vera said and jumped to her feet. 'Ooh, give me that case. You shouldn't be carrying anything heavy.'

Ivy smiled. 'I'm okay; it's only small and not heavy at all.'

'Right,' Vera said, kissing her on the cheek. 'It's good to see you. We'd best get in the queue for a bus to Levenshulme.' Vera still lived in her old family home on Dickenson Road near where Ivy had grown up before moving to Liverpool when she'd married her late soldier husband, whose family were from Toxteth. 'I hope your journey was okay.'

'It was fine. I read most of the way and almost fell asleep.'

They stood in the queue in Piccadilly Gardens for a while and waited for the number 92 bus. They were at Vera's house in no time, passing places on the way that Ivy recognised from her younger years.

The Victorian detached house, in its own large garden, was now in a shabby state on the outside with peeling paint on the frames around the stained-glass windows and the brickwork crumbling in places. It was comfortable enough inside, with tall-ceilinged rooms that must cost a fortune in coal to keep warm. Ivy looked around the drawing room, as Vera called it, while her friend made tea in the kitchen. It was years since she'd last been in here; she used to come back with Vera after school. The marble fireplace spoke of grander days when the house had belonged to Vera's father, a wealthy factory owner who had become seriously ill. The family had fallen on hard times following his death.

Vera came back with a tray of pots and a plate of home-made scones, and put the tray down on the coffee table. Ivy remembered that, like her, Vera had always been good at domestic science at school and loved to cook. Ivy had made a career of her skills, but Vera had chosen to stay at home, forgoing marriage *and* a job, to help her late mother look after her ailing father.

'You'll have to tell me all about this new man in your life,' Vera said, pouring tea into dainty china cups and pushing the matching sugar bowl in Ivy's direction. 'I see he's given you a ring, so hopefully his intentions are honourable, considering your condition.'

Ivy felt her cheeks heating. 'Yes, we'll be getting wed shortly. We need to decide on a date and make the arrangements.'

'And you said he was a divorcé?'

'He is almost. Another couple of weeks and it will all be done with.'

'Well, when you weigh up what's happened to you it's a good job he is.' Vera pursed her lips disapprovingly.

'Quite.' To her knowledge, Vera had never even had a boyfriend, so was hardly qualified to give advice on relationships. Ivy changed the subject. 'I was thinking that while I'm over this way we might have an afternoon or two out, maybe go and see a film and do a bit of shopping in the city.'

'That would be lovely,' Vera said. 'I never go anywhere. I've no one to go out with.'

'You could maybe join a club through the church or the WI or something to meet new people. You're only thirty, like me. It's a bit too young to do nothing with your life. Perhaps you could go to night school and learn a skill and then get a job. You'll meet people to go out with then.'

'I'll think about it.' Vera raised her cup to her lips and took a sip.

Ivy realised she was wasting her breath and changed the subject. She patted her stomach gently. 'Shame about this really. We could have gone to Belle Vue Zoo and had a few rides on the fair. I love the Bobs and the Caterpillar.'

'Oh no, it would be most unsuitable. You can't take that sort of risk,' Vera said.

'Have you ever considered selling this big house and buying something more suitable for one person?' Ivy asked.

Vera sighed. 'I've thought about it, often; but I haven't got around to doing anything about it yet. This house needs money spending on it and I simply haven't got any apart from a small endowment left to me by Mother. When that runs out I'll have to do something.'

Ivy nodded, wishing she and Joe had a big house to sell. It would set them up nicely in an area well away from Dora and his kids.

On Wednesday evening, Ivy told Vera she was going upstairs to pack her case in readiness for her trip home tomorrow. Vera had bought a couple of tiny nightgowns when they'd been shopping yesterday and had given them to her for the baby. Ivy felt a bit guilty as her friend was short of money and the gowns would never be worn. But she'd managed to assuage her feelings by treating them both to fish and chips in a local café for dinner today, followed by a matinee at the ABC Ardwick. They'd both enjoyed Doris Day in *Calamity Jane* and had laughed and slapped their thighs as they'd sung along to 'The Deadwood Stage'.

'Vera,' Ivy called downstairs. 'Is it okay if I have a bath? My back's aching a bit. It might help ease it.'

'Of course,' Vera called back. 'The heater's been on so there should be enough hot water for you.'

Ivy ran a bath and lay back in the warm water, putting her plan into action. She'd complain of stomach pains later as well as the backache, and during the night would 'miscarry' down the lavatory; not wishing to wake Vera, she'd 'manage' on her own until her friend was up. Then she'd involve Vera tomorrow by asking her to get her some sanitary towels from the chemist, which she could burn on the parlour fire that was always lit to take the chill off the cold house. She'd ask her to ring Joe at work from a phone box and tell him that she'd lost the baby and would be staying here until the weekend to recover. Vera would no doubt want to call the doctor but Ivy would tell her there was nothing to be done other than rest for a few days and that she'd rather see her own doctor when she got home. Joe could do the explaining to management and hopefully he would drive over here on Saturday and pick her up. It was an easy enough plan; fingers crossed it all worked in her favour.

'Oh, Dora!' Esther exclaimed as Dora apologised for being late into work and explained about the burglary and that she and Jackie had to get the bus and tram from Knowsley this morning. 'Oh you poor girl. Get on the phone right away and tell the council you don't feel safe any more. I'll leave you to do that while I just pop upstairs to have a quick word with Sammy.'

Dora settled Jackie at the table with her crayons and a colouring book and then phoned the council offices. She was eventually put through to the right department and, after pleading her case once more, she waited patiently as she was passed on to a more senior housing officer. But the end result was the same as before. She would be offered a new property in due course.

'I'm sorry, I can't tell you when that will be, Mrs Rodgers,' the man on the line said as Dora protested that she thought she'd been waiting long enough and didn't feel safe in her own home any more. She burst into tears and slammed down the phone as Esther, followed by Sammy, came down the stairs. They were both looking secretive.

Esther put her arm around Dora's shoulders and sat her down on a chair. She made a pot of tea and, when they were all holding steaming mugs and Jackie had her juice and biscuits, Sammy cleared his throat and looked at Esther, who nodded.

Dora looked at the pair, hoping they weren't going to tell her they no longer required her services.

'We've been having a bit of a think over the last week or so,' Sammy began. 'And we've come up with what we both think is a wonderful idea.'

Dora frowned and put her mug down on the table. She placed her hands together on her lap.

'Don't look so worried,' Esther said. 'You might not think it's as good an idea as we do, but we'll tell you anyway.'

Sammy nodded. 'Stop me if you think I'm getting carried away,' he said, smiling. 'The top floor of this building is not used for anything useful. Everything that's stored up there, and it's only a few boxes of junk, can be put on a garden bonfire. There are three rooms; two large ones and a small one at the back. The windows are in decent condition and the wiring was done when we had electricity put in a few years ago. We had the gas mantels up until then. The small room at the back is over the cloakroom, so we could get water plumbed up there and it would make a nice little kitchen area with a sink and some cupboards fitted. The other two rooms would do nicely as a sitting room and a big bedroom that could be split by a screen for privacy. The only thing missing is a bathroom, but there's the toilet and sink in the cloakroom on the floor below to use.'

Esther smiled at Dora's puzzled expression. 'What Sammy is trying to say is that we wondered if you'd like to live up there and we'd help you turn it into a nice little flat. It's very private and you can use the back door to come and go and then just slip up the stairs, so there's no need to worry about coming to and fro through the shop when we're closed. There's room to have Carol visiting because we've got a bed settee at home that has hardly been used, so it could go in the sitting room for you, and the girls would have the bedroom to themselves. If you like the idea, once we've got it ship-shape, you could tell that man from the welfare that this is your permanent residence and he might say yes to you having Carol back for good and she could go to the school off Scottie Road where Jackie will be going. No need for either of them to change then, is there?'

Sammy nodded enthusiastically. 'And of course we've got the garden at the house for them to play in. You can always pop over at the weekend. There's still the swing from when Sonny was a little boy and the pond with fish, and we always get frogs in the spring.' Sammy looked so excited at the prospect of showing the girls the frogs that Dora flung her arms around him and gave him a hug.

'It all sounds wonderful. You need to tell me how much rent you'd like me to pay.'

He shook his head. 'No rent. You being on the premises is a good thing for us. Call it caretaker's perks, my dear.'

Dora smiled, feeling tearful. 'I don't know what I've done to deserve you two in my life,' she said. 'You're like an extra set of parents to me. I love you both so much.'

'So, is that a yes then?' Esther beamed. 'Oh, Dora, I'm so thrilled. We'll go up and take a look now and decide what we need, make a list, and then we can get it cleared out and cleaned and painted, and you can move all your stuff in.'

'I'm coming up there too,' Jackie said, jiggling from foot to foot.

Sammy swept her into his arms and ran up the stairs with her, both giggling.

'He's in his element,' Esther said, smiling, as they followed.

Dora nodded. 'So am I. You've no idea. I have to admit I was getting really quite scared living on Wright Street and now the thought just terrifies me. There are huge rats running about and strange men hanging around. As soon as a house is empty they're in stripping the lead pipes out and anything else they can sell on. I'm worried they'll go in mine while I'm at work and steal what precious little I have left. Frank's put new locks and bolts on, so hopefully that will help for now until upstairs here is ready. I'll get my brother and some of his big strong mates to help us with the decorating and they can carry the furniture up the stairs. Thank you so much. I'm really grateful, and I haven't felt this excited for ages.'

*

'Dora, Joe's on the phone,' Esther called up the stairs to the workroom on Friday morning. 'Are you coming down or shall I tell him you're busy?'

'I'm here,' Dora said, running down to take the call. 'Wonder what *he* wants? Hope there's nothing wrong with Carol.' She took the phone from Esther. 'Hello, Joe. What's up?' She listened quietly as he spoke and then, 'Of course you can. Jackie will be happy that she's staying overnight with us. And, yes, I'll have her while you get things sorted out. Don't forget we'll be at Mam's. Okay, good luck… and Joe, I'm sorry about the baby.'

She hung up as Esther raised an eyebrow and shook the kettle in her direction. She nodded and sat down next to Jackie, who was colouring dresses for the paper dolls that Esther had cut out for her. 'Joe wants to bring Carol tonight so he can get an early start tomorrow. He's got to go and get Ivy from her friend's in Manchester. She's, er, apparently lost the baby.'

'Oh dear,' Esther said, raising an eyebrow. 'You don't sound very convinced.'

Dora shrugged. 'Hmm. Don't you think it's a bit *too* convenient that she goes away for a few days, miscarries while she's there having a rest, and yet she lugs massive heavy pans around in the ROF canteen, mops the floors and stacks the chairs and seems to be just fine on it? Knowing that she'd miscarried previously, don't you think she'd have been taking more care of herself this time around?' Dolly, ages ago, had told her the story of Ivy's loss of her husband and baby, which wasn't common knowledge. Joe had never mentioned it but Dora assumed he knew Ivy's past history too and would have expected her to take care of herself.

Esther nodded. 'Maybe she's had a fall downstairs or something.'

'Maybe,' Dora said and then, before she could stop herself, blurted out what had been in her mind all along, but she'd been unsure how to voice without sounding like the jealous ex-wife. 'Or *maybe* she was just out to trap Joe and was never pregnant in the first place. I told him he was naïve to trust her. She conveniently waited until we were getting back together, in March, to tell him even though she'd supposedly been pregnant since December. Any other unmarried woman would be out of their mind and dying to share it with the father, wouldn't they?'

Esther pursed her lips. 'In my experience, yes, I agree with you. It's not something you worry about alone if a father is around. But who knows what goes on in Ivy's head.' She handed Dora a mug of tea. 'Well at least you get extra time with Carol this weekend. That will be lovely for the three of you.'

Dora nodded. She couldn't wait to see Agnes at dance class tomorrow and ask what *she* thought.

Chapter Twenty-Six

'I want to go home to my flat,' Ivy announced as Joe drove through Kirkby towards the prefab estate. He'd picked her up as requested, turning up first thing, but had hardly said two words to her after a quick peck on the cheek and a short hug on Vera's doorstep. Vera hadn't invited him in and Ivy took it to mean that she didn't approve of him. All she'd said was '*He* took his time. He should have come right after I phoned him.' But Ivy pointed out that he had a job he couldn't just walk away from at will and a little daughter to see to and there was nothing he could have done anyway. And besides, she hadn't wanted him there any sooner than Saturday, otherwise her acting skills would have needed to go into overdrive. As it was she'd enjoyed Vera waiting on her hand and foot and a catch-up with the latest Agatha Christie novel she'd brought with her. Taking the odd aspirin and having a hot water bottle behind her back for the imaginary pain while lying on the sofa listening to *Housewives' Choice* was a small price to pay for a bit of peace and quiet. And by insisting Joe wait and not come rushing over, she hoped she had made him feel anxious and suitably worried about her, enough to still want to marry her.

Joe frowned and pulled the car over to the side of the road. 'Why? I thought you'd be coming back to the bungalow with me. Somebody needs to look after you.'

'I can look after myself. My landlord and his wife are just downstairs if I need anything.'

'Ivy, you're my fiancée, I insist. Let me look after you. You've just had an awful experience again. Who knows how it will affect you as time goes on? I'm taking you to my place and tomorrow I'm bringing your doctor in to see you, no arguments.'

Ivy chewed her lip. That was the last thing she'd been expecting, or needed. When Joe had asked her earlier what Vera's doctor had said she'd told him she hadn't seen him as her own doctor knew her better and she'd rather see him on Monday. She'd assured him there was nothing a doctor could have done anyway.

She took a deep breath. 'Joe, I want to go home and if you won't take me I'll get a taxi to come for me when we get to yours. And I don't want to see your kids this weekend. It would be too upsetting for me and unfair on you if you don't spend some time with them tomorrow. And it won't affect me as time goes by. I know what you're thinking, but being pregnant doesn't do the same to me as it did to Dora. I just need some peace and quiet and my own bed, that's all.' She stopped and took a deep breath. He looked so worried and she felt a bit sorry for him, remembering that he'd suffered the loss of his newborn daughter, Joanna. To him this new loss was real, not fake like it was for her. She softened her tone and stroked his arm. 'Look, maybe you could pop around tonight for an hour. I might feel a bit brighter by then.'

'Well, if you're sure? I really don't like leaving you in case something goes wrong and you can't get down the stairs to your landlord.'

She patted his hand. 'Joe, stop fretting, I'll shout for him if I need to. Take me home and with your spare afternoon maybe you could go and watch a match with one of your pals.'

'So, what do you reckon?' Dora asked as she and Agnes sat with mugs of coffee and flapjacks in the café area of the hall in Kirkby where Marjorie Barker ran her dancing classes. Their daughters were having a tap lesson today and the strains of the Billy Cotton

Band Show with singer Alan Breeze performing the old wartime song, 'The Fleet's in Port Again', drifted through the open door. Carol had gone with Uncle Frank to get a few things from the shops for Mam and he was picking them up later. Dora had just put Agnes in the picture about the news of Ivy's miscarriage and her thoughts on the matter.

'Oh, Dora, I don't know,' Agnes said, putting her mug down on the table. She broke a corner off her flapjack. 'While it sounds feasible, surely to God she wouldn't do something like that to him. Not when she knows how awful it is to lose a baby and she also knows *he* knows that too. She wouldn't be that cruel, would she?'

'Hmm, I think she would. But I can't say anything to him, can I? He looked upset and worried when he dropped Carol off last night. He apologised for bringing her over before Saturday, but he said he needed to be with Ivy and dashed away before I could question him further. Anyway, we'll see. Time will tell. He won't marry her if he finds out she's been lying, will he?'

'I don't suppose he will, but Dora, that shouldn't make any difference to the decision *you* made, should it? Joe still wanted to be with you, baby or no baby. You said you didn't want him – *again* – remember?'

Dora raised an eyebrow. 'Yes, I do. Oh, I don't want him back. I've made my choice. I'm quite happy to be moving into my new flat soon and with my job and everything. Things are working out right for me at last. And I'm keeping my fingers crossed that Mr Oliver says yes to me having Carol back as soon as we're settled in.'

'There you go then. It's a shame it all went wrong for you and Joe, but sadly these things happen. And as long as you and the girls are all right, that's all that matters.'

Dora settled her daughters in bed, warning them not to be noisy and disturb Granny, and then ran downstairs. She unpacked a bag she'd brought some sewing in. She was unpicking a pair of curtains and altering them to go in her new sitting room. There were two long slim windows with Georgian panes and she'd bagged a lovely pair of floor-length curtains from Paddy's market the other day. There was enough fabric, which was a beautiful William Morris golden lily design, to make curtains for both windows and matching cushion covers too. Dora had snatched them up as another woman, who'd also been eyeing them, had turned to talk to her companion.

The bed settee that Sammy and Esther had given her was already upstairs in the new flat and was brown hide with curved wooden arms. It was immaculate and the mattress was spotless. A much nicer piece of furniture to sit on than the uncomfortable old sofa she'd been given when she'd moved into Wright Street. That could stay down there when she moved in. The new curtain fabric had the same shades of green and gold in it as her carpet squares that were coming with her. Her brother and his mates had worked really hard each night this week after work and had painted the walls in cream and white-glossed the woodwork. Another day or two and everywhere would be finished.

She felt really excited at the prospect and couldn't wait. She would be able to invite Agnes and Sadie round for a cuppa without feeling embarrassed by her surroundings. She hadn't seen either of her friends for a while now, apart from Agnes briefly at the dancing classes. It would be lovely to catch up. Frank, who was out in Liverpool with his docker mates tonight, was meeting her down there tomorrow to do some more painting and she was hoping to move in next weekend. She'd given her landlord a week's notice along with her final week's rent. He'd wished her well and told her she could take the old gas stove if it was of any use to her. But the new flat had no gas since Sammy had had the electrics done, so Dora would be leaving it behind. Frank's mate had got hold of an electric stove for her. That was the beauty of a brother who worked on the docks. He could get his hands on almost anything.

Joe hadn't been quite as enthusiastic when she'd told him she had a new place that she'd shortly be moving into, although he'd sympathised over the burglary. She went over their conversation in her mind as she pinned the hems of her curtains.

'New place?' He'd frowned. 'I didn't know you'd got a new place. So, the council have pulled their finger out at last. Not before bloody time either.'

Dora shook her head. 'It's not a council place, Joe. I'm moving into rooms above the draper's shop where I work. We're just in the throes of getting it ready for next weekend.'

'Oh, right. Well, that'll be better than Wright Street for you both.'

'Hmm,' she said. 'For all three of us actually. It's a really big flat. There's plenty of room for Carol too. It's permanent, so there'll be no moving schools, apart from the one time when she comes back to me. She'll be going to the school Jackie starts in September, All Saints. I've written to Mr Oliver. I'm just waiting for his reply. So, you can concentrate on your new family with the lovely Ivy now, can't you? You can forget all about ours.'

He'd frowned at the sarcasm in her voice. 'I don't want to forget about our family, Dora. How can you even think that? Those girls are my life. And where will they play on Homer Street? It's too busy outside and I bet there's nothing at the back of the place either. Maybe you should have waited for a council house.'

'I was sick and tired of waiting. I think they'd forgotten all about us. It could have taken months before I was offered anything. There's a small private yard around the back of the shop, and Sammy and Esther don't live too far from there. They have a lovely garden the girls can go to play in.'

Joe had shaken his head. 'We'll have to see what Mr Oliver says then, won't we?'

Dora shook the fabric and folded the curtain she'd been working on. She felt a bit mean now when she thought about what she'd said. There would be no new family for Joe now. He'd need his daughters more than ever and she knew he wouldn't give Carol up without a fight.

Dora moved into her new flat the following week on the Friday evening after work. Frank's mate had borrowed his dad's van and between them they'd brought the rest of the furniture over from Wright Street. It didn't take long to arrange what little she had in the two rooms and she and Jackie slept like logs that first night. She didn't feel worried or insecure the way she had at Wright Street and the bedroom at the back was quiet and peaceful with no noisy neighbours to disturb their slumbers.

Frank brought Carol from Joe's on the Saturday as Joe said he couldn't leave Ivy. Once she'd settled the girls in bed, Dora popped downstairs to use a sewing machine. They'd done their usual giggling and messing about but were sleeping now. She wanted to finish making some cushion covers. With her own machine stolen in the burglary it was handy having these to use. It would have been nice to invite Mam and Frank for Sunday dinner tomorrow, but Mam would never have been able to get up the two flights of stairs so Frank was picking them all up from here mid-morning to have their usual Sunday in Knowsley. She wondered if she should ring Joe from the downstairs phone and see how Ivy was, then thought better of it. The woman had never shown consideration for *her* so why should she bother? If she was honest with herself it was Joe she was most concerned about. Ah well, she'd see him tomorrow when he came to collect Carol. With a bit of luck she should be hearing something from Mr Oliver soon and then they could get Carol settled down here once and for all.

At least the flat would look really nice if Mr Oliver chose to visit her at home, and no doubt he would. She snipped the thread, turned the last cushion cover right side out and gave them all a press with the iron. Back upstairs she slipped the four covers over the cushion pads, arranged them on the bed settee and stood back to admire her efforts. She checked on the girls, who were flat out side by side with angelic expressions on their faces, long hair fanned across the pillows, one blonde, one dark; chalk and cheese.

She made herself a mug of Horlicks in the little kitchen area, kicked off her shoes, switched the wireless on for a bit of background noise and picked up a copy of *Woman's Weekly*. She looked around her new sitting room with a feeling of pride. It didn't half look posh with her William Morris curtains. Even Agnes couldn't afford William Morris fabric and she and Alan weren't short of a bob or two. Sammy had got her an electric fire that was set into a wooden mantel surround and the fire part glowed like lit coals when it was plugged in. It made the room feel lovely and cosy. Dora felt a rush of contentment wash over her for the first time in months. She had somewhere decent to live and was in control of her life again, and it was a good feeling to have.

Chapter Twenty-Seven

'So what do you think, Mam?' Dora linked her arm through her mam's as they walked around the large, well-kept gardens of Ashley House Elderly Persons Home. It was one of three run by the authorities that could offer Mam a place and it was just outside Kirkby, so not too far to visit her. So far this one seemed the nicest. The smell of home baking had met them on entering. The communal lounge and dining room were clean and the furniture was of good quality. Music was playing quietly from a wireless set, there was a television in the lounge and some of the residents were seated around a large table playing board games with members of staff. Miss Smart, the middle-aged warden who'd shown them around, had suggested they take a stroll and left them to it.

Mam nodded as they sat down on a bench under a tree. 'It's not a bad place, chuck. I know I'm losing my marbles, Dora, I've known it for a while now. It was funny at first, finding my glasses in the fridge with my library book, and forgetting when I put things in the oven to bake that I hadn't lit it. I'd be safer in a place like this. And the other old dears seem quite nice. It's time to admit that I can't look after myself properly any more. Our Frank's put his life on hold for me and you're always worrying about me and can't keep running over to Knowsley, you've got them little girls to think about. Both of you have got your lives to live. I've had mine and it's been a good one.'

Dora smiled and squeezed her hand. 'We'll come and see you every week, you know. And Frank can come and get you in the car so we can have an afternoon at the park when the weather's nice. So what do you think? To me this one is the best of the three. It's a bit livelier.'

Mam laughed. 'The other two felt like God's waiting room if I'm honest, chuck. But I like it here and this garden is lovely.'

'Shall we go back in then and tell Miss Smart it'll do?' Dora got to her feet and helped Mam up. 'Dad would have loved this garden, wouldn't he?'

'He would that. The flower borders are beautiful; so colourful and not a weed in sight.'

Back inside Miss Smart showed them into her office and arranged for tea and biscuits to be brought in. 'I'm so glad you think we're right for you, Mrs Evans. We try and make it a home from home for our residents. All the meals we serve are home-cooked, even the bread is baked here. Every other Sunday we have a chap comes in and he plays the piano and we have a lovely sing-song. We do a bit of gentle keep fit mid-week to stop joints from seizing up and if there's a good film on nearby we arrange a private bus to take us to the picture house. We also have a hairdresser coming in on a Wednesday for shampoo and sets.'

'Be like stopping in a posh hotel,' Mam said. 'I won't know I'm born.'

Miss Smart smiled and reached into a drawer in her desk for a set of keys. 'Shall we go and take a look at the room we've reserved for you, Mrs Evans?'

As they waited at the gates for Frank to pick them up, her mam squeezed Dora's arm. 'I am doing the right thing, aren't I?'

'Mam, of course you are. It's time you took life a bit easier and let people look after you for a change. If I had a big enough house with a downstairs bathroom you could live with me and the kids, but I haven't.'

Mam nodded. 'You will make sure our Frank gets himself set up, won't you, love?'

'I will, Mam. He's going to come and stay with me on odd nights and his mate's on others. He said he'd put his name on the list for a one-bedroomed council flat once you've given notice on the house. Here he is.' She waved at her brother as he pulled up, then helped her mam into the front passenger seat. 'We'll go and get our Jackie from Joe's place now and then go back to yours for a couple of hours,' she told Frank. 'This weekend's flown. Can't believe it's work again tomorrow. We're getting really busy with wedding orders and young lads wanting their trouser legs tapering. It's a new fashion from America apparently.'

'You can do my jeans, Sis,' Frank said. 'Remind me to give them to you before I take you home.'

Joe brought Jackie to the door when Dora knocked. He didn't invite her in as he usually did. 'Where's Carol?' she asked. 'I want to say goodbye to her.'

He looked over his shoulder, seeming nervous. 'Er, she's with Ivy learning to knit,' he muttered. 'She doesn't want to come to the door. Best not to disturb them. Ivy's not feeling too good. The girls have been scrapping and the noise gives her a headache.'

'Does it now?' Dora pursed her lips. 'Funny that. They haven't scrapped for ages. You should tell Ivy she'd better get used to the noise if she wants to be part of this family.'

Joe pulled the front door closed behind him and walked to the car with them. 'Can I pop in with Carol for ten minutes tomorrow night after you've finished work? I, er, need to have a word with you. Not now,' he added hurriedly as Jackie looked up at him, her blue eyes curious. 'Tomorrow would be better.'

Dora shrugged. 'Yes of course you can.' We close about six so any time after that. You'll have to come to the back door. Sammy's had a doorbell fitted.' She helped Jackie onto the back seat and climbed in herself. Joe shut the door and waved as Frank pulled away. Dora looked out of the back window as he walked back up the garden path, his shoulders hunched. She wondered if he'd had a letter or something from Mr Oliver. She hadn't yet but whatever he wanted to talk about, she didn't think it was going to be something she would like.

Dora stared at Joe as he looked down at his hands and twiddled his fingers. The girls were playing in the bedroom and he had just dropped the news on her toes that he and Ivy were getting married next month. Of all the months he could have chosen it had to be June. Their twins had been born in June and their daughter had died the same day. She felt sick that he hadn't even considered the month before making the arrangements.

'Dora,' he said. 'Are you okay?'

She sat back on the sofa and stared at the ceiling for a few seconds to compose herself before replying, determined not to break down in front of him. 'Well, I have to be, don't I? But couldn't you have chosen another month than June? Not like you have to rush her up the aisle now she's no longer expecting, is it?'

She saw a flash of pain cross his face and wondered if it was for their lost baby or for his and Ivy's. 'Shit, I'm sorry, Dora. It's not that I forgot or anything, I never will, but Ivy chose the date.'

'Why doesn't that surprise me? Anyway, I'll tell you this. If and when you marry her,' she couldn't bring herself to say Ivy's name, 'I'm changing my name back to my maiden name. Mine and Jackie's surname will be Evans and if I get custody of Carol I'll change hers too.'

'You can't do that; change your name and theirs, I mean.'

'Yes, I can. I don't quite know how, but if I can do it I will. I couldn't bear to be Mrs Rodgers when *she* is.' She blinked hard so that the threatening tears didn't start.

Joe got to his feet. 'Will you give Carol a call for me please? I need to get her home for bed now.'

She went to the bedroom and called Carol, who came running with Jackie on her heels. 'See you at the weekend, sweetheart.' She kissed Carol. 'Just a thought, has *she* moved in with you now?'

'Not fully,' Joe replied. 'She's still not right in herself, so she stays at her own place most nights. She's, er, left her job. She didn't go back in after, well, you know… She's looking for something with fewer hours.'

'Really? Thought she loved working at the ROF. So if she's out of work, how's she paying her rent and bills?'

Joe blushed slightly. 'She's got a bit of savings and I'm helping her out.'

Dora shook her head. 'Joe, she really saw you coming, didn't she? You are such a mug.'

'Dora, that's not fair. She's gone through a lot.'

'Yeah.' Dora nodded. 'So she says. Did you ever go with her to the doctor's after she lost the baby?'

Joe frowned. 'No. She went on her own. Why?'

Dora shrugged. 'It might have been to your advantage if you did go, that's all.'

'I'm not sure what you're implying,' Joe said.

'Think about it. Now you'd better get Carol home.'

Dora settled Jackie into bed and made herself a cuppa. She sat with her feet up on the sofa and went over her conversation with Joe. Maybe she was barking up the wrong tree and Ivy *had* been expecting. But somehow she doubted it. Ah well, he'd made his bed, as Mam would say. It was up to him what he did with his life; she just knew he was about to make the biggest mistake ever. But there was no way Ivy was having her daughter. She'd be right on that phone to Mr Oliver in the morning and ask him to hurry up with his decision.

It was going to be a busy few months coming up, getting her mam settled in the home, Frank in a new flat and moving Carol in here. Sammy had mentioned the other day that his neighbour's cat had recently had kittens. If he and Esther were in agreement, she might ask if she could have one of them for the girls when they were ready to leave their mother. Carol would love that and it might help her settle in better. A bit of bribery never went amiss.

Chapter Twenty-Eight

May 1954

Mr Oliver placed the mug of tea Dora had made him on the coffee table and smiled. He laced his fingers together and looked at Dora over the top of his spectacles.

She took a deep breath and waited, staring at him, her heart pounding so loud she was sure he could hear it.

He cleared his throat and began to speak. 'Well, I think I've seen all I need to see, Mrs Rodgers. The accommodation is very suitable and well set out. My only concern is that Carol will be sharing a bed with her sister and not have one of her own.'

'Like I already told you, Mr Oliver,' Dora said, 'the double bed will be going and I will put in an order for two single beds. However, my girls love to share and sometimes they sleep better snuggled together.'

He ignored her comment and consulted his notes. 'Er, you don't have a bathroom either.'

'Neither do half the families of Liverpool, Mr Oliver,' Dora replied pointedly, trying her best to be patient. 'When the children visit their father they will take a bath there and the public baths are a stone's throw from here. We use them all the time. I have an inside lavatory and hot running water. I can assure you my children will be kept spotless.'

Mr Oliver smiled. 'I have no doubts about that, Mrs Rodgers. I'll compile my report today with the recommendation that in due course Carol is to be removed from the custody of her father and put into your full-time care. We will notify Mr Rodgers of this. You've already addressed the issue of schools, I believe?'

Dora nodded; relief flooded her veins, but mixed with concern over what Joe would say when he got the notification letter. He'd go absolutely mad, but he knew this would happen sooner or later, and she'd waited long enough. 'Her name is down at All Saints; the same school that Jackie will be starting in September.'

'Right, what I'm going to suggest is that due to the reports of her unsettled behaviour in class, I feel Carol should finish the term at her current school. It will be an easier transition for her to accompany her sister to All Saints at the start of the new September term. I'm sure she will settle in better.'

'Okay.' Dora nodded. What he said made sense. 'What if I have her for full weeks in the school holidays? It will give her time to get used to being with us all day.' The holidays weren't that far off and it would give her a chance to arrange for new beds and to prepare Carol for the change.

'I was about to suggest that,' Mr Oliver said. 'How will you manage for child care while you work?'

'I'll be fine. I've already agreed to work part-time during the school holidays and when they go to their father's at the weekend I can make up my hours.'

Mr Oliver got to his feet. 'In that case, I'll bid you good day. My reports will be in the post shortly.'

Dora saw him out through the shop and turned to Esther with a big grin on her face. Jackie was in the back room doing her number practice and singing softly to herself.

'What did he say?' Esther whispered, pulling the door to and looking as excited as Dora felt.

'He said yes.' Dora jigged up and down. 'I can't believe it. She's got to finish the term at her old school, which is fair enough, and then she'll start the new school with Jackie in September.' She looked around. 'Where's Sammy?'

Esther shrugged. 'Just popped out for a while,' she replied airily, a secretive smile on her face. 'He shouldn't be too long now.'

As she spoke, Sammy arrived back, carrying a small cardboard box that appeared to be making a scratching sound. He placed the box on the counter and lifted the lid, which had holes punctured in places. A chunky black kitten with enormous ears, big green eyes and long whiskers stared at them.

Dora clapped her hand to her mouth. 'Oh my goodness, he's beautiful.'

'He's a she,' Sammy said. 'Meet Topsy. She was the last in the litter to go and I'd already staked a claim for you. I rather thought that if the powers that be say yes to Carol coming back, Topsy might help her settle in here.'

Dora's eyes filled with tears. 'Oh I'm sure she'll be thrilled. She loves animals. Thank you so much, Sammy.' She flung her arms around him and gave him a hug as Jackie, disturbed from her work by all the noise, appeared at her side.

'There's a bag of kitty bits and pieces in the van. I got a basket and some special food and my neighbour gave me a list of things she likes to eat. Seems she's partial to pilchards.' The kitten did a squeaky meow as though she recognised the word. Dora picked her up and showed her to Jackie, whose face lit up with a gleeful smile. 'You are going to be so spoiled by my two,' she said to the kitten. 'What do you reckon, Jackie? Do you think Carol will love her?'

As Dora had predicted, Joe was not happy about losing Carol. She actually felt a bit sorry for him in that he would only have Ivy for company during the week and was really going to miss his little girl. As he brought Carol's case up the stairs and helped her unpack her things and put them in a drawer, Dora saw tears in his eyes that he hurriedly dashed away.

She felt nervousness, mixed with excitement, at having both her girls under one roof for longer than a night and hoped Carol would settle quickly. She'd had the two single beds delivered and Frank had picked up matching bedspreads in pink and white candlewick, so the room looked girly and pretty with a pink and white rug in-between the beds. The pink flowery curtains had been a bargain that Dora had picked up on the market and altered to fit. Topsy was the centre of attention and Carol adored her on sight, squealing with delight as she picked her up.

'Can we keep her, Mammy?' Her hazel eyes were wide with delight as she cuddled the little cat. 'I love her so much already.'

'Of course we can, sweetheart. She wanted to come and live here when she heard you were coming to live here too.' Dora crossed her fingers behind her back as Carol made no protest against that statement.

She sat the girls at the table with beans on toast for tea and made Joe a brew. 'Would you like a sandwich with your cuppa?' she asked as he parked himself on the bed settee with a despondent sigh. 'I've got cheese or corned beef.'

He shook his head and looked away. 'I'd better not. I said I'd pick fish and chips up on the way home. Ivy will be waiting.' He finished his drink and got to his feet, looking wistful. 'I'll see you on Sunday, girls. Uncle Frank will bring you for tea while Mammy goes to see Granny. Now be a good girl, Carol. Look after Topsy for Mammy.' He left the room and Dora saw him off downstairs. 'I hope she settles for you,' he said huskily. 'You'd best phone me if not and I'll come for her.'

Dora nodded. She locked up behind him and made her way slowly back up the stairs. He'd looked like he'd really wanted to stay longer and have tea with the girls. Jackie had got the big boxed compendium of games out ready to play and Joe always enjoyed a game of Ludo or Snakes and Ladders with them. It was such a shame he had to dash away, but maybe it was the right thing to do. Start as they mean to go on.

After a noisy card game of Happy Families that Carol won, Dora packed the pair off to bed with the promise of Uncle Frank taking Carol swimming in the morning while Jackie had her dancing lesson. Topsy meowed at the bedroom door and Carol called out, 'Mammy, can she sleep on my bed, please?'

Dora chewed her lip. She scooped up the little cat and took a towel from the cupboard. She spread the towel on the end of Carol's bed and sat Topsy down. Carol beamed as the kitten settled down and began to purr.

'Don't have her up near your face, now,' Dora warned. 'She might make you sneeze with her fur. I'll leave the door ajar in case she needs to wee.'

When she checked on them all an hour later Topsy was curled up by Carol's head on the pillow as spark out as both girls. She smiled and shook her head. The bond between kitten and child was already firm. It felt good to have her little family complete again. Sammy had been right about the cat helping Carol to settle. There'd been no crying as Joe left tonight, thank goodness, and if there ever was in the future, she'd no doubt it would get easier as time went by.

Chapter Twenty-Nine

December 1954

Dora snipped the thread of the wedding dress hem she'd just finished and cocked an ear. Was that the back door? She was expecting Joe to bring the girls home any time soon from their weekend visit to the prefab. Since Carol had moved back in with her and Jackie, Joe now saw them from Saturday afternoon after Jackie's dancing and Carol's swimming lessons, and he brought them back in time for tea on Sunday. Dora missed her weekends with them, but the free time gave her the chance to keep on top of the orders coming in through the shop and to do a regular visit to the care home to visit her mam with Frank. She got to her feet and hung the white lace dress over a mannequin as footsteps sounded on the stairs.

'Mammy!' Jackie burst in and flung her arms around her mother. Carol ran in behind her and Dora held out her arms but, ignoring her mother, Carol's eyes searched the room, seeking out Topsy, who was lying on an old feather cushion on top of a box in the corner. She hurried over, dropping her bag on the floor, and stroked the little cat's head, her face softening into a smile. Dora shook her head as Joe, carrying the girls' small overnight cases, came up behind them. He raised an eyebrow as his daughter squealed with delight at being reunited with her pet.

'She's done nothing but talk about the cat the whole weekend,' he said. 'There's a tin of pilchards in her bag.' He smiled as Dora laughed. 'I took them to the shops for sweeties and a comic yesterday and all Carol wanted to buy was a treat for Topsy.'

'Ah well, Topsy has been the clincher in helping her to settle in here,' Dora said. 'I might as well as be invisible, but that cat's been a life saver many times over.' Dora hid the hurt she still felt at Carol's occasional rejection of her, but she would never give up trying to make up for them being apart. 'Come on, upstairs now, and I'll put the kettle on and make Daddy a drink. Carry Topsy carefully, Carol.'

Up in the flat Joe sat down on the bed settee while Dora made mugs of Camp coffee and the girls went to the bedroom to put their things away, Topsy on their heels.

Joe cleared his throat. 'How's your mam doing?'

Dora shrugged. 'Okay, I suppose. She's settled in well enough, but I think she misses Sugar Lane. Hard to tell though as she's away with the fairies most of the time.'

'Sorry to hear that,' Joe said. 'As they say, there's not much fun in old age.' They finished their coffee in companionable silence and he got up to leave. He called for the girls, who came rushing out of their bedroom. Carol flung herself at him and burst into tears.

'Don't go, Daddy,' she sobbed. 'I want you to stay here with us tonight.'

Dora looked away as Joe's eyes filled. She took the empty coffee mugs into the kitchen, leaving her girls and Joe alone for a few minutes. When she came back into the room Carol was on her knees tugging at Joe's trouser leg.

'Come on, Carol,' she said gently, pulling the little girl into her arms. 'Let's find that tin of pilchards you bought for Topsy, she needs her tea. Daddy has to go now. Shall we ask him to come for tea one night in the week after work?' She looked up at Joe and nodded towards the door for him to leave. 'She'll be fine in a few minutes,' she whispered.

'Noooo,' Carol screamed. 'I'm going home with my daddy. I'll get my bag.'

Joe stood by helplessly as she pushed Dora away and ran into the bedroom, slamming the door shut.

Jackie burst into tears as Carol came running back out, shoving things into her bag, her coat flung over her shoulders. 'I don't want Carol to go to Daddy's, Mammy,' Jackie sobbed. 'She lives with us now.'

Dora took a deep breath. It was the same most Sundays when Joe brought them home. As soon as he'd gone, Carol settled down again as quickly as she'd got upset. But Dora hated this scenario. It made her feel like the wicked witch. She spoke, a slightly firmer edge to her voice this time. 'Carol, come on now. See how upset Jackie is, and you're scaring Topsy with all that noise. She's run under the settee. We have to let Daddy go. Ivy will be wondering where he is. He'll come on Wednesday for tea, won't you, Daddy?' she finished, looking meaningfully at Joe. It was easier for him, to a point. They didn't cry after *her* when she dropped them off at the prefab; they were so happy to see him. And if agreeing to come for tea caused him a problem with Ivy, well tough. His daughters should come first, like they did with her.

Joe nodded, looking her in the eyes. 'Yes, I'd love to come for tea. But only if Carol stops crying right now.'

Carol looked up from beneath her thick fringe and nodded. She wiped her eyes on her cardigan sleeve and gave a watery smile. 'I promise,' she said, reaching for Topsy, who had warily ventured out from her hiding place.

'Good girl,' Dora said, breathing a sigh of relief. 'Kiss Daddy goodbye and we'll go and feed Topsy.'

After she'd settled the girls for the night, Dora sat with a mug of tea, reflecting on the events of the last few months. It would be Christmas in three weeks; time was flying. Carol had settled well in her first term at All Saints School alongside Jackie, and during the week, after school, was a willing little helper to Esther in the shop. She'd proudly arranged all the bobbins of thread in the correct shades and had sorted out the bundles of ribbons and lace, stacking them neatly. She helped to reckon up the cost when customers made purchases of several items, and Esther and Sammy praised her constantly in their efforts to make her feel as welcome as Jackie was. Apart from the regular crying scenes when Joe was leaving, and Dora put that down to Carol's attempts at trying to control the situation in the only way a child would know how, all seemed to be well. Hopefully it would be easier as Carol got older.

Over the next twelve months Joe came regularly for tea mid-week and Carol seemed to be settling much better. Dora knew it caused him problems with Ivy, but it helped Carol and, as far as Dora was concerned, their daughter's happiness was far more important than his marriage.

'There's something we need to talk about,' Dora said to Joe after they'd finished tea one Wednesday night and the girls had gone to their room to get ready for bed. They'd all had a nice time, played a couple of board games, and while Dora washed up, Joe had listened to the girls reading their school story books.

He looked at his watch and sighed. 'I really need to get going. Ivy will pull her face if I'm much longer. Can it wait until the weekend?'

Dora chewed her lip. Something had been bothering her for several months now and she'd been putting off saying anything for fear of causing an argument. But if she didn't do it soon, she'd *never* do it. 'Not really. I want to get the ball rolling and the sooner the better. I already told you I want to change my surname back to Evans, and I want to do the same for the girls, so that it doesn't look awkward at school if they have a different surname from me.'

Joe stared at her, his jaw dropping. 'I didn't think you were serious about that. They're my daughters. Why do you want to change their names – and yours as well, come to that?'

She folded her hands on her lap and looked him in the eye. 'I don't want the same name as Ivy. I hate sharing Mrs Rodgers with her.'

Joe shook his head, staring at her as though she'd gone mad. 'Well, I can understand *your* reasoning for a change, but I don't want you changing *their* names. That's completely wrong,' he finished as Carol appeared at his side, her eyes wide and questioning. 'And anyway, it's against the law to do that, isn't it?'

'It isn't. It's perfectly legal if you do it right. I can do it by deed poll. Frank told me he'd read about it somewhere. We should ask the girls what they think,' Dora suggested. 'Carol is old enough to understand and make up her own mind.'

Carol planted her feet firmly apart, hands on her hips. 'I don't want to change my name. All my friends at school will laugh at me. I want my name to be the same as Daddy's.' She stamped her foot and pouted.

Dora sighed, wondering why on earth she'd assumed this would be easy. 'What about you, Jackie?' she asked as her youngest sat down beside her, thumb in her mouth. 'Do you want the same name as Mammy or Daddy?'

Jackie pointed at Dora. 'Mammy's name,' she whispered.

Joe shrugged and raised his hands in a helpless gesture. 'Okay. If that's what you both want. Carol stays a Rodgers and you two can change to Evans.' He got to his feet and sighed. 'I'll leave it with you, Dora. Now I really must go.'

'Kiss Daddy goodbye, girls.' Dora stood back as they enveloped Joe with hugs and kisses. She saw him to the door.

'We'll see you soon,' she said as he turned at the top of the stairs. His eyes were moist and she felt a rush of sympathy for him.

'This still isn't easy for me, you know,' he said. 'I hate goodbyes and being apart from them. But then, you know how that feels, don't you?'

Dora nodded. She patted his arm gently. 'I do, Joe. It's hard, but it gets easier to cope with after a while. Just keep on looking forward to the weekend. It was all I ever lived for, for a long time.'

Joe took a deep breath before getting out of the car. Ivy would be in a right mood – again. He was sick and tired of the way she moaned constantly about his daughters while they were at the prefab, and then even gave him the cold shoulder *after* he'd taken them home. Punishing him, almost. She hated him going for tea on a Wednesday too, but if it kept the kids happy it was a small price to pay.

He went indoors and called out, 'Only me,' as he put his keys on the hallstand and hung his jacket up on the pegs.

Ivy was in the kitchen, stirring something on the stove, her back to him. She ignored him as he knew she would. He sat down at the kitchen table and lit a cigarette. He took a long drag and blew smoke into the air. 'What's that you're making?' he directed at her back. 'Smells nice.'

'It's for tomorrow's tea,' she snapped. 'Mince and onion. Saves me time. I want to go shopping in town tomorrow morning and I've got a hairdresser's appointment in the afternoon.' She turned the light off from under the pan and removed her frilly pinny. 'Right, I'm having a bath and an early night.'

'It's only just gone half eight,' Joe said, frowning. 'I thought we might watch a bit of telly together now I'm home.'

Ivy shot him a withering look. 'I'm surprised you're not tired yourself, working and then rushing over there to see *her* and the kids. Dancing to her demands every week instead of spending time with me. I'm stuck at home on my own all day. It's not fair. Don't you think you see enough of them at the weekend?'

Joe rolled his eyes. 'No, I don't. I'd see them every day if it was possible. As far as I'm concerned, I don't spend anywhere near enough time with them.'

'And how do you think that makes me feel?' Ivy's lips trembled, but there were no tears. 'After what happened to our poor baby and knowing it's unlikely I can give you any more children. Don't you think it upsets me?'

'I'm sorry, love.' Joe sighed. She always pulled that one out of the bag and made him feel guilty for being a father. 'Let me finish my fag and I'll run your bath for you. Why don't you go and relax in the sitting room and I'll pour you a nice glass of sherry.'

Ivy stared at him and then shuffled away in her slippered feet. He jumped up and got a glass out of the cupboard, tipping a generous amount in. A drop of sherry usually made her a bit less grumpy and maudlin. Joe shook his head as he handed her the drink, wishing for the millionth time at least that he'd never met her and was still living with Dora and his precious daughters.

Chapter Thirty

January 1957

Dora hurried back to Homer Street and banged the snow off her boots on the shop mat. She'd just rushed the girls to school, at the last minute as always happened on a Monday after they'd had two lie-ins in a row. Esther and Sammy had arrived while she was out and had put the paraffin heaters on to take the chill off the large room.

It had been really cold since Christmas and even now, the first week of January, it showed no signs of letting up, although the snow wasn't *too* heavy. 'Roll on summer,' Esther said as she gingerly removed her woolly hat and then put it back on again. She coughed and held her sides.

Dora frowned. 'That cough sounds worse than it was last week. You need to see a doctor, Esther. You should be home resting. Me and Sammy can manage here.'

'I'm all right. Don't fuss. I'm better here than sitting moping about at home. And someone needs to be in the shop while you two are in the workroom.'

Sammy looked at Dora and rolled his eyes. 'She won't be told. I suggested she stay in bed and I'd pop back and get her a bit of dinner later. We can manage. The panto season is over so we've little theatre work in at the moment, barring a couple of quick repairs, and the wedding season won't be on us for at least a couple of months. The main work at the minute is the youngsters wanting these new styles they can't get in the usual shops. Maybe we can offer a bespoke tailoring service for the young men. What do you think? Like those jackets I've seen some lads wearing, drape jackets, they call them. Your brother's got one.'

'Hmm,' Dora said with a grin, thinking of her brother strutting around in his red velvet jacket with the black lapels and denim drainies, thinking he looked the bee's knees. 'Frank sees himself as a Teddy Boy now, except he's a bit older than the usual age group. It's all this new Rock 'n' Roll music coming over from America. The dresses the girls are wearing now are lovely. Very full skirts with lots of net petticoats to make them stick out when they do that new dance they call a jive.'

Sammy nodded. His face screwed into a frown and his eyes looked as though he were miles away. 'Just popping out for a minute,' he announced. 'Get that kettle on, ladies. I won't be long.'

Esther stared after him. 'Wonder what's got into him?'

Dora shrugged. 'No idea. Not like him to dash off when we've just opened.'

'It's far too quiet in here without our Jackie,' Esther said as she brewed a pot of tea.

Dora smiled. 'But she loves school and Carol's well settled so it couldn't be better. Took a bit of time, and at one point I thought it would never happen, thank God for Topsy. The girls are such good company for each other. Very competitive as well. That little monkey Jackie runs rings around Carol. It's all down to you though, Esther, all the teaching you did during those few years before she started school.'

Esther poured them a mug of tea each as Sammy dashed back in, bringing a blast of cold air. 'Hurry up with that door,' she yelled as he banged the snow from his shoes on the mat. He dropped a handful of magazines onto the counter and smiled.

'What have you bought magazines for?' Esther said, picking up a copy of *Woman* and staring at the cover.

'To get an idea of the latest styles,' he said. 'See, that young girl on the cover there, well she's wearing a dress like Dora described. We should be aiming at a younger customer. We've got our own designer on site. There are hundreds of kids in this city who go out dancing at weekends. They want to dress up a bit, not go out in styles their parents wear. Am I right, Dora?'

She nodded, liking the way the conversation was going, but at the same time wondering how she could possibly make hundreds of dresses. They'd need a factory of their own. Or at least to get one involved with production of her designs. That's where a place like Palmer's would have come in handy.

'What I thought as I walked back from the newspaper shop was that we need a new window display now Christmas is done with. We'll get the wedding stuff out again in March, but Valentine's Day is coming up and that would be a nice theme for a fresh display. Do you think you'd have time to knock up a sample dress like that one, Dora, if I nip to the wholesalers and try and get some similar fabric?'

The dress, made in a striking red and white polka dot design, had a sweetheart neckline, button-fronted bodice with cap sleeves and a full skirt with the white net petticoats just peeking out from below. The waist was tiny and cinched in with a shiny white belt. Dora flicked through the magazine and saw that it was called a waspie belt.

'I'll get my pad and pencil,' she said, excitement running through her veins at the prospect of a new challenge. The bodice and neckline were similar to another design she used to make and the skirt would just be masses of gathered fabric attached at the waist.

'That's my girl,' Sammy said, a delighted smile on his face. He rooted in his pocket for his van key. 'Right, I'm off to look for some spotty fabric and waspie belts. See you later.'

'And I'll get cracking on cutting out some paper hearts for the window and when the girls are home from school we'll colour them red. A real team effort,' Esther said as Dora's black cat, tubby now, appeared at her feet and wrapped herself around her legs, rubbing her face on Esther's fur-topped boots. 'Hello, Topsy. Wait until you see what a nice treat I've brought in for you today.'

'You spoil her,' Dora said, 'just like you spoil me and the girls. No wonder she's fat. But we love you for it.'

'Not half as much as we love you lot,' Esther said, blinking rapidly.

Dora opened the back door and let the cat out. No doubt she'd be back in seconds on a day as cold as today was. Just as she'd expected, Topsy wanted back in within a few moments. Dora shut the door and went to put her coat upstairs, taking her mug of tea with her.

She switched on the wireless and turned the dial to the *Light Programme*. The good thing about all this new music and fashion coming over from the USA was the singers were good-looking and the songs were exciting, compared to most post-war music. Big swing bands like Joe's were falling out of style and soon there'd be no work for them in the social clubs. She wondered how he'd manage without his extra weekly income now he was providing her with money for both girls. Ivy would just have to get off her fat backside and find a job. How long did it take to get over a miscarriage, if there even had been one? She was milking it for all it was worth. Nearly three years. What a joke.

Dora thought back to how *she'd* coped with the death of her newborn, two bouts of severe depression and another birth in less time than that. That woman had really seen Joe coming. Dora almost felt sorry for him. But he'd been stupid to marry her when there had been no need. Ivy didn't seem to like him spending time with his girls either. Although Joe wouldn't let anything stop him from having them at the weekend and his Wednesday teatime visits.

But Jackie had told her just before Christmas that when Daddy went for a paper or popped out to the shops, Aunty Ivy shouted at them, and she always moaned at Daddy that she had a headache because *they* were there and she said that he should take them home.

Dora had asked Jackie what did Carol say about Aunty Ivy shouting at them and Jackie had shrugged her shoulders. 'She said nothing. I don't like Aunty Ivy, Mammy. I wish she'd go out when we're at Daddy's.'

Dora resolved to mention this to Joe next weekend before things got to the point where Jackie didn't want to go and see him. It was so handy to have the time to herself while Joe looked after them. She loved going to visit her mam at the home and catching up with Frank, who'd told her she should come along to the Grafton one night with him and his mates and he'd teach her how to jive. One Saturday she planned to do just that, so that she could see first-hand what the young people were wearing to go out in.

Dora sat at one of the cutting-out tables and began to sketch dresses like the ones in the magazine. As if on cue, the latest singing sensation Elvis Presley began to warble a song that sent a thrill through her. 'I Want You, I Need You, I Love You'. The words sent a shiver down her spine and she imagined being in Joe's arms and him singing along, whispering in her ear. She took a deep breath, before the tears that were never far away could take hold, and carried on sketching.

Dora snapped out of her trance as she heard Esther calling her name, and ran down the stairs. 'Wait until you see these,' Sammy said, laying two huge rolls of cotton fabric on the counter. He dashed back outside to the van and came in carrying two wrapped bales of white netting for the underskirts. He took the wrappings off the fabric rolls and Dora gasped as she ran her hand over the surface.

'Those are fabulous,' she said. One roll was red with white polka dots and the other black. The polka dots were the size of a shilling piece and the colours really striking.

'And look.' He held up a small box that contained an assortment of shiny waspie belts in white and red. 'Thought the red would look good with the black dress. Adds that bit of colour. Maybe girls could match their shoes to it. What do you think?'

Dora smiled at his enthusiasm. 'They're absolutely perfect. Everything is. My designs are upstairs for you to look at, just rough ideas at the moment, but I can already see in my mind's eye that they'll look fabulous in these fabrics. Oh, I can't wait to get started.' The phone rang and Esther went to answer it.

'I've been thinking about how we can make the window look really special,' Sammy said, his eyes twinkling. 'Two dresses, one either side in each colour on the mannequins, and what about if I bring my new-fangled gramophone from home and maybe your brother could lend us a few records to go in the display and then we could have a few red hearts and maybe some black musical notes dotted around. The youngsters would see that we're moving with the times.'

Dora nodded, her creative mind working overtime. 'Yes, that sounds great.' She stopped as Esther came back into the shop, a worried expression on her face.

Sammy frowned and put his arm around Esther's shoulders. 'What is it? What's wrong?'

She took a deep breath. 'That was Sonny,' she began. 'He's having marriage problems and wants to come home for a few months. He said he's getting a transfer from his bank up to Liverpool while he sorts himself out.'

Sammy rolled his eyes. 'I hope you let him know he can only stay on a temporary basis,' he said.

Esther started to cough uncontrollably. Sammy sat her down on a chair behind the counter and Dora got her a glass of water. 'If he's going to come back and start causing trouble he can bugger off home,' Sammy growled. Esther looked like she was going to cry.

'Would you like me to leave you alone while you discuss this?' Dora asked, moving towards the stairs. She'd been aware there was a problem between them and their son, although they spoke little of him and in all the time she'd known them he'd never been to see them or they him, which had seemed a bit odd. She wondered briefly what had caused the rift between them. But with everything that had been going on in her own life, she didn't like to pry into theirs.

'No, sweetheart, you might as well as hear the truth about our wastrel of a son,' Sammy said. 'If he's going to be around for a while, the more you know the better.' Sammy went on to explain that Sonny had disgraced their family by getting involved with the wife of one of their, at the time, best friends. 'He'd always had the best of everything, nice home, private schooling, we spoiled him rotten and he was always an ungrateful little sod. He treated me and his mother like shit on his shoe, if you'll pardon my French, Dora. He was clever and passed all his exams and we had high hopes he'd go to university but he decided he wanted to go to London and try and get a job in banking. We said we'd support him and threw him a going-away party, and it was during that party that our friend accused him of seducing his wife. Not that the woman would take much seducing, mind, but that's by the by. This all happened in front of family and friends from our synagogue where we are – or were – highly respected. Sonny told everyone that it was *he* who'd been seduced, that she was old enough to be his mother, and all hell broke loose. The couple involved are now divorced and our name is mud in certain Jewish circles.' Sammy took a deep breath.

'He swanned off to London, got a decent job and eventually met a nice girl, Marylyn, through work. We were invited to the wedding. He told us they wanted to buy a house and asked if we could lend them a deposit. We agreed to help them get a good start and lent him several hundred pounds; a deposit for a modest home, as we were led to believe, furniture and a car so that they could visit us. The money was to be paid back as both had good jobs in the bank and could afford it. Esther and I had planned to retire early and to travel abroad to spend time with family that we still have left in Israel and the USA with that money. We haven't seen a penny back yet as the house they bought is practically a mansion compared to ours, and that's not small, as you know.

'They say they have no spare money each month, even with the discounted mortgage they got from the bank. And to be honest that is the first time he's phoned in I don't know how long – months, near enough a year. He only ever rings when he wants something. So now he's having marriage problems, which could well mean we'll never see our bloody money ever again. I bet it's his fault. He's got a wandering eye; think he's a ladies' man. Marylyn's probably had enough and chucked him out.'

Esther patted his arm. 'We don't know that yet, Sammy. It might be *her* fault.'

Sammy raised his eyebrows. 'Don't you dare go soft on him. You know what he's like. When's he coming?'

'He's driving up on Saturday,' Esther said. 'He can start work on Monday.'

'Good. I don't want him swanning around the house doing nothing while we're working our backsides off.'

Dora shook her head. She'd never seen Sammy angry before. It was beyond her to understand how anyone, least of all their own flesh and blood, could treat this lovely couple in such a thoughtless way. They didn't deserve it. They worked so hard and had been so very kind to Dora and her daughters. She wanted to help them as much as she could. 'I don't know what to say,' she whispered. 'That's just awful.'

Sammy puffed out his cheeks. 'Let's put him out of our minds for now while we get on with sorting out our window display. Come on, Dora. Let's go up and see your new designs then.'

Chapter Thirty-One

Ivy pulled the pillow over her head and ignored the door-knocker. No doubt it would be Dolly again, making sure she was up. Nosy cow, she was. Pretending to see if she was okay when all she really wanted to do was pry. She'd get up when she felt like it and not when Dolly thought she should. She'd only invited her in a handful of times and then she'd felt as though Dolly was quizzing her about the miscarriage, trying to trip her up almost. Better to keep her out of the way. Once Joe was out at work she had all day to do her chores and prepare him a nice meal for when he came home. She held her left hand in the air and admired her rings. She still couldn't believe she was married to the man of her dreams. Even though she got the impression that *he* didn't seem to think he was married to the woman of *his* dreams.

She could count on one hand the times he'd made love to her since their wedding night. Not that it really bothered her. He'd at least consummated the marriage and it wasn't as if they were trying for a baby. She could take it or leave it, all that messy palaver. All she'd wanted was Joe on her arm officially and the rest she wasn't that bothered about really. Carol had told her yesterday that Aunty Dolly had asked if Ivy was poorly as she never came out of the house. She told Carol to tell Aunty Dolly to mind her own business next time she said anything. Those kids of Joe's were driving her mad. The weekends were becoming a nightmare. They were so bloody noisy. That little one never stopped singing and dancing. If she heard the Christmas alphabet song one more time she'd swing for the little madam. She and Joe never had a minute to themselves. She hadn't bargained on spending all this time with his kids when she'd accepted his proposal.

She stuck a foot out of bed to test the air. It still felt cold, although Joe had told her he'd lit a fire before he left for work. If she didn't get up and shove some coal on it now it would go out, and she really hated all that messing about with cinders and ash and what have you. That was man's work. She might give Flo a call later at the ROF after the dinnertime rush. It was time she invited her over for her tea one night. She hadn't seen her since their wedding day when Flo had been her witness and a random bloke from the factory floor had been Joe's. It wasn't the wedding she'd anticipated, but it was better than nothing and the outcome was the same as Dora's fancy white wedding; she'd got her man and that was what mattered. And, unlike Dora, she wasn't letting him go. She lived in dread of the day he might find out her secrets and the damage they'd done to him and Dora, but all being well he never would and she could take them to the grave with her.

She swung her legs out of bed and went into the kitchen to put the kettle on. There was a note on the table. A curt note in Joe's handwriting. *We are out of margarine and bread. I'm working overtime. You will need to go to the shops. Joe.* No 'love Joe' or kisses. Damn it. She'd need to hurry up and get dressed then before Dolly went shopping later and collared her. Joe was narked with her again for complaining about the kids. She wished he'd find another job now he didn't have Carol living with them. He'd had long enough. He'd talked of a car company over in Crewe, but said it was too far if there was an emergency with the girls and he was needed to pick them up from school, that he'd wait until the car trade took off in Liverpool as there were rumours it would do.

Then again, if they did move she'd need to find a job as this house was subsidised by the ROF and anywhere else would be more expensive. That was the trouble with him having to keep Dora and the brats in the style to which they'd become accustomed. And Ivy was buggered if she was getting up at the crack of dawn to help support them on any measly wage she could earn in a job that required no skills. She wasn't going back to factory cooking again; it was too much like hard work. She'd married Joe for an easier life.

'Dora,' Esther called as she came back into the shop with the girls after school. 'Your friend Agnes called while you were out. Would you ring her when you've got a minute, please?'

Dora nodded. 'I'll just sort these two out with a snack and put the fire on for them upstairs. And then I'll give her a ring.' She ushered Carol and Jackie up the stairs and, on the landing, nearly fell over Topsy, who was weaving in and out of the six legs she loved best. 'Silly puss, move out of the way. You'll have one of us breaking our neck on the stairs if you're not careful.' She switched on the electric fire to take the chill off the room, poured the girls some orange juice and made a stack of jam butties. She put the tray on the coffee table and told them not to go near the fire. 'I'm just going down to phone Aunty Agnes and when you've finished your snack you can both go and help Esther with a very important job.'

'Oooh, what job is it?' Carol asked, her hazel eyes wide with anticipation.

'Wait and see. Take your school clothes off and put them neatly on your bed. Put your play clothes on and then come downstairs.'

She hurried down the two flights of stairs and dialled Agnes's number, wondering why her friend had called her at school picking up time. She was usually out picking Patsy up. Her friend answered after a few rings, sounding anxious. 'Hiya, Agnes, what's up?'

'Oh, Dora, didn't Joe give you my message on Sunday when he dropped the girls off? Obviously he didn't, or you would have called me. He was actually in the bathroom when I rang and Ivy said she'd pass on a message to him to ask you to call me.'

'No message, I'm sorry, but you know that one and messages,' Dora replied. 'What's wrong, anyway?'

'It's my mam; she's fallen down the stairs and fractured her hip. She's in Fazakerley hospital and it looks like she'll be in for a good few weeks. What me and Alan were wondering is, would you recommend the home your mam is in? We'll need to do something – those stairs are so steep, she won't be able to manage them again.'

'I'm so sorry to hear that, Agnes. Joe can give that bloody woman an earful when I see him. And yes, I would recommend Mam's home, but your mam's not losing her marbles yet and it's mainly for people who are. I can ask when we go next weekend, if you like.'

'Oh, would you? Thank you, that would be a big help. I've phoned the council and asked what the waiting lists are like for ground-floor flats and they said there's quite a wait, but they've listed her anyway. And they also said they were building some little bungalows on various estates as well for elderly people, so he's put her on the list for one of those, but it will have to be somewhere close enough for me to see to her. That's why I thought a home would be best; she's got someone there with her all the time then. It's peace of mind, isn't it?'

'It is, and that's worth its weight in gold, Agnes. I'll call in and see you after we've been to visit Mam next week.'

'Thank you, I look forward to seeing you again,' Agnes said.

Dora put the phone down as her daughters appeared behind her. 'Go and see Esther while I finish the work I'm doing.'

Esther sat the girls at the table and gave them a handful of cardboard hearts she'd cut out and some musical notes, with instructions to colour the hearts red and the notes black. 'These have to be coloured very neatly because they are going in the window, so everyone in Liverpool who walks past the shop will see them.' She smiled as they ooh-ed with importance.

Jackie knew immediately what the notes were, while Carol looked puzzled. Jackie explained and danced the notes up and down the table. 'They make tunes, Carol. I think these ones make my new favourite song, "Que Sera Sera."'

Dora stopped halfway up the stairs to listen to Esther and her girls singing the Doris Day song. She swallowed the lump in her throat as she thought what valuable times these were for her daughters and their surrogate grandmother, and hoped that her girls would remember them always as they grew up and had their own children. Just like the girl in the song.

Sammy was wiping his eyes as she walked into the workroom. He'd been listening at the top of the stairs. She gave him a gentle hug. There was no need for words.

After school on Friday, Carol and Jackie excitedly arranged the hearts on the floor near the front of the window and Dora and Sammy stood the two mannequins either side. Dora fluffed out the skirts of the hastily sewn dresses and fastened the belts around the waist of each one. Sammy set his gramophone in the centre and fanned out several records on the floor around it. He'd already stuck some of the musical notes on the glass, but the condensation would eventually peel those off so the rest had been glued to white card and arranged around the side walls of the window. They all stepped outside to take a look. The display lights were on and the evening dusk was gathering along with a thick Mersey mist.

'That looks wonderful,' Dora said, clapping her hands over her mouth.

'Those dresses look the business,' Sammy said. 'They look expensive. Well done, Dora, and thanks for sitting up at night to get them finished. I know we can't get any made in time for Valentine's Day as such, but if it brings people in to place orders, then that's good enough for me.' He turned as a horn tooted behind him and

Frank pulled up on his motorbike. He clambered off and nodded his head with approval.

'Rock 'n' Roll, eh? That looks great, Sis. Well done, all of you.'

'Uncle Frank,' his nieces said in unison and started to pull him inside. 'Come and see what we did for the window.'

'I'm staying tonight, Sis,' Frank called over his shoulder. 'Mersey mist is rolling in thick and fast and I don't fancy riding back to my mate's in Woolton on that.' He nodded at his bike. 'Wish I'd come down in the car now. But hopefully it'll clear by the morning and I'll go home and get the car ready for madam's dancing class and our visit to Mam. Is that okay, by the way?'

Dora laughed. 'You know it is. You can have my bed settee and I'll top and tail with these two and the mad cat.'

'Right, we'll get off,' Sammy said. 'Will you lock up, Dora? Frank will need to take his bike around to the backyard and he can come in that way.'

'Of course. See you both on Monday. Try and get some rest, Esther, see if you can shake that cough off. Oh, and good luck tomorrow.'

Sammy rolled his eyes. 'Thank you, we'll need it.' He and Esther gave Dora hugs and waved to the girls and Frank.

'Right, I'll take the bike around the back. Shall I grab fish and chips from up the road for tea?'

'Oh, yes, that would be wonderful. Don't waste your money on a full fish for those two though, they won't eat it. Just get them one portion of chips and a fishcake each. I'll go and put the kettle on and butter some bread.'

She locked the door behind Frank and turned off the big shop lights. The window display looked so fashionable and she felt really proud of herself for the part she'd played. Working here was the best thing to happen to her in a long time. She just hoped that the arrival of Sammy and Esther's son wouldn't hurt his lovely parents in any way.

Chapter Thirty-Two

February 1957

Esther slammed the phone down and laced her fingers together to stop her hands from shaking. Sammy was on a theatre run and Dora was upstairs with a customer taking measurements. Sonny's wife, Marylyn, had just called to ask that a message be passed on to him as he wouldn't accept a call from her at work. The message – that their London home was about to be repossessed – needed to be passed on as soon as possible. Sonny had apparently emptied the joint bank account, leaving her with nothing, and the mortgage hadn't been paid for several months.

Well, there was bugger all she or Sammy could do to help. He was getting nothing more from them. She put her hand to her chest as she felt a faint fluttering near her heart. That boy would be the death of her and Sammy. He'd only been home a week and already he'd argued with them both, causing Sammy to tell him he had to be out by the end of the month. There'd be fat chance of that now – he'd have no home to go back to. But that wasn't her or Sammy's problem. Sonny was old enough and daft enough to sort things out for himself.

She'd wait until they got home before she told Sammy of the phone call. Dora was seeing their customer out and would be picking up the children from school soon. And she didn't want

Sammy going round to the bank and causing a scene and getting all worked up about it in a public place either.

On the way home, unable to keep it to herself any longer, Esther told Sammy about the phone call. He agreed that they'd talk to Sonny after their evening meal and try to get to the bottom of what had gone wrong.

As Sammy tidied the dishes away, Esther brought a pot of coffee through to the dining table and poured three cups. Sonny rose to his feet and announced he didn't want any as he was going out.

Sammy told him to sit back down as he needed to talk to him. Esther patted his hand as Sonny frowned at them both. Sammy had kept quiet over their meal, wanting to eat in peace, but now he was ready to do battle.

'I hope this isn't going to take long,' Sonny grumbled. 'I've arranged to meet a friend.'

'A friend?' Esther muttered scornfully. 'You mean a woman?'

Sonny shrugged. 'A colleague from the bank, and yes, she's a woman. But what's that got to do with you?'

'Everything, when your wife was on the phone this afternoon in tears, telling your mother that your house is about to be repossessed and you've left her with not a penny to her name,' Sammy snapped as Sonny stared at him but remained silent.

'Is it true?' Sammy demanded. 'That the mortgage hasn't been paid for quite some time? I'm surprised the bank has allowed that situation to happen,' he continued. 'Considering you both work for them.'

A nervous twitch started in Sonny's cheek as he stared at them. He drew a deep breath. 'Marylyn stopped working when we started having marriage problems. Said she couldn't cope. To keep us going I borrowed against the house. I struggled to pay it back. She wouldn't agree to us selling it, *I* knew we couldn't afford to hang onto it but she wouldn't listen. I took all the money out of the account as I knew she'd spend it like it's going out of fashion. But I *did* leave enough in to pay the mortgage this month. *She* must have spent it on clothes or something.'

'That's not what she told me,' Esther said. She knew he was lying; he didn't meet her eye as he spoke, a childhood trait he'd never grown out of. 'She also said that you'd told her *we* would sort it out. Well I'm sorry, but that is not going to happen.'

Sammy nodded his agreement. 'Not a cat-in-hell's chance,' he growled. 'Now I suggest you go and pack your bags and get back down to London and deal with your mess. You're not welcome here.'

Esther took a sip of her coffee. She felt sick inside and Sammy looked worried to death. She hated what their son was capable of. It went against everything they stood for and believed in. He cared about no one but himself and she knew he was living for the day when they both popped their clogs and he'd inherit all that they'd worked hard for, and he'd dance happily on their graves. Well, that wasn't going to happen if she had anything to do with it. She and Sammy must talk about changing their wills.

'I have nowhere to go,' Sonny said, a hint of panic in his voice. 'You can't just throw me out like this. And I can't afford to lose my job. If I go back to London now I might get the sack and then no one will benefit. Okay, if you don't want me here, I'll find somewhere to stay, see if a colleague at the bank can put me up, or something. I'll get my things together and make a couple of phone calls.'

He left the dining room, slamming the door behind him. Sammy shook his head. 'What a bloody mess.'

Esther pursed her lips. She could hear Sonny in the hall now, talking to someone on the phone, hopefully his wife. His voice rose a couple of octaves but she couldn't tell what he was saying. Then he was back in the dining room, a pleading expression in his brown eyes.

'Well?' Sammy asked.

Sonny shrugged. 'She's drunk and I can't get any sense out of her. She's always drunk. You've no idea how hard it's been for me the last few months, coping with that. And the friend I was hoping would put me up isn't in. I'm not sleeping on the streets like a vagrant.'

Esther sighed, thinking his behaviour had probably driven the poor girl to drink.

'I wouldn't expect you to,' Sammy said. 'But I'm telling you now, by the end of the week, your mother and I want you out. Either clear off back to London, or get yourself a flat or lodgings in the city. I don't care what, as long as you are gone from our home.'

Sonny's half-smile didn't reach his eyes. 'Thank you.' He turned, walked towards the door and stopped. 'Er, what about the rooms above the shop? The top floor. I could easily turn it into a flat; then I'd be out of your hair. I'll be at work all day and home after you close, so I won't get in your way or anything.'

Sammy shook his head. 'I'm afraid that won't be possible. The flat is already occupied.' He said no more as Esther raised a warning eyebrow in his direction.

Sonny frowned. 'I didn't realise that. You never told me.'

'Why would we? It's got nothing to do with you,' Sammy said. 'Now if you don't mind, your mother and I have a few things we'd like to discuss in private.'

Dora's first meeting with Sonny Jacobs was not a good one. Sammy was out buying more dress fabric for all the orders their window display had brought in, and Esther was doing her usual Monday morning trip to the bank to pay the takings in, and she always called at the market too – to check out the bargains, as she put it. Dora was standing behind the counter leafing through another of the magazines that Sammy had bought, looking at pictures of the dirndl skirts and shell tops that also seemed to be popular with the young women today. The doorbell rang and a young dark-haired man stepped inside. He was smartly suited and carried a briefcase. Dora stared at him as he scrutinised her, looking her up and down. 'Can I help you, sir?'

'Is this what my father pays you for? To stand around reading when you should be working?' His tone was curt, with none of the nasal twang of Liverpool about it. His voice was cultured and his eyes dark like his father's, but lacking the kindness that shone in Sammy's brown eyes.

'I beg your pardon? How dare you insinuate I'm doing nothing?' Dora spoke with a bravado she wasn't really feeling.

He raised his chin slightly.

'You are, are you not, my father's employee?'

'I'm his designer, yes.'

'Ah, right. So shop girls have fancy titles now, do they?' he sneered, his voice loaded with sarcasm.

'Excuse me; I am *not* a shop girl. I design and make clothes. I'm a fully trained seamstress, I'll have you know. Sammy is out buying fabric and Esther is at the bank. They won't be long, if you'd like to take a seat. I'm just holding the fort for a few minutes.'

His shifty eyes flicked around the salesroom, taking in the stock and the window display. 'Did you make the dresses in the window?'

She nodded, trying to think who he reminded her of. 'I also designed them and custom-made the patterns.'

He narrowed his eyes. 'And there's just you that makes them up?'

'Yes.' She wondered what he was getting at.

'And do you have orders for the dresses?'

'We do.'

'Hmm. It seems my father is missing a trick here.'

'What do you mean?' Dora folded her arms as he put down his briefcase.

'He could be raking it in, but he needs more than one seamstress. You're a designer; he needs more women to do the donkey work, the cutting out and stitching.'

Dora frowned. 'There isn't room for more people and machines. We're not a factory. And I think your dad is happy enough as things are.'

'Humph, he doesn't have a business head on him. *How* can he be happy in this back-street shop when he could be a millionaire if he put his mind to it? He needs a factory and *you* could help him run it.'

Dora frowned and stared at him, and then it struck her who he reminded her of. George Kane. The son-in-law of Gerald Palmer, who'd founded her old place of work: Palmer's Ladies Fashions of Distinction. Kane had run the business into the ground in no time after Gerald passed away. Taking constantly and putting nothing back took its toll. Thinking for a moment of Joanie, who would still have been here but for Kane, Dora felt a huge angry rush. How dare this man come into his parents' shop and criticise what they'd built up over the years when he'd practically stolen their savings to feather his own comfortable nest. He showed little respect for the privileged upbringing they'd given him.

'Factories cost money,' she snapped.

He waved his arms around. 'He owns this place. He could borrow against it. My bank would be happy to lend money to a new business. That's what this decade is all about. The war's behind us. Regrowth, we're building a future for tomorrow's generation.'

Dora shook her head. He sounded like one of those newsreaders on the telly. 'We're just recovering from the war in Liverpool, or hadn't you noticed? We've still got bomb-damaged houses near the docks. Things take time to get back to normal. All that stuff you talk about is okay for you London folk but it means little to us up here yet.' She stopped as the doorbell rang and Esther hurried in, bringing a blast of cold air with her.

'Still a bit parky out there,' she said, then stopped as she saw Sonny. 'What do *you* want? Shouldn't you be at work?' She glared at him as she put her bags down on the counter and pulled off her hat and coat.

Dora took the bags through to the back room for Esther and left mother and son alone while she put the kettle on. She could hear raised voices, Esther telling him to get out now, and then the bell ringing and door slamming. Esther popped her head around the doorframe. 'Are you okay?' Dora asked. She looked pale and tired and still hadn't recovered from the cough that had plagued her for most of the winter.

'Just got a bit of a headache. Did he say anything out of order to you?'

'No, he just gave me a lecture on looking at magazines instead of working. Said you don't pay me to do nothing.'

'Cheeky so-and-so,' Esther muttered through gritted teeth. 'He's done nothing but bring trouble home since the minute he came back to Liverpool. Upset me and his father constantly. He's moved out and is sharing a flat with an old friend in Walton Vale for the time being. We don't want him around. We'd rather he went back to London and we've made that quite clear, but he said he's staying in Liverpool.'

Dora nodded. She didn't blame them. 'He, er, suggested that Sammy gets a factory up and running and the bank will loan the money.' Dora picked up the kettle as it started to whistle and poured water into the tea pot.

Esther shook her head. 'Oh he did, did he? He lives in cloud cuckoo land. Does he ever stop to consider the age of me and his father, I wonder? I was nearly forty before he was born and Sammy was forty-five. We would have been long retired if he'd paid us back his debts, but we can kiss goodbye to that money now. He's got into a mess financially, his house is being repossessed and we still haven't really got to the bottom of his marriage troubles and what went wrong either. But I tell you one thing, Dora, there'll be no factory. Sammy is happy with the set-up we've got now. It keeps him and me busy enough.'

'It does, and me – I love working here for you,' Dora agreed. '*And* it gives me a home too.'

'I've got you a job,' Joe announced as he took off his work clothes in the bedroom. Ivy was in the kitchen dishing up his tea. Home-made steak and kidney pie; his favourite. She was a fabulous cook, there was no doubt about it, but her talents were wasted on him alone. He made his way to the table as she appeared with a laden plate in her hands. He rubbed his growling stomach as she placed it in front of him. 'Did you hear me?'

'What?' she asked, bringing in her own plate and sitting down opposite him.

'I said, I've got you a job,' he repeated.

She frowned. 'What do you mean? You know I'm not well enough to go out to work yet, Joe.'

He raised an eyebrow. 'It's part-time work. And I tell you what, why don't I take an afternoon off and we'll both go to the doctor's and ask him how long he thinks it should take you to get over that miscarriage.' He watched her face as her cheeks flushed slightly and she looked down at her plate. 'I mean, it's what, three years? If you're still not right yet then there must be something they can do at the hospital.' He tucked into his pie, relishing the taste of the rich gravy, waiting to see if he'd called her bluff. He needed her working. He was struggling unless he did overtime. Band work was drying up due to the clubs wanting solo singers like Johnny Ray, and even Elvis Presley now this new Rock 'n' Roll music was catching on.

'What's the job?' she asked, pushing her food around her plate.

'Back at the canteen. But they said you can do part-time to start. The replacement cook isn't a patch on you. The management will be happy for you to come back and give her a hand. The new cook wants to retire as soon as they find another.'

'I'd be too embarrassed,' she muttered.

'Why? A lot of water's gone under the bridge since then and everyone knows you're my wife now. People ask about you. You've nothing to hide, have you?'

'Of course not,' she snapped. 'It'd just feel a bit strange. That's all.'

'Right, well they said call in tomorrow and talk about it. The bottom line is, I need you working, Ivy. I've got a family to support as well as you. We all need to pull our weight. Dora does her best but I like to help her out where I can with the girls. They always need something new at that age.' He finished his meal and got to his feet. 'Right, I'm relaxing with the *Echo* for five minutes now we've sorted that out.'

Joe walked away, aware of her eyes burning in his back. He now knew she'd snared him under false pretences and he wasn't about to let her get away with it. A band mate of his had a wife who worked in Ivy's doctor's surgery. She'd put her job on the line to get him the information he'd asked for and he'd be forever grateful. Ivy's records had showed no sign of a recorded miscarriage. A premature baby had been born dead several years ago, and following that she'd had an emergency operation that meant there'd be no more children for her, ever. While he'd half felt sorry for her when that was confirmed, the crafty cow had lied and destroyed all he had going with Dora for ever. Joe could hardly bear to look at Ivy now, never mind go near her. But he had no choice other than to grin and bear it for the next few years; he couldn't possibly afford another divorce and to support yet another ex-wife.

Chapter Thirty-Three

July 1957

Dora smiled as Carol hurled a ball at the coconut shy. It hit the spot and a coconut fell from its perch onto the grass below. She leapt around like a mad thing as Jackie and Frank cheered and clapped their hands.

'Well done, gel,' Frank said, retrieving the coconut for her and handing it to Dora, who shoved it into an already laden shopping bag. 'Do you want a go, little Jacks?'

Jackie shook her head and pointed to the donkey rides.

'Okay, a quick ride then we'll get your mam a cuppa; she looks like she needs it.'

They strolled across the grassed area to a line of tired-looking donkeys.

'This lot look like they've retired from New Brighton beach,' Frank joked as he lifted the girls up onto the saddles. He ran alongside them as they bounced along, laughing as they giggled.

Dora sat down on the grass, tucking her full skirt around her. She was wearing one of her own creations in the same polka dot fabric as her window display dresses; except hers was turquoise with white spots and she'd left off the net underskirt. A perfect colour for a glorious summer's day with the white patent waspie belt cinching in her neat waist and matching her peep-toe shoes.

She lay back, propped up on her elbows, and looked around to see if she could spot Agnes and her family. It felt warmer today than it had all week and she shaded her eyes as she looked over to the tea tent, where the queue seemed to be getting bigger. Woolton Church Fete, held annually in the grounds of St Peter's Church, was proving more popular than ever this year according to the man on the coconut shy.

There were several groups of young lads hanging around; all dressed smartly in their drainies and shirts, sleeves casually rolled up, quiffs immaculate, ciggies dangling from lips, eyeing up several groups of young girls, who were dressed to kill with their hair in the new-style ponytails swinging from side to side as they walked around the field, wiggling their backsides and swivelling narrow hips. Promenading, her dad had called it, when young people made eyes at each other. Fancying their chances, her brother called it. Whatever it was, Dora would give her right arm to be that age again and have Joe eyeing her up across a room like he'd done many times in the past.

The familiar lump rose in her throat and she swallowed it. He'd been annoyed that he couldn't have the girls this afternoon as he'd wanted to bring them to the fete himself. But she and Frank had promised Mam that they would pop in with them later as Mam hadn't seen her granddaughters for a few weeks and had complained last week that no one bothered to visit her any more. Which wasn't true; she and Frank went every week. Sadly her memory was getting worse. Agnes had got her mam into the care home on a temporary basis while her hip healed and until she was mobile again. So the pair were company for each other.

Joe had agreed he'd just have the girls tomorrow, although he'd said Ivy would pull a face as he'd promised to take her over to Southport for the afternoon and she wanted them to go alone. Dora suggested he take the girls too and he'd looked embarrassed and told her Ivy wouldn't like that. She sighed. It was bloody tough. She'd come into the family through her own choice and by doing so she needed to get used to the idea that Joe had kids and that was that. She looked up as someone called her name and Agnes strolled into view, holding Patsy's hand. They were alone; Alan must be on shift. Agnes flopped down beside her and lifted Patsy onto her knee. She rooted in her bag and pulled out a hanky, wiping Patsy's snotty nose and adjusting her sun hat.

'Think she's got a bit of hay fever,' she said. 'She's streaming today. It's because it's so dry and dusty. Beautiful though, isn't it. Oh look, Patsy, the band's starting to play.'

As she spoke Carol and Jackie came running across to Patsy and the three of them ran off to watch the brass band play. Dora smiled proudly. Each girl wore a sundress made by her in pretty pastel and white prints, and white sun hats. She wondered how many people here today were wearing one of her creations from the shop. It made her feel really proud. One day, when she was rich, she might even have her own label. Well, she could dream.

'Afternoon, Agnes,' Frank said as he drew level. 'I'll go and get you two a brew and find out what time that skiffle group are playing. They're really good, according to one of my docker mates. He knows the drummer, Colin Hanton. He's seen 'em having a practice. Says they're better than Lonnie Donegan.'

Agnes looked suitably impressed. 'What a shame Alan had to work today. He likes that Lonnie Donegan fella. I do too, but he's not a patch on Elvis, eh, Dora?'

Dora grinned. 'Nobody's a patch on Elvis. He makes my toes curl and my knees go weak when I hear him singing and he's so ruddy good-looking. Anyway, what's this new group called, so Agnes can tell Alan?'

'The Quarrymen,' Frank called as he walked away.

'How was your mam?' Dora changed the subject.

Agnes sighed. 'Oh, you know, all right I suppose, but she's not ready for coming back to the house yet. She actually said last week that she wants to stay where she is. She enjoys the company. But it's whether the home will *let* her stay. I mean, she's walking about using a stick, but if she falls again that will be it. Back to square one. Stairs are out of the question. It's been a long job getting her to this stage, so I don't want her being set back with another accident. And while we're waiting, we're paying her rent on the house as well as helping out with the home's fees. It's costing us a fortune. I'm glad I managed to get that job at Patsy's school now. I nearly didn't take it, but I'm so glad I did. It helps.'

Dora nodded. Agnes had recently started working as a school secretary at Fazakerley primary school. 'Nothing doing with the council for her? Bungalow or flat?'

'Nope.'

'They're rubbish. That's just how I was. Waiting ages for nothing. I honestly think they'd forgotten me. I'd have been the only person left on that street. Thank God for my guardian angels. I don't know what I'd do without them.'

'How's that horrible son of theirs?'

'He's still in Liverpool. Flat-sharing with a mate. They don't say too much about him in front of me, but I can tell that him even being in the same city upsets them.'

Frank came back with two cups of tea and sat down beside them. 'The Quarrymen are on when the brass band have finished in about ten minutes. They're playing on the back of that lorry over there.' He pointed to a flatbed lorry draped with bunting.

Dora could just about make out a name painted in red on a sign fastened to the side of it. Probably the name of the group, she thought. She watched the girls holding hands and dancing, Jackie and Patsy trying to teach Carol a few simple steps but failing. Carol went and stood away from them with her arms folded and a mutinous expression on her face. If things didn't go her way she could be a stubborn little madam. 'Frank, go and fetch our Carol over here, looks like she wants to thump those two.'

Frank scooted across the grass as Dora spotted two familiar figures walking towards her daughters. 'Bloody hell,' she muttered to Agnes and pointed. 'Joe's here, with *her*.' She stared as Carol flung herself at Joe's legs and Frank stopped to speak to them.

'Oh no. Fancy bringing her with him. I mean, I can understand him wanting to come to the fete and to see the kids, but look at the face on it.'

Dora nodded. 'Miserable bugger. She's about twenty paces behind him as well. She obviously doesn't want to be here, so why bother?'

Agnes raised an eyebrow. 'I know why.' She grinned. 'She knows *you* are here. She's keeping an eye on him.'

Dora laughed. 'Silly woman. She's got nothing to worry about, I can assure you.' She got to her feet, smoothed the skirt of her dress down and fluffed out her long freshly washed hair that gleamed gold in the sunlight, framing her face and falling in soft curls to her shoulders. She could feel her cheeks heating slightly as Agnes laughed at her.

'Nothing to worry about? Have you looked in a mirror lately? You're absolutely blooming with all this new-found independence and talent, lady. And that blush has given a pretty colour to your cheeks.'

Dora drew in a deep breath as Frank waved her and Agnes over. 'Oh God,' she mumbled as Agnes linked her arm and pulled her along.

'We need to be in place for the group coming on,' Frank said. 'They'll bring the truck over here for the stage.'

Dora nodded. Joe was looking at her. She smiled. 'Afternoon, Joe, er, Ivy. How are you both?'

'We're fine, thank you,' Ivy snapped before Joe could open his mouth. He had hold of Carol's hand and was watching Jackie and Patsy taking a bow to an appreciative audience who were clapping their dancing session.

'Never one to miss an opportunity, that girl of ours, eh, Dora?' He laughed, bending to greet his youngest, who gave a delighted squeal when she saw him.

Frank nodded. 'She's destined for the stage, I've said it before and I'll say it again.'

Ivy sniffed and turned away. She looked hot and bothered, her face shiny with perspiration, dark hair sticking to her head and her choice of a tight black skirt and long-sleeved top not really practical for a hot sunny day. Agnes nudged Dora. 'Did you see her face when Joe said *that girl of ours*,' she whispered. 'Spoke volumes. Jealous, of the kids as well as you. That must make life very difficult for Joe.' She shook her head. 'I feel really sorry for him.'

'Right, come on. The truck's coming over this way. Step back a bit, kids,' Frank ordered. 'Should be a good one,' he said, as Joe nodded.

'I've been looking forward to this,' Joe said. 'See what sort of music is stopping my band from getting gigs. Work's really drying up, so I might have to look at doing something different.'

As the group of young lads climbed on board the back of the truck, two picked up guitars and one picked up a banjo as several young girls surged forward, their faces animated with anticipation. The lad Frank's mate knew sat behind the drum kit, another stood behind what Frank called a tea-chest bass and yet another picked up a washboard. Dora noticed he had thimbles on his fingers.

'There's quite a few of them,' Joe said with interest. 'No brass section though. I suppose that's with them being skiffle.'

Frank nodded. 'Saw that film *Blackboard Jungle* the other night. The song "Rock Around the Clock" comes from it. Bill Haley's Comets have got a sax player, Joe. Might be worth thinking about starting your own Rock 'n' Roll group.'

Joe smiled. 'I'll have a word with the lads. We're probably all too old now, though. The kids want youngsters like the lads here.'

An announcement blared from the overhead speakers that The Quarrymen were about to play, causing a flurry of last-minute audience members to flock around the truck. One of the lads, dressed in denim jeans and an orange-checked shirt, stepped towards the microphone stand and ran his hands through his thick dark hair, smoothing his large quiff into place. He had a cheeky grin that he flashed to his audience, clearly loving the limelight. The group struck up with 'Maggie Mae', a Liverpool folk song about a Lime Street prostitute who robbed her clients. The upbeat tune soon had Jackie and Patsy dancing again. Dora watched the lad with the washboard running his thimbled fingers up and down it, fascinated by the rat-a-tat noise he made. She found her hips swaying and dropped her bags on the floor, as did Agnes, and the pair danced together, laughing and giggling like their daughters. Joe and Frank grinned at one another and rolled their eyes. No one saw Carol and Ivy slinking away hand in hand as they were all enjoying the music.

The singer, who'd told them his name was John, flashed a cheeky grin and cracked jokes with the audience before announcing the next song. The group launched into their own rendition of Lonnie Donegan's 'Puttin' on the Style'.

A dark-haired, hazel-eyed lad, wearing a white jacket with a pink carnation in his buttonhole, stood close by watching the group. Dora reckoned he looked about fifteen; she observed how he never took his eyes off the singer, watching his fingers moving up and down the neck of the guitar, and nodding in time to the rhythm as though mesmerised. She heard the boy next to him say 'You okay, Paul? Not bad, are they?' as Paul quietly nodded his approval.

Dora smiled; The Quarrymen had many fans amongst the youngsters at the fete. She felt an arm snake around her waist as she danced in time to the music and was conscious of Joe pulling her close. She whipped around as he pressed his lips close to her ear. 'Don't panic, Carol has disappeared, but so has Ivy, so they've probably gone to find a lav, or something.'

'Okay.' Dora nodded, conscious of his closeness and the scent of Brylcreem. He made no effort to remove his arm from her waist and she in turn made no effort to pull away. 'That young lad's good, isn't he?' She nodded towards the cheeky singer in the orange-checked shirt. 'What did he say his name was?'

'He's *very* good,' Joe replied. 'He's one to watch out for, if you ask me. If he carries on like that, one day he'll be more popular than Elvis.'

Chapter Thirty-Four

Ivy reappeared with Carol on her heels just as Dora was starting to get a bit worried. 'You should have told us you were taking her somewhere,' she said to Ivy.

'She said she needed a wee, but no one took any notice of her,' Ivy said. 'So she asked me instead. I do know how to look after her, you know. You lot were too busy listening to that racket.' She inclined her head towards The Quarrymen, who were taking a bow and leaving their makeshift stage.

'They were very good,' Joe said, 'but thanks for seeing to Carol for us.'

Dora saw Ivy stiffen at Joe's use of the word *us*.

'Not my cup of tea,' Ivy sniffed.

Joe shrugged and shook his head. Dora got the impression from the look on his face that not many things *were* Ivy's cup of tea. She turned to Frank. 'We'd better get going now. Then we can have an hour with Mam before her teatime. Agnes, is it okay if I come over to yours tomorrow afternoon when we take the kids to Joe's?'

'Course it is,' Agnes said, grabbing Patsy by the hand. 'I'll be glad of your company. Alan's on shift again. You can measure me up for a dress like yours while you're there.'

'Smashing. I'll bring some samples of fabric as well. Right, come on, kids. Say 'bye to Daddy and Ivy.' Dora picked up her bags and Jackie ran to Joe for a kiss goodbye. Carol stood close to Ivy, her arms folded, a sulky expression on her face.

'I don't want to see Granny. It smells horrible in there. I want to go home with Daddy and Ivy and sleep at their house tonight.'

'Carol,' Frank admonished. 'That's a rude thing to say. And Granny hasn't seen you for a few weeks. She's looking forward to it.'

But Carol wasn't happy and started to cry. 'I want to stay with Daddy,' she howled.

Joe bent down beside her. 'You're coming to me tomorrow. We'll see you then.'

Carol flung herself onto the grass and sobbed and screamed for all she was worth. People passing by stopped to look and then hurried on, shaking their heads. One woman muttered something about people having no control over kids these days.

'Carol, what's wrong with you?' Dora said, feeling embarrassed. 'Get up, now. You're making a right show of yourself in front of all these people.'

Ivy knelt down beside Carol and pulled her close, whispering something in her ear. She stopped crying instantly and rubbed her hands across her tear-stained face.

'What did you say to her?' Dora asked, feeling shocked by her daughter's sudden and unexpected outburst. Carol hadn't had a temper tantrum like that for years.

'That if she stopped making all that noise we'd take her to see Roly at my old landlord's on the way home and that she can stay with us tonight.' Ivy got up off her knees and brushed the grass from her skirt. 'That's if it's okay with everyone,' she finished, looking around.

Joe held up his hands. 'It's fine by me. Dora?'

She sighed. 'I suppose so. But Granny will be disappointed, so you will have to go next week. Be a good girl and we'll see you tomorrow night.'

'She'll be fine,' Ivy said, taking Carol by the hand. 'I've got plenty of clothes for her, so no need to worry about bringing anything over later.'

Dora nodded. In other words, Ivy was letting her know, she wasn't welcome. She shook her head, gave Carol a kiss and she and Frank made their way to the car park alongside Agnes. Jackie and Patsy were strolling hand in hand just in front, singing 'Maggie Mae' at the tops of their voices.

'Oh, dear, now why couldn't they have remembered the words to one of the other songs,' Dora said with an embarrassed grin.

Ivy and Joe held Carol's hands as they walked back to the car after watching a dog show on the field and cheering for the lovely black spaniel who won the cup and a rosette. Ivy's little chat in private with Carol on the way back from the lavatory earlier had worked. Never mind Jackie being theatrical, Carol had excelled herself with that little performance. She smiled as Carol skipped along between them. Joe looked happier and that pleased her.

She felt like any other family going about their business today. She couldn't give him any babies herself, so it was time she bucked up her ideas and made an effort to make his children feel welcome in their home. Otherwise, she'd be losing him and she didn't think she could bear that. She'd seen the longing in his eyes when he'd looked at Dora today. She could cope easily with Carol; she looked after her often enough.

She'd been selfish, wanting Joe to herself, and it had backfired as he seemed to want to spend less time with her as the months went by. It was that little one she found hard to deal with. So noisy and full of herself, just like her mother. Since she'd been back at work Joe had been a bit more relaxed about things, although at times she'd catch him staring at her with an unfathomable expression on his face, as though he wanted to say something but couldn't bring himself to do it. So it was a case of a little effort at a time to try to win his love, because there was no way she wanted to end up on her own again after she'd waited a lifetime to have him by her side.

*

Dora glanced with envy around Agnes's beautiful front room with the sun streaming through the large bay window. 'It's so nice in here. You've got it lovely.'

'Thank you. Wish I had your gorgeous curtains though. They'd look smashing with this green carpet.'

'My pride and joy, those curtains,' Dora said. 'Oh, dear, me and Joe would have loved to live on The Avenues. It was something we'd talked about and he said it's where he would buy me a house when he'd saved up.'

Agnes nodded. 'My mam's might be empty, given time. I don't think she'll be coming back because of the stairs. I could ask the landlord if he'd give you first dibs on it. It's not as big as this one, and no front garden, but it's a lovely little house and it would be great for you and the girls. And it would be so nice to have you a few avenues down.'

Dora chewed her lip. Agnes's mam's place was on Fourth Avenue, just a stone's throw away. 'I might not be able to afford the rent. I don't pay any now, but it has meant I've been able to save a little. Maybe Joe would help a bit more if we moved there. It's school though. They'd have to change. Carol might not be happy about that. She goes to secondary school next year, so that would be a good time to move. I bet Sammy and Esther won't like it either. But I know someone who would love to go to school with her best pal.'

Agnes smiled. 'Oh, Patsy would be thrilled to be at the same school as Jackie. Ah well, give it time, it's not happening yet, with Mam I mean, we need to get her somewhere first, but we can dream, can't we?'

Two weeks after the Woolton fete and a week before the end of school closing for the summer term, Dora was late picking up the girls. She dashed along Scotland Road towards the entrance to All

Saints playground and spotted Jackie, her arms full, standing by the gates. 'Sorry I'm late, chuck,' she said, relieving her daughter of school and swimming clothes bags. She looked hurriedly around but could see no sign of Carol. 'Where's your sister? Trust her to be missing when I need to get back. Aunty Esther isn't feeling well and Sammy's going to take her home early.'

'Don't know.' Jackie shrugged. 'She hasn't come out yet.'

Dora frowned as the remaining parents and children went on their way. After another five minutes waiting patiently, she grabbed Jackie by the hand and marched into school. There was no one around in the main corridor, which stank of carbolic soap, so she popped her head into a nearby classroom and called to the cleaner who was swabbing the floors with a large mop. 'Excuse me; are there any teachers still on the premises?'

'Try the staffroom down the end, queen, or Mr Storey's office next to it,' the woman called and went back to her mopping.

Dora hurried down the corridor, a feeling of panic rising in her chest. The staffroom door stood open but the room was empty. The headmaster's study was next door, so she knocked and the door was opened by a tall, bespectacled, grey-haired man wearing a grey suit. Mr Storey held a pipe in his hand and the smell of strong tobacco hit her as he exhaled and smiled, although not with recognition; she could have been any parent.

'Yes, can I help you?'

'I'm looking for my daughter, Carol Rodgers. She hasn't come out of school yet and she doesn't appear to be anywhere in here.' Dora realised she was gabbling as a feeling of terror clutched her heart. What if someone had taken Carol? There were some odd types who hung around the area at times.

'What is your daughter's name and age?'

'She's Carol Rodgers and she's ten,' Dora said.

Mr Storey frowned and beckoned her inside before going over to his desk. He picked up a piece of paper and looked at it, then

went to a filing cabinet in the corner, opening the third drawer
down and pulling out a card. He ran his finger down the card and
nodded. 'I thought the name rang a bell. We sent Carol home at
dinnertime. Complained of a tummy ache, so according to this
information her mother was informed by telephone and she came
and collected her.'

Dora stared at him as though he'd gone mad. 'But *I'm* her mother
and I got no such call,' she said, her voice rising. 'There must be
some mistake. What phone number do you have on there?'

'I'm afraid that's confidential information, Mrs Rodgers.'

'I'm Ms Evans,' Dora shrieked. 'Who has got my daughter?
What have you done with her?'

It was Mr Storey's turn to look worried now. 'All I can tell you
is that Mrs Ivy Rodgers came and took her home after we called
to let her know that Carol was unwell. Carol went away quite
happily with her.'

'Ivy, you called *Ivy*?' Dora realised she was yelling now and took
a deep breath. 'Ivy is *not* Carol's mother; she is her stepmother.
How dare you let her take my daughter? Why is *her* phone number
on Carol's record?'

Mr Storey looked down at the card he was holding. 'It says
here that the contact number was changed recently, following
information sent to the school via a letter brought in by your
daughter.' He looked up. 'I really think you need to take this
matter up with Mrs Rodgers, er, Ms Evans. There appear to be
some crossed wires.'

'Oh, don't you worry, I *will*,' Dora snapped. 'And get that
number changed back to mine right away.' She grabbed a pen from
his desk and wrote the shop number down on a piece of paper
and thrust it at him, before grabbing Jackie's hand and marching
out of the office. Anger carried her back to the shop. She'd swing
for that bloody Ivy. What the hell did she and Joe think they were
doing, undermining her parental authority like that?

As they approached the shop she saw an ambulance, its bells ringing, pull up outside and her heart sank. Esther? Oh my God, she'd taken so long and promised she'd be quick, with her being poorly and Sammy wanting to take her home. She dashed inside to see Sammy wringing his hands, a white-faced Esther lying on the floor by his feet, a cushion under her head. She dropped down beside her as the ambulance attendants hurried in. She heard Sammy explaining what had happened. Esther had just collapsed onto the floor in front of him and he'd been unable to get any response from her. He'd panicked and called an ambulance.

Chapter Thirty-Five

It was one of the longest nights of Dora's life as she sat with Sammy and held his hand. They were waiting for news in the family area of Fazakerley hospital. Sammy had gone with Esther in the ambulance and Dora had told him she would get Frank to bring her to join him as soon as he called in on his way home from work. Sammy had called out as the ambulance doors closed that she wasn't to tell Sonny what had happened. Frank was looking after Jackie and told them not to worry about anything. He'd lock up the shop and it would remain closed for the time being.

The problem of Carol being taken out of school Dora would let Frank deal with. She'd called the prefab after Sammy left but no one answered the phone and her loyalties were torn; she knew Sammy needed her and the school had assured her that Carol had been happy to go off with Ivy. Frank had said he would call Joe and speak to him when Joe got home from work. Frank was as angry as Dora and agreed it was out of order for Ivy to do such a thing.

A young nurse disturbed her thoughts as she wheeled a trolley in. It was set with a snack and a pot of tea. 'Thought you'd be ready for some refreshments.' She smiled and poured two cups for them. 'Let me know if you need anything else. The sandwiches are cheese or egg.'

'Is there any news yet?' Sammy asked, his voice wavering. All they'd been told so far was that the doctor who'd examined Esther suspected a bleed in the brain and was operating immediately.

'Not yet, I'm sorry.' The nurse smiled sympathetically. 'Your wife is still in theatre. A doctor will be with you as soon as we have some news.'

Dora sniffed back tears and took a sip of the hot sweet tea, just like her mam used to make for shock. She hadn't thought she'd be able to eat anything, but her stomach growled as she lifted the lid off the plate of sandwiches, reminding her that she'd had nothing since dinnertime and it was now two thirty in the morning. 'Come on, Sammy,' she cajoled as he protested he wasn't hungry. 'We both need to keep our strength up for Esther. You know how much she likes to make us eat.'

At three fifteen a young doctor came to them and led them to a side ward where Esther lay on a bed, her face as white as the pillow she rested on. 'I'm afraid it's just a matter of time,' the doctor whispered. 'The bleed was extensive and there was nothing we could do to stop it. I'm so sorry.'

Sammy wept uncontrollably in Dora's arms. Her own heart breaking, she found the strength from somewhere to comfort this man who'd become as dear as a father to her. How he would cope without his darling Esther, she couldn't imagine. The pair were inseparable. She took a deep breath. 'Sammy, do you think it's time we let Sonny know what's happened? I could call him at his friend's or ask Frank to go and get him.'

He pulled away from her, wiping tears and snot on his shirt-sleeve. 'Over my dead body,' he growled. 'This is all his fault. Him coming home and upsetting her made her ill. She's not been right since the day he walked through that front door, fretting and worrying about what he'd be up to next. I won't have him around when I'm saying goodbye to her. The only person I want by my side is you, Dora.'

Dora nodded, too choked to speak.

Esther passed away just before Frank arrived at the hospital to tell Dora he'd taken Jackie to school and that he'd put a notice up on the shop door. He went to find a phone to let work know he wasn't coming in today due to a bereavement. When he came back to them Sammy asked if Frank could take him home and requested that they come into the house with him. He couldn't face it on his own.

Dora felt her stomach lurch as Frank pulled onto the drive of Sammy's beautiful detached home. Sonny's car was parked there.

Sammy tutted and shook his head. 'What the bloody hell is *he* doing here?'

The front door flew open and Sonny stood on the doorstep, a look of anger on his face as he saw Frank and Dora helping his father from the car.

Dora was thankful her brother was with them. Frank would stand no nonsense from this one.

'What's going on?' Sonny demanded as Frank pushed past him, supporting Sammy, who ignored his son. Sonny stumbled backwards and cracked his elbow on the doorframe. 'I asked you a question?' he yelled, angry at being ignored. 'I called at the shop and there was a notice on the door about not being open today. I come here to see what's wrong and find the house empty and no sign of you or Mother.'

'Get inside, boy,' Sammy growled. 'Showing me up on my own doorstep.'

Frank took Sammy to the back of the house as instructed and sat him down on a sofa in a large sitting room that overlooked the well-tended back garden.

'Dora, would you make us some tea while I speak to my son, please? Perhaps you could help her, Frank?'

They nodded and left a stony-faced Sonny standing in front of the fireplace, glaring at his father.

'Shout if you need us,' Frank said, giving Sonny a look that dared him to put a foot out of place.

'Why would he need you,' Sonny yelled after him. 'I'm his flesh and blood, not you.'

Dora filled the kettle and placed it on the gas hob. She looked around the huge kitchen where Esther had made all her beautiful cakes and biscuits and felt the tears running down her cheeks. Frank put his arms around her and held her tight.

'I can't believe she's gone,' she sobbed. 'She wasn't well, but I never expected this… How are we going to cope without her? She was Sammy's life, his world.' She stopped as she heard raised voices from the sitting room and then the door opened and Sonny barged his way into the kitchen. His face was white, but he looked angry rather than upset.

'Why didn't one of you call me?' he demanded. 'She was my mother, I should have been there. Now he's blaming me, saying it was my fault she died. You two had no right to be with her at the end.'

'I wasn't,' Frank said quietly. 'And Dora was there because your father asked her to stay. She's been there for both of them for a long time now and them for her. It's called respect. You should try it sometime.'

'Oh, she's been there all right, wheedling her way in, living rent-free in the flat that should have been mine when I came home. Well, things will change now, I can tell you. He's in no fit state to make decisions. That will be down to me from now on. I want you and your brats out of that flat by the end of next week.' He turned at a noise from the hallway and next thing his feet left the ground and he was on the floor, flat on his back, holding his nose.

'That's for your mother,' Sammy said, rubbing the back of his hand. 'And Dora stays put. Give me back your key, get out of my home and my life. I don't ever want to set eyes on you again. You are not, and never will be, welcome. Go and sort your mess out in London. And I don't want you at the funeral either.' He looked at

Dora. 'I'll have that cuppa now if you don't mind, my dear.' He shuffled away as Dora looked at Frank and shrugged her shoulders.

Following Jewish tradition, Esther's funeral was arranged within twenty-four hours and a service held at the Sefton Park Hebrew Congregational Church. Dora had never seen a church so packed. The couple still had many friends, in spite of losing some over Sonny's past indiscretions, and were popular in Liverpool as their business had served the community for many years. Word had quickly got round after Frank put an announcement up in the shop window about Esther's death, along with an apology for the shop still being closed. Dora had been shocked by the speed of the arrangements. The funerals she'd been involved with for baby Joanna, Joanie and her dad had taken several days to prepare for.

Esther's graveside burial service was held at Long Lane Jewish Cemetery in Fazakerley and Dora was touched to see Agnes standing by the gates as the procession passed by. Agnes caught up with them as Dora and Frank parked their car and made their way to the grave.

'Thank you for coming,' Dora said as Agnes linked her arm.

Agnes smiled. 'I couldn't not come. And it's only a few minutes' walk from my house. How's Sammy holding up? He looks very smart.'

'Yes, he does,' Dora said proudly. Sammy wore a dark suit and a tall black hat with his beard and hair neatly trimmed. She was so used to seeing him covered in bits of cotton thread and wearing his usual skull-cap. 'He's okay. Still in shock. They do things differently to how we do them. It's been so quick. We've not even had time to think properly. Certainly no time to grieve yet.'

'No sign of Sonny Jim then?'

'Nope. And hopefully he won't come back. Sammy's washed his hands of him. He wrote a long letter last night to tell him that the money he was loaned when he got married will be written off, but he will get nothing else. If he tries any funny business Sammy will take him to court for it. I posted the letter first thing this morning to the bank where Sonny works. Sammy said to make sure I asked for it to be signed for so we know he's got it. I stayed at the house with him last night and so did Frank. Joe's looking after the kids today; he's taken a day off work so he can take them to and from school.'

'And you sorted that mess out about the phone number?'

'Yes,' Dora replied. 'Ivy said that she'd asked in her letter for their number to be added to mine in case of emergencies when the school couldn't contact me. Joe apparently thought it was a good idea too. But of course that isn't what the letter actually said, and I was never contacted because they thought it was a genuine number change. She lies through her teeth, as we know. But short of asking for that letter back, which I know Joe won't do as he'd rather keep the peace, what can we do?'

They joined the other mourners at the graveside, but stood well back, as Dora wasn't too sure about Jewish protocol and didn't want to offend anyone by doing the wrong thing. They were there to see Esther laid to rest, and that's all that mattered. She sent a little silent prayer to heaven in her mind, sure that Esther would know they were all thinking about her.

Frank handed Dora a mug of Horlicks as she stretched out on the bed settee at the flat. His sister looked pale and exhausted. It had been an eventful last few days. Topsy twisted around his legs and he stroked her ears affectionately. She purred and rolled onto her back. 'Soft old thing,' he said, tickling her tummy. He was staying here while the shop was closed as he felt Dora was vulnerable on her own. There were some right scallies around, like them that had burgled Dora that time. She'd never got her rings back; the scuffers never did get to the bottom of it. Frank always kept a look out in pawn shop windows and the like for them, but he'd had no luck so far. He felt better knowing that if he stayed here he could keep his eye on things for Sammy too so he had some time to grieve for Esther. Frank knew exactly how he would be feeling right now. Even though he and Joanie had only had a few months together and Sammy and Esther had shared a lifetime of marriage, the pain was just as bad and it never went away. Thank God they'd both got Dora and her kiddies to look after.

Chapter Thirty-Six

While the shop was still closed during the week following Esther's funeral, Dora caught a bus over to the pleasant suburb of Allerton to visit Sadie in her new home. It was ages since they'd seen each other. With school holidays looming, both would be busy with their kids, so today was an ideal time for a catch-up.

Sadie, looking well, and as slim as anyone who'd carried five babies in quick succession could, welcomed her into the spacious hallway with open arms. 'Oh, it's so good to see you. The little ones are out in the back garden so come through. We can do the tour as we go.'

Dora admired Sadie's light and spacious sitting room with its bay window and new carpet, and the first three-piece suite she'd ever owned. 'Brand new as well,' she said. 'It's on the never-never from Epstein's. It was the only way we could afford to buy things, but Stan's got overtime most weeks so we're managing. Better than all that mismatched stuff from Wright Street. And look,' she said as they reached the kitchen at the back that overlooked the garden, 'a fridge!'

'Oh lovely. That's what I miss. I loved my fridge at the prefab. I could have had Mam's, but Frank's taken it to his mate's for when he gets offered a flat. He half-paid for it when they bought it, so it was almost his anyway.'

'And see,' Sadie pointed through a hatch in the wall, 'there's a dining area, but we've shoved the table right up to the wall so the kids have got space to play. Saves them taking their stuff into my posh room and making a mess. I'll show you upstairs when we've had a brew. There are a couple of deckchairs outside. We can sit out and get some fresh air while it's nice. Belinda and Steven are on the lawn. I can't believe our Lindy starts school in September. Time flies.'

'It does,' Dora agreed. 'Our Carol goes up to secondary school next year.'

Sadie brought two mugs of coffee out and they relaxed in the warm sunshine.

'Your garden is lovely,' Dora said, admiring the neat lawn and well-stocked flower beds.

'My dad comes over at the weekend and looks after it for us. It was covered in builders' rubble and weeds when we moved in but it's a good size. The bottom end is a lost cause because I've got two would-be Anfield players on my hands. They have to practise somewhere I suppose. Don't want them out on the front in case they break any windows. The neighbours are a bit classier round here than Wright Street – present company excepted,' she finished with a grin as Dora raised an amused eyebrow.

'Wonder how the Smyths are getting on? Bet that Lenny one is in prison now or the army, *if* they'd have him. Did you ever hear anything else about your jewellery?'

Dora shook her head. 'No, those are long gone by now. For all we know, Lenny could be married and his new wife wearing my rings. It's a shame in a way; I'd like to have given one each to the girls when they're older, but it wasn't meant to be.'

'How's Sammy doing? We saw the news about Esther in the *Echo*. Bet it was a shock for you both. So sudden like that.'

'It was awful.' Dora sighed and chewed her lip. 'I spoke to Sammy this morning before I left home. He said he's okay, just putting his paperwork in order while he's got the chance, but he sounds lost. I don't know if we can carry on with the business to be honest, if he'll have the heart to do it, and I know this might sound selfish, considering, but I'm really concerned about my future. It's my home as well as my job. I have to admit that I feel quite scared when I allow myself to think about it.'

'Are you still on the council list?' Sadie asked.

Dora stared at her. 'I don't know, I never gave it a thought. They won't have my new address though. Do you think I should ring them to find out?'

'Definitely. I mean, if Sammy decides to sell up, where would you go? A buyer might want the flat for storage or to live in. You'd be on the move again.'

Dora nodded. 'I'll do it as soon as I get home. Oh God, the thought of having to uproot again makes me feel ill. I can't go back to Knowsley because there's nowhere to go back to. And finding somewhere private to rent that's big enough for me to earn a living out of as well would cost the earth.'

Sadie patted her arm. 'It might not come to that. Sammy may decide to carry on. But he's past retiring age, so you should get yourself prepared, just in case. And look on the bright side, you've got Carol now, so you get extra points, and if you were homeless you'd be at the top of the list.'

The thought of being homeless with two kids and a cat in tow hadn't even entered her head, but now it filled Dora with dread. The kids would have to go to Joe and Ivy and maybe *she'd* have to camp out at Agnes's for a week or two. But what if she lost Carol again? And both girls might be removed from her care this time around if she had nowhere to live. If Joe and Ivy could give them a stable home and she couldn't, then there was every chance that they'd get custody. Life had been so good for a long time now and she'd got used to it. The idea of things spiralling out of her control again scared the life out of her. Then she thought of poor Sammy and how life was for him at the moment, and felt selfish. At least she still had those she loved around her and she'd get through it – she'd got through worse in the past.

*

With Sadie's words echoing through her mind, Dora went to collect the girls from school. She hurried them home and gave them a snack while she went downstairs to use the phone.

The council worker who took her call explained that her previous application for rehousing had lapsed and she would need to fill in the forms again. He said he would put them in the post after she told him that her needs may prove to be urgent very soon, and told her to fill them in right away and to bring them to the town hall for processing so that there was no danger of them being lost in the postal system. Dora thanked him and hung up.

She was tempted to ring Sammy to ask what his future plans were, but she didn't feel it was her place to mither him. No matter how many times he and Esther had told her she was like a daughter to them, she wasn't flesh and blood and his business decisions were nothing to do with her. She'd just have to wait and see. She'd discuss her thoughts with Frank once the girls were in bed. She didn't want anything getting back to Joe and Ivy via Carol until she knew for certain what her position would be.

She felt at a loose end with no sewing to do; all their orders were dealt with and there was nothing new recently. Back upstairs Jackie was on the floor in floods of tears. 'What have you done to her?' Dora asked Carol, who was slouched on the bed settee looking glum.

'Nothing,' Carol said, her bottom lip pouting. 'Why do you always think it's my fault when she's upset? She's crying because she misses Esther, and so do I,' she finished as fat tears ran down her cheeks.

Dora sighed and pulled her close. 'Jackie, come up here, sweetheart. I'm sorry. I know you two are missing her as much as I am.' Jackie clambered up beside her and snuggled close. 'And it's okay to cry. Tears are good for you. But we need to be brave in front of Sammy when we see him. *He* needs lots of love too.'

*

As Dora walked slowly up Homer Street after taking the girls to school, the day before they broke up for the summer holidays, Sammy was pulling up outside the shop in his van. She waved and smiled as she drew level with him. She noted how pale he looked and the dark circles under his brown eyes. He unlocked the door and picked up some post from the doormat, and handed Dora a large buff envelope bearing the council's stamp across the top. She blushed as he raised an eyebrow, and put the envelope down on the counter. He looked through his own post, throwing it down on the counter when he saw it was mainly advertisements from wholesale companies. He went to open the door to let in some fresh air. 'Everything okay with you, Dora?' he asked.

'Yeah, not bad. How about you, Sammy? Come here, you look like you need a hug.'

'Don't show me any sympathy,' he said, 'you'll have me blubbing. Make me a brew instead.'

She nodded and went into the kitchen. Esther's glasses were still there, on top of a magazine she must have been reading when she got up to go into the shop. Had she maybe felt a bit strange and gone to look for Sammy before she collapsed? They'd never know now and maybe it was best they didn't. Dora filled the kettle, and moved the glasses to a shelf so they wouldn't upset Sammy if he came through and saw them. He had enough reminders at home. It felt very empty without Esther chattering away in the background. The heart and soul had gone out of the place. Dora made two mugs of strong, sweet tea and carried them through to the shop. A woman had come in and was talking to Sammy, her head on one side in that sympathetic manner that people use for the newly bereaved. She meant well, but when she left Sammy rolled his eyes and shut the door after her and dropped the catch. Dora put the mugs down on the counter and caught his eye.

'I can't be doing with that all day,' he muttered. 'Maybe it was a mistake to come in, but I've done all I can do at home for now. And we need to have a talk about the shop and things, Dora.'

Dora nodded, her stomach lurching as he blew out his cheeks and took a sip of tea. 'Just what I needed, my own tea is not as nice.'

Dora smiled and picked at the envelope from the council. Sammy pointed to it. 'What's that all about then?'

'It's an application form to be rehoused,' she said. 'I thought I'd better get my act together, in case I need to move out of the flat.'

He nodded. 'A wise move, my dear. I think we should take things a bit easier over the next few weeks. Maybe have a sale, get rid of some of the stock. We won't take any further orders for now. I need to have a think about the future, the same as you're doing.'

'Has Sonny been in touch?' she asked.

'He responded to my letter. Thanked me for writing off his debt and said he'd do his best to pay back a little of what he owes me. Empty gestures, that's all. I won't be replying in a hurry. He's back in London to sort out his mess, for the foreseeable future.'

Dora breathed a sigh of relief. Hopefully he wouldn't show his face in Liverpool again for a long time, but deep down she had a feeling that wasn't the last they would see of Sonny Jacobs.

Over the next two weeks Dora worried about her future as she and Sammy halved the price of the stock and had a big sale. She looked around at the depleted shelves and sighed. Although he'd said nothing to her yet, Sammy had been preoccupied, wandering around in a daze. She'd made sure he'd eaten with her and the girls at night before he drove home. That way she knew he was getting at least one cooked meal a day.

She'd had a letter of response from the council about her placement on the housing list, but it would seem that while she still had a roof over her head and had not been given notice by her landlord, she still wasn't considered a priority. She felt in limbo. It was almost like being back at square one on Wright Street, but without the horrible neighbours and rats. The only alternative to staying on in the flat was to try to rent privately in the clearance areas, build up a list of private sewing clients again and hope for the best. But the slums would be her very last resort.

Four weeks after Esther's funeral Dora boxed up what little was left of the lace and trimmings and felt even more despondent. There was now hardly anything left to sell. The window display was almost empty and people had stopped looking in as they hurried by. Sammy was still paying her a wage, but she missed making garments and the fun side of the business with the theatre work. She placed the boxes on the floor behind the counter as the doorbell rang out and Sammy hurried into the shop.

'Good morning,' he called. 'Is that kettle on?'

'It will be in a minute,' Dora said, pleased to see him smiling. She made two mugs of tea and carried them through to where Sammy had parked himself on a chair behind the counter.

Sammy took a welcome sip of tea and sighed. 'I need to talk to you about my plans for the next few months, Dora,' he said. 'Take a seat.' He pointed to the other chair. Dora felt her stomach contract with nerves. This was it, end of an era, a time she'd been dreading.

'I'll start at the beginning,' he said, a faraway look in his eyes. 'I told you a while ago that Esther and I had plans to travel and to visit family in Israel and the USA and we had to put everything on hold when we lent Sonny that money.'

Dora nodded. 'You did.'

'Well, it's still something I'd like to do in honour of her memory and before I get too old to enjoy it. We both lost family in the Holocaust; my two younger brothers died at Auschwitz, as did Esther's dear mother and father and one of her sisters. Her other sister is in New York and there are nieces to meet that I've never seen before. I have two older brothers who are still alive and living in Israel and I also have nephews. This is my time to travel now. I feel she is urging me on to do it and I must obey that urge. I've put the house up for sale. It's too big for me now she's gone. I'm also retiring. I can't run this business without her. My heart isn't in it. I know it's not what you want to hear, Dora, as you love working here and we've loved having you and the girls as part of our family, but it's run its course. You're a very talented young lady and you *will* find work. Places need good designers. I will give you the best of references and you'll be snapped up. Or you can set up on your own again and work from home. I will pass on your details to our clients and I'm sure they will follow you.'

Dora took a deep breath and nodded. It was what she'd prefer rather than working for someone else. 'I'll need to wait until I've got a new place to live and then maybe I'll do that. Wherever I work it has to fit in with my girls and school, of course. So working from home would be better for me. But it will take ages for the council to rehouse us. The last time I think they forgot my family even existed. If it hadn't been for the kindness shown by you and Esther I'd have gone crazy down on Wright Street. I'll start looking for somewhere right away. If you could write a letter that I can forward to the council to tell them that you want me out of the flat, it will help my case.'

Sammy nodded. 'I will do that. But for now you can stay upstairs until I get an offer on the place. You might want to put your name on a few things so that you've got a head start for working from home again: a machine, a mannequin and what have you. By the way –' He took a sip of tea. 'Don't think I'm nosy, but I couldn't help overhearing what you were saying to Agnes when she called you recently. Something about her mother, wasn't it? I do hope it's not more bad news.'

'Oh, no, not really, just that her mam was offered a bungalow from the council, so Agnes has persuaded her to accept it and is now busy sorting out the things she's taking from the old rented house and putting them in the new place before she comes out of the care home. She's all right for a while though because she gave a good month's notice to the landlord—' Dora stopped and a slow smile spread across her face – and then vanished just as quickly, because she just knew she couldn't afford to pay the rent on anything as nice as that. It would be so much better than living on a big council estate though – and if only it were possible, she'd jump at the opportunity, save all the waiting and anxiety that being on the council list brought with it.

'And is the empty house near Agnes, by any chance? In Fazakerley?'

'Yes,' Dora replied. 'It's on Fourth Avenue and Agnes's is on Second Avenue, but she and Alan are buying theirs.'

Sammy nodded and chewed his lip thoughtfully. 'See if you can get Agnes on the phone right away,' he said. 'Tell her that if it's still available, you will have the house. Go on, quickly before it's offered to anyone else. And we'll go over there now and have a look at it.'

Dora shot off her seat and ran to the phone, her legs shaking and her hands trembling as she dialled Agnes's number. 'It's Dora,' she said. 'Is your mam's house still up for grabs? It is? I want it, Agnes. I'm coming over with Sammy now,' she finished as Agnes squealed excitedly that she'd ring the landlord right away. Dora hung up as though in a trance. Sammy shook the van keys at her and they left the shop.

'Sammy, stop,' Dora cried as he sped off up Scotland Road. 'I can't do this; it's just a pipedream. I can't afford that house.'

'Yes, you can,' he said. 'I will help you with the rent until you get on your feet work-wise, on two conditions.'

She stared at him. 'I can't let you do that. And what conditions do you mean?'

'Yes, you can, and the conditions are that, when I come home occasionally from my travels, I can beg the odd night's bed and breakfast from you while I catch up with my beautiful surrogate granddaughters. And that you promise to keep Esther's grave supplied with fresh flowers while I'm away. You'll be so close to the cemetery, you're practically neighbours.' His eyes twinkled and he smiled at her.

Dora laughed. He really was the most wonderful stand-in father. She was so lucky to have walked past his shop that day and spotted the card in the window. 'Of course you can. And as regards looking after Esther's grave, it goes without saying.'

Sammy smiled, and although there was still a sadness in his eyes that Dora knew would take for ever to go away, he said softly, 'New beginnings, eh, Dora?'

She nodded and swallowed the lump in her throat. 'Joanie once said that to me,' she said, remembering, and so had Joe, she thought, but she didn't voice it; she didn't want to drag up any painful memories on this happy day. 'Take the next turn on your right,' she said. He turned into Fourth Avenue and halfway down was Agnes, waving excitedly from the front step of a bay-windowed, mid-terrace house. Dora smiled at the thought that this was to be her and her daughters' dream home for the foreseeable future.

AUTHOR LETTER

To my loyal band of regular readers who bought and reviewed *The Lost Daughter of Liverpool*, thank you so much for waiting patiently for the sequel. You all know who you are and your support is so much appreciated. Thank you for all your daily contact on FB and the Notrights group. If you enjoyed *The Forgotten Family of Liverpool*, I'd be so grateful if you could write a review and let me know what you think.

You can also sign up here to receive an email whenever I have a new book published. You can unsubscribe at any time, and your email address will never be shared. www.bookouture.com/pam-howes

I'd love to say a big thank you to the dedicated team at Bookouture who never fail to turn out a great book. Thanks especially to Abi and Vicky, my fabulous editors, for guidance and for all their editorial support and encouragement. You've helped make my story something special.

A big thank you to the wonderful Kim Nash for everything you do for the Bookouture authors. It is so appreciated. And thank you to the gang in the Bookouture Authors' Lounge. The best bunch of authors on this planet. I feel honoured to be amongst you all.

Much love to you all. Pam.

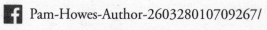 Pam-Howes-Author-260328010709267/

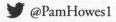 @PamHowes1

ACKNOWLEDGEMENTS

For my man, daughters and grandchildren. My own loyal support system. Love you all very much. xxx

Thank you once more to my FB friends on our little group – 60's Chicks Confidential – for their undying friendship and support. Thanks also to my lovely friends and Beta readers, Brenda Thomasson and Julie Simpson, who read an early draft of this story and gave me the thumbs-up. Thank you also to the awesome bloggers who shared my first novel in this trilogy with a blog tour. You all do such a fabulous job in spreading the word.